Cowboy Country

The indicator stick turned blue,

and sheer, utter panic clamped down on her.

But there was no time for that now. In seven and a half months, she, Virginia Marie Bradford, would be somebody's mother. She had to *think,* dammit.

"For once in your life, be logical," she muttered. "What are you so afraid of?"

The list seemed endless. At forty-two, she was too old to be a mother. She didn't know how to be a mother. Shoot, she was probably too much of an airhead to be a mother.

The second she started to show, the kids at the high school would laugh themselves sick. Her family would be appalled. Her friends would know she'd lost her mind.

And local sheriff Andy Johnson would think she'd lied about not being able to get pregnant that wonderful, insane night of passion she'd shared with him....

Dear Reader,

Welcome to Silhouette **Special Edition** . . . welcome to romance. Each month, Silhouette **Special Edition** publishes six novels with you in mind—stories of love and life, tales that you can identify with—as well as dream about.

And this wonderful month of May has many terrific stories for you. Myrna Temte presents her contribution to THAT SPECIAL WOMAN!—our new promotion that salutes women, and the wonderful men who win them. *The Forever Night* features characters you met in her COWBOY COUNTRY series—as well as a romance for sheriff Andy Johnson, whom many of you have written in about. Ginny Bradford gets her man in this gentle tale of love.

This month also brings *He's the Rich Boy* by Lisa Jackson. This is the concluding tale to her MAVERICKS series that features men that just won't be tamed! Don't miss this tale of love at misty Whitefire Lake!

Rounding out this special month are books from other favorite authors: Barbara Faith, Pat Warren, Kayla Daniels and Patricia McLinn—who is back with *Grady's Wedding* (you remember Grady—he was an usher in *Wedding Party, #718*. Now he has his own tale of love!).

I hope that you enjoy this book, and all the stories to come. Have a wonderful month!

Sincerely,

Tara Gavin
Senior Editor
Silhouette Books

MYRNA TEMTE

THE FOREVER NIGHT

SPECIAL EDITION®

Published by Silhouette Books New York
America's Publisher of Contemporary Romance

To my editor, Mary Clare Kersten.
Thanks for all the encouragement, patience and humor.
You're a joy to work with.

ACKNOWLEDGMENTS
My sincere thanks to: Dr. Sharon Cathcart and Kathy Jones
from the North Spokane Women's Clinic, and Sandi
Ludescher, Spokane, Washington. And to my nephew, Brian
Gum of Hamilton, Montana, for inventing the word
Schnoodle.

SILHOUETTE BOOKS
300 East 42nd St., New York, N.Y. 10017

THE FOREVER NIGHT

ISBN: 0-373-09816-2

First Silhouette Books printing May 1993

Printed in the U.S.A.

Books by Myrna Temte

Silhouette Special Edition

Wendy Wyoming #483
Powder River Reunion #572
The Last Good Man Alive #643
For Pete's Sake #739
Silent Sam's Salvation #745
Heartbreak Hank #751
The Forever Night #816

*Cowboy Country Series

MYRNA TEMTE

grew up in Montana and attended college in Wyoming, where she met and married her husband. Marriage didn't necessarily mean settling down for the Temtes—they have lived in six different states, including Washington, where they currently reside. Moving so much is difficult, the author says, but it is also wonderful stimulation for a writer.

Though always a "readaholic," Ms. Temte never dreamed of becoming an author. But while spending time at home to care for her first child, she began to seek an outlet from the never-ending duties of housekeeping and child rearing. She started reading romances and soon became hooked, both as a reader and a writer.

Now Myrna Temte appreciates the best of all possible worlds—a loving family and a challenging career that lets her set her own hours and turn her imagination loose.

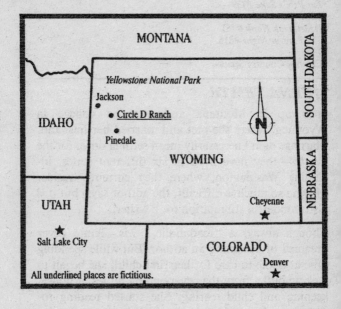

MONTANA

SOUTH DAKOTA

Yellowstone National Park

Jackson

● Circle D Ranch

IDAHO

● Pinedale

WYOMING

NEBRASKA

UTAH

Cheyenne
★

★
Salt Lake City

COLORADO

Denver
★

All underlined places are fictitious.

Chapter One

"Bluuue?" Ginny Bradford shrieked. "No! Don't you *dare* turn blue. Don't even *think* about turning blue, you dirty, rotten, miserable, son of a... biscuit eater!"

The indicator stick that had come with the home pregnancy test didn't appear to be the least bit intimidated by threats. Ginny changed tactics.

"Aw, come on, sweetie, don't *do* this to me," she begged. "It was just one night. One little indiscretion in all these years. As God is my witness, I'll never do it again."

The indicator stick remained unimpressed by either her pleading or her Scarlett O'Hara imitation. The wretched thing had turned blue the second she'd dipped it into the little cup that had been included in the kit. Before her horrified eyes, it turned bluer and bluer. Did that mean she was carrying twins? Triplets?

The thought made sweat break out on her forehead. Her fingers trembled. She dropped the stick into the trash can and set the cup on the toilet tank. Leaning her fanny against the wall, she covered her face with both hands and slid down until she was sitting on the bathroom carpet.

"Dummy, dummy, dummy," she chanted, banging the back of her head against the plaster in rhythm with each word. "How could you *be* such a dummy?"

Hugging her knees to her chest, she gazed at the vivid purple shower curtain. She tried to picture herself holding an infant. She couldn't. That dream had died so hard, it was as if she'd erased all such images from her brain.

Her heart raced. Sheer, utter panic clamped down on her lungs like two giant fists and she couldn't breathe. Black dots danced in front of her eyes.

"Cut it out, Ginny! Just stop it!"

The sound of her own voice wavering out of control brought her up short. She shuddered. Hysterical laughter surged up inside her. Gulping in long, deep breaths, Ginny forced it back down.

There was no time for that now. In seven and a half months, she, Virginia Marie Bradford, would be somebody's mother. She had to *think*, dammit.

"For once in your life, be logical," she muttered. "What are you so afraid of?"

The list seemed endless. At forty-two, she was too old to be a mother. She didn't know how to be a mother. Shoot, she was probably too much of an airhead to be a mother. She didn't have health insurance. She didn't even have a regular job, and she seriously doubted the school district in Pinedale, Wyoming, or anywhere else would be willing to hire an unwed mother.

The second she started to show, the news would zip from one end of the county to the other. She might as well call the *Pinedale Roundup* office and tell them to publish the story. What kind of headline would they use? Local Sheriff Knocks Up Substitute Teacher?

Lord, the kids at the high school would laugh themselves sick. Her family would be appalled. Her friends would know she'd lost her mind. Andy would think she'd lied about not being able to get pregnant.

Ah, yes, Andy Johnson. Dealing with him would be the real kicker. Oh, she liked him—she liked him a lot. In fact, she felt downright affectionate toward the man.

He'd been a generous, uninhibited lover—the kind of lover most women dream about but are never fortunate enough to meet. During the past six weeks, Ginny had frequently found herself daydreaming about that wonderful...all right, *insane* night of passion she'd shared with him. She still didn't know what had possessed her.

Until her old buddy Sam Dawson's birthday party back at the beginning of September, she hadn't had sex in three and a half years. For the last six months of his life, her husband had been too sick and weak to want sex. She hadn't missed it a whole lot, and she'd thought whatever needs and desires she'd once possessed had died with Charlie Bradford.

Well, she didn't believe that now. How could she when memories of the things she had done and felt with Andy haunted her, making her heart pound and her palms sweat?

If Andy had been interested, she wouldn't have minded doing a few of those things...well, maybe *all* of those things with him again. Not to mention a few new things that had occurred to her during a steamy daydream, too.

Unfortunately the passion hadn't lasted past sunrise. Talk about the morning after from hell! Since she'd never gone to bed with anyone besides Charlie before, she hadn't had a clue as to what she should say or do. Andy hadn't appeared to be a whole lot more comfortable.

He'd practically jumped out of bed, yanked on his rumpled uniform and taken off like a rooster with his tail feathers on fire. She'd only seen him twice since then—once at the bank and once at the post office—and she doubted that was an accident on Andy's part. In a town as small as Pinedale she could have reasonably expected to run into him once or twice a week.

What really bugged her was that he'd been polite at both encounters, but he sure hadn't lingered to chat, and he'd kept glancing over his shoulder as if he expected her dad to come after him with a shotgun. She'd considered marching into Andy's office and telling him to his face that he might as well relax because she didn't expect him to ask her for a date or anything else. She felt a little hurt and rejected, but hey, she wasn't stupid.

Much as she liked, admired and even lusted after Andy Johnson, the last thing she needed was another tough, macho, opinionated man in her life. Andy qualified for all three adjectives. In spades.

For cryin' out loud, the man was a sheriff. Sure, he was handsome and sexy, and she'd had a wonderful time dancing with him. And making love with him. But she knew as well as she knew her own shoe size, that she could never have a good relationship with him over the long haul.

In an argument, Andy could roll over her like a tank. He wouldn't do it to be mean, but because he had utter confidence in his own convictions. To a man like him, right was right and wrong was wrong, and there was no use in trying to get him to see any sort of middle ground.

Well, she'd lived with a man like that once. For almost twenty years she'd done her level best to be a good little corporate wife, and she wasn't about to put herself in the position of having to live by anyone else's standards again. Uh-*uh*. No way. Forget it.

She'd rather romp with a rattlesnake. Swim in raw sewage. Eat ground glass.

It wasn't that she wanted to do anything outrageous, not by her definition of the word. But her definition and Andy's were bound to be miles apart on any number of issues.

Dang it, she'd stuck by Charlie to the bitter end. Then she'd worked and sweated to finish four years of college in three. Now it was supposed to be *her* turn to do what *she* wanted. She'd come home to Pinedale to start a new life. On her own terms.

"And by God," she said, pounding the floor with her fist, "that's exactly what I'm gonna do."

Ginny sighed and closed her eyes for a moment. In the privacy of her tiny bathroom, her words sounded great—full of fire and determination. But what would happen when she told Andy she was pregnant? Oh, *damn*.

He was bound to be furious. Beyond that, she couldn't even begin to imagine how he would react. After the way he'd been avoiding her, *surely* he wouldn't want to get married. Please, God, no.

But on the other hand, he was a pretty straight-arrow kind of a guy. A hidebound, traditional, honorable kind of a guy who just might decide it was his duty to give his child his name. And if he got an idea like that into his brain, there'd be hell to pay getting it back out again.

"Well, maybe I just won't tell him," she whispered.

You'll never get away with that unless you leave Pinedale, a quiet voice inside her head said.

"But I just got home," Ginny wailed. "I don't want to move again, and I'm going to need all the help I can get. My family and friends will eventually come around."

Do you really want this baby, Ginny?

A warm, sweet glow ignited in her womb. She laid one hand over the zipper on her jeans, as if covering the tiny life inside her would somehow protect it. Oh, yes. She wanted this baby. At her age she might never have another chance to have one. Despite all her worries, fears and insecurities, she wanted this baby more fiercely than she'd ever wanted anything in her entire life.

Then face it, the voice insisted. *Andy can count months as well as anybody else in this burg. He'll be furious if you don't tell him.*

Ginny couldn't deny the logic in that. Well, maybe she could convince Andy that he wasn't the father. She could tell him there'd been someone else in her life before she moved back to Pinedale. Yeah. That might work.

What if the baby has red hair?

"Shut up, will ya?" Ginny grumbled at that nagging little voice.

Unfortunately she couldn't dismiss it. She came from a family of blondes. Over the past twenty years, Andy's hair had darkened to a rich, cinnamon shade like his father's, but it had been a bright, carroty color when he'd been a kid. The other kids had enjoyed teasing him about it and his freckles. Rats. She wished she'd paid more attention to the genetics lectures in the biology course she'd taken.

Lord, what a mess. Her eyes burned and her throat ached. Shuddering with the effort, she willed the threatening tears away. They wouldn't do her any good.

Intending to bounce it off the bathtub in a temper tantrum, she grabbed the box the pregnancy test had come in. She started to crumple the flimsy cardboard, then paused when a sentence at the very bottom caught her eye.

Wait a minute. The test could be wrong. The box said it was 99.6% accurate, but maybe she was getting ahead of herself. Other than a late period, she didn't have any symptoms. There was no sense in alarming Andy until she'd actually seen a doctor. Right? Right.

She struggled to her feet, rushed into the kitchen and finally located the phone book under the pile of laundry she hadn't taken the time to fold. Flipping to the yellow pages, she found the list of obstetricians in Jackson and started dialing. The earliest appointment she was able to get was on the third of November.

That was fine with Ginny. It would give her two weeks to get used to the idea of having a baby and think through all of her options. Surely she'd be able to come up with something. In the meanwhile, she would continue to substitute in the Pinedale schools and see if she couldn't develop some other sources of income. Just in case.

"Hi, Barb. How're ya doin'? Where's your boss?"

Sheriff Andy Johnson grimaced at the sound of that familiar voice coming from the vicinity of the dispatcher's desk. Hank Dawson had been his best friend for more years than Andy cared to remember, but he didn't have time to shoot the bull with his buddy tonight. He had a pretty good idea what Hank wanted, and he just plain wasn't in the mood. Not that it would do him any good.

Sure enough, without waiting for an invitation, Hank stepped into Andy's office, closed the door and plunked himself down in the straight chair across from the desk. "You still holed up in here hidin' from Ginny?"

"I'm on duty, Hank," Andy replied. "Halloween's always crazy."

"Oh, yeah? How many calls have you had?"

"None so far, but it's Friday night. I figure every teenager in town'll be out raisin' hell before long."

Hank laughed and shook his head. "I don't think so. Just about everybody in town's over at that haunted house Ginny helped the kids design. You seen it yet?"

"Nope."

"C'mon, Johnson. You can't miss it. You won't believe some of the stuff they've rigged up."

"Thanks, but I'll pass."

"Don't give me that. I know something happened between you and Ginny after Sam's birthday party, but it's not like you to hold a grudge for two months."

"I'm not holding a grudge."

"Then what the hell's wrong?"

"I just don't want to get involved with her. And I don't want to talk about her, Hank."

Hank nudged his Stetson back on his head, then propped the heels of his boots on the corner of Andy's desk. Lacing his fingers together over his belly, he studied Andy for a long, nerve-stretching moment.

"Well, that's tough, 'cause we *are* gonna talk about her. Dammit, Johnson, tell me what happened."

Andy rubbed the back of his neck and let out a snort of disgruntled laughter. "It's none of your damn business."

"Bull. You and Ginny are both practically part of the Dawson family. But all of a sudden, you're both avoidin' us, 'cause you're afraid the other one's gonna be visiting. I'm sick of it, Johnson, and so is Sam. Now start talkin'. What did that woman do to you?"

"She didn't do anything."

"Okay, then you must have done something. Takin' a wild guess, I'd have to say maybe you slept with her, and now you're afraid she'll expect some kind of a relationship. Is that it?"

"You're a nosy son of a buck, Dawson."

"Yeah, but I'm right, aren't I? And I can't help feelin' a little bit responsible since I goaded you into askin' her to dance in the first place. Tell you the truth, I was kinda surprised when you two hit it off so well."

Andy laughed. "So was I. I mean, she's older than me, and I thought she was the biggest flake in Wyoming. But I really got a kick out of her."

"Yeah, Ginny's quite a gal. I always thought Sam was an idiot to turn her into a pal, but go figure." Hank tipped his chair onto its hind legs. "What I wanna know is, how'd you ever wind up in the sack with her?"

"It just...happened," Andy said with a shrug that didn't even begin to convey how confused he still felt about the whole thing. "We were having a great time dancing, you know? And then all of a sudden, she got upset and ran out of the house. So I chased her all the way out to your old foreman's house to find out what was wrong. One thing just sorta led to another. That's *all* I'm gonna tell you."

"Oh, *I* get it now," Hank crowed, slapping his knee. "You caught her at a vulnerable moment and now you're feelin' guilty about it."

"Spare me the psychology, Dawson. Your wife does it better. For your information, I didn't seduce Ginny. She's a big girl, and she wanted it as much as I did."

"So why avoid her now? Wasn't she any good in bed?"

Remembering just how hot Ginny had been in bed, Andy felt his groin start to tingle. Thank God he had the desk in front of him or Hank would never let him hear the end of it. He shook his head, hoping the movement would erase the tantalizing images forming in his mind.

"No," he said gruffly. "That wasn't a problem, but any fool could see we're not right for each other, Hank. We're just too different."

"That's the wrong excuse to use with me," Hank said. "Look at Em and me, will ya? The preacher's daughter and he black sheep. Lots of folks think we're the mismatch of he century, but I've never been happier. Maybe you oughtta sk Ginny out. See where it might lead."

"No way."

"Look, Johnson, it's not like you've got much of a crop f fillies to choose from. You and Ginny had fun together. Vhere's the harm in taking her out a few times?"

"I'm not gonna start anything with a woman until I hear ack from the Drug Enforcement Administration."

Hank's feet hit the floor with a thud. "Don't tell me you vent ahead and applied for that job?"

"Damn right. It'd be a helluva lot more exciting than 'inedale and I'm ready for a change. Why shouldn't I?"

"Because this town needs you, that's why. And you're li- ble to get yourself killed."

"Oh, yeah?" Andy demanded, leaning forward with his lbows braced on the desk. "Well, the DEA boys seemed to hink I handled myself okay when I helped them before."

"Hey, I know they'd love to have you, but your roots go retty damn deep here. You're the last guy I ever thought 'ould leave."

"Then it's high time I did. My mind's made up, Hank. If hey offer me a job, I'm *gone.*"

"You're not doing this because of what happened with Ginny, are you?"

"Nah." Andy sighed and shook his head. "Well, not ompletely anyway. But you said it yourself, Hank. There ren't many single gals around here. If I'm not gonna have wife and kids, I might as well try something new."

"All right," Hank grumbled. "But at least talk to Ginny nd get things straightened out so you can be in the same oom without climbin' the walls, will ya?"

"I'll think about it."

Hank checked his watch, then pushed himself to his feet. "Think fast, bud. They'll be closin' up the haunted house

in another hour or so. Get your butt over there and do it tonight. Catch ya later.''

Andy waved his friend off and tried to get back into the
report he'd been working on before Hank had interrupted
him. Five minutes later he threw down his pen, shoved back
his chair and grabbed his coat and hat off the coat rack.
After telling his dispatcher, Barb Brinker, where she could
reach him, he hurried out to his patrol car.

He didn't know what he could say to fix the situation with
Ginny. Hell, he knew he'd handled the morning after with
about as much finesse as a boar hog in rut. He should have
at least called her on the phone and apologized or something. Let her know he still respected her.

Hank would have snickered until he choked if Andy had
told him the whole story about what had happened out at
the old foreman's house. The truth was, he did feel guilty.
Ginny *had* been vulnerable that night. And so had he.

They'd been surrounded by people they'd grown up with,
all of them married and raising families. He and Ginny had
had a great time dancing and laughing and carrying on like
everybody else. He'd been glad she was there so he didn't
have to dance with the other guys' wives for a change.

But there'd come a moment when someone had dimmed
the lights in the kitchen. Everyone had gathered there to
dance and to play all their old high school make-out songs
on the stereo. It was then that he'd suddenly realized just
how empty his life had been since Denise had walked out on
him.

He'd looked into Ginny's eyes and had seen the same
stark, aching loneliness that was gnawing at his gut. When
she'd bolted out the back door, he couldn't have left her to
suffer alone any more than he could have left an injured deer
to die in agony in the middle of the highway.

The truth was, memories of that night with Ginny had
haunted him for the past eight weeks. Making love with her
had touched him in a deep, indefinable way he'd never experienced before. He hadn't wanted to examine the feelings
she'd roused in him, so he'd taken the coward's way out and

given her a mighty wide berth ever since. But dammit all, he *did* want to see her again.

He found a parking spot three blocks away from the abandoned store the kids had taken over. Then he walked down the street, greeting folks who were on their way home. The funny thing was, he still didn't completely understand why he felt so drawn to Ginny.

Although he liked her long, straight, wheat-colored hair and her big, dark brown eyes, it wasn't like she was drop-dead gorgeous. She was more on the skinny side than slender, and her features were more striking than pretty. And, then, she was every bit as tall as he was, which was kinda unusual, since he stood only an inch shy of six feet.

It must have something to do with her personality and that old saying that opposites attract. While he'd always followed the rules and been quiet and reserved, Ginny had a reputation going back to high school for being the life of any party and a rebel to boot. The kids around town still talked about the pranks that woman had instigated, and they probably didn't know half the stuff she'd actually done.

Take the time she'd convinced a bunch of girls to sneak into the boys' locker room, for instance. They'd smeared petroleum jelly on the toilet seats and stolen all the toilet paper. Moose Jorgensen, the football team's biggest, meanest lineman, had been ready to kill Ginny for that one. Only Sam Dawson's intervention had saved her hide.

Chuckling at the memory, Andy stopped walking for a moment and looked up at the star-studded sky. Yeah, Ginny was quite a character, all right. She had a kind of childlike enthusiasm and curiosity he found fascinating. While he'd been with her, he'd felt younger, more connected to the folks he usually socialized with, less aware of the burden of responsibility his job loaded on him. He'd just plain felt . . . happier.

Yeah, he'd had a good time with Ginny, in bed and out. They'd come together in mutual need and shared some moments he'd never forget. But that had been one special night.

They didn't have enough in common to keep a relationship going in the long run, no matter what Hank said.

Still, Hank was right about one thing. Whether the DEA offered him a job or not, he'd still have to stay in Pinedale for another year to finish out his term of office. He couldn't go on avoiding Ginny for that long.

Eerie music, accompanied by rattling chains, blood-curdling screams and maniacal laughter, echoed on the air every time the old store's front door opened. Andy stepped inside, smiling when he heard startled shrieks coming from the back of the building.

After paying the five-dollar admission to a petite ghoul who had a bloody hatchet sticking out of the middle of her back, he followed a green fluorescent arrow painted on the floor through a black, filmy curtain. As he walked down a darkened hallway, the walls appeared to close in on him.

Hands grasped at his coat. He heard furtive rustling noises down around his feet. Something that felt like cobwebs brushed against his cheeks, making him shiver. Ginny was such a nut, he wouldn't put it past her to have rounded up a whole herd of spiders for this event.

He turned a corner. Dim lights allowed him to see a steaming cauldron and a tall, silent figure draped in black. Its head slowly came up, revealing a pasty complexion, deeply sunken eyes and a pair of pearly white fangs.

"Good evening, Sheriff Johnson," it said in a gravelly voice. "We've been waiting for you."

Recognizing the basketball team's starting center, Andy chuckled. "That's quite a getup, Billy."

"Knock it off, Sheriff," the boy said, his voice half an octave higher. "You're not supposed to recognize me."

"Sorry."

Billy grinned, pulled himself up to his full height and drew the cape open with his right hand. His voice dropped back to its original note. "Come in. Join the party."

For the next fifteen minutes Andy continued through the maze, confronting first a werewolf, then a skeleton and next a body reclining in a coffin. Lights flashed. Thunder rumbled. The eerie music grew louder.

The kids were having the time of their lives, and he cheerfully played along with them. Then a witch who looked an awful lot like one of the varsity cheerleaders blindfolded him and led him through a doorway.

"We must feed our guests." She cackled. "What would you like, Sheriff?"

Taking a firm grip on his wrist, she plunged his hand into something warm, wet and squishy. "Some nice, fat, juicy intestines?"

Andy jerked his hand back. The witch giggled. "You don't want that?" she asked. "How about an eyeball?"

She shoved his hand down, into what he hoped like hell was a bowl of peeled grapes.

"Or maybe some fresh meat, straight from our dungeon?"

Andy yelped at the cold, slimy thing under his fingers and pulled away from the witch. He heard thumps, bumps and more giggles while he yanked off the blindfold. Then he looked at the table and told himself that only Ginny would think of providing such grisly props.

He'd seen worse, of course. Shoot, he *knew* the bloody things in those dishes were parts of a cow or maybe a pig, and he hadn't even really touched them because his hands were clean. The cheerleader laughed and patted his back.

"It's a pity you're not hungry, Sheriff Johnson. Why, Igor gave his all for this party."

Shuddering, Andy moved on. After passing a row of pod people, he encountered a giant-screen TV that was flashing scenes from classic horror movies and more recent slasher films. The soundtrack set up a rhythm to the images, drawing him in for one instant, repelling him the next.

"High-tech Halloween," he muttered, shaking his head.

"Pretty good display, isn't it?" a deep voice said from behind him.

Andy started, glanced over his shoulder and found Sam Dawson grinning at him. Then he laughed and shook the hand Sam offered him. "I'll say. Whoever did this one is demented," he said, nodding at the television.

"Thanks. My stepson will love hearing that," Sam replied with a wry smile.

"Colin did this?"

"He's been workin' on it for weeks. The kid's a genius when it comes to computers and electronics. Dani's been threatening to lock him in the barn if he doesn't stop givin' us all nightmares with this stuff."

A teenage girl on the screen let out a terrified whimper. A hand clasped around a hunting knife advanced toward her. "I don't blame her," Andy said.

He followed Sam through a doorway and saw a well-lit area up ahead. A crew of costumed teenagers sold caramel apples, popcorn balls, cookies and soft drinks. Sam's wife, Dani, and her daughter, Kim, flanked a Frankenstein monster while the high school newspaper's photographer prepared to take their picture.

"You're just in time, Sam," Dani called. "Take off your hat and get in here with us."

Andy ambled over to watch, and found himself chuckling at the monster's clowning for the camera. The creature draped one arm around Sam's shoulders, the other around Dani's, as if he were just another member of the family. Then he leaned down, stuck his face beside Kim's and whispered something that made the little girl giggle. He held up two fingers behind Sam's head, making rabbit ears. When the photo session ended, the monster peeled off his mask, revealing a laughing, disheveled Ginny Bradford.

Andy's heart contracted at the sight of her. She looked utterly pleased with herself and the world around her, as if she were soaking up sunshine on a perfect spring day instead of standing in a drafty old store full of gruesome displays, wearing a man's suit that was so ugly, the local charities would have burned it. The kids behind the refreshment table whistled and applauded. Ginny gave them a bow and a grin.

"Show's over. Get back to work, you guys," she said.

Wiping the back of one hand across her forehead, she tossed the mask aside and turned back to the Dawsons. The whole group started walking in Andy's direction.

"Whew, that thing's hot," she said. "So, what did you think of our haunted house? Did you have fun?"

"It was wonderful, Ginny," Dani said with a laugh. "Gross, but wonderful."

"Yeah, it was great, Gin," Sam agreed. "Didn't you think so, Andy?"

Ginny whipped her head around and stared at him. Something close to fear flickered in her wide, surprised eyes. Her smile drooped. The color in her cheeks faded. "Oh, uh . . . hi, Andy. I didn't see you standing there."

Andy shoved his hands into his coat pockets and tried to smile at her. "I agree with Sam and Dani. About the haunted house, I mean. It's really amazing."

"Thanks."

An awkward silence fell over the group. Ginny's complexion paled even more. Feeling about as welcome as a cockroach at a dinner party, Andy opened his mouth to make an excuse and leave. He'd never get a second alone with Ginny in this crowd anyway. Before he could say a word, however, her eyes rolled back in their sockets, and she pitched forward, falling like a sack of rocks.

Dani and Kim gasped. Sam shouted Ginny's name. Andy managed to yank his hands out of his pockets and catch her before she hit the floor. Abandoning their posts, the teenagers gathered around, laughing and shoving each other for the best view of the action.

"Way to go, Mrs. B.," one of the boys said. "What're you gonna do for an encore?"

"Hey, Sloan," another boy yelled. "Get a picture!"

The photographer ran over. With Ginny's deadweight pulling him off balance, Andy swore when the camera's flash went off two feet from his face and nearly blinded him.

"She's out cold, you damn fools," he shouted, dropping to his knees. "Get back and let her have some air."

The kids obeyed immediately. An anxious hush filled the room. Ignoring everyone else, Andy turned Ginny onto her back and stretched her out on the floor. After loosening the top two buttons on her shirt, he stripped off his heavy coat, rolled it up and used it to elevate her feet.

To his relief, Ginny's color improved. Her eyelids fluttered, then opened a second later. She looked up at him, her dark eyes cloudy with confusion.

"What? What happened?"

"You fainted," Andy told her, his voice sounding more gruff than he'd intended.

"Well, that was silly," she said, trying to get up.

Andy pushed her back down. "Lie still, Ginny. Let your brain get some oxygen. Do you hurt anywhere?"

"No. I'm fine. Really."

"When was the last time you had anything to eat?"

"I don't know. Lunch, I guess. We've been busy here ever since school got out this afternoon."

Andy glanced up at Dani. "Would you get her a Coke and a cookie?"

"Of course. I'll be right back."

Sam squatted down on one heel, his forehead wrinkled with concern. "Maybe I should call Pete," he suggested, referring to his brother-in-law, who was a doctor.

"No way," Ginny protested. "Don't make a fuss, Sam. I'm okay."

"Well, maybe you are, but what about little you-know-who? You can't be too careful, Gin."

Pushing herself to a sitting position, Ginny darted a look at Andy, then sent Sam a glare that was hot enough to melt the fillings in his teeth. "Will you shut *up*, Dawson?"

Sam glanced at Andy, looked back at Ginny and shrugged. Her face flushed a deep, vivid red. An uneasy, suspicious tingle raced the length of Andy's spine.

"What are you talking about, Sam?" he asked.

"It's not my place to tell you," Sam muttered.

The tingle intensified. Mentally counting off the weeks since Sam's birthday party, Andy turned his attention back to Ginny. "Does this 'little you-know-who' have anything to do with me?"

Her gaze dropped to her lap. In a voice so low he could barely hear it, she said, "Maybe. Could we discuss this somewhere else? Please?"

Dani arrived with a cookie and a can of Coke. After giving Ginny a long, hard stare, Andy clamped his mouth shut and stood. Stunned by the possibility of what he thought she had just admitted, he pushed his way through the crowd of worried teenagers and walked over to study a huge papier-mâché spider dangling from the ceiling.

As the shock receded, anger surged in to take its place. Just what the hell did that woman think she was trying to pull? She'd said she couldn't get pregnant. Had she lied? Had all her talk about not wanting to get married again been a line of bull to lull him into a false sense of security so he'd have to marry her? Well, he had plans, dammit, and she wasn't gonna mess 'em up.

And why had she answered his question with a maybe? Maybe she was pregnant? Maybe he was the father? Didn't she *know?* Had she slept with somebody else?

Swearing under his breath, Andy smacked the spider and sent it spinning in a wild, erratic circle. That was exactly how he felt at the moment. Crazy. Confused. As if his life had suddenly started spinning out of control.

Chapter Two

Feeling incredibly foolish, Ginny climbed to her feet. She gave the applauding kids a distracted smile and shooed them back to their posts, then scanned the room for Andy. Her heart sank when she spotted him standing next to Simon, the big spider she'd had so much fun making.

Simon was bouncing and spinning on the end of his string. It didn't take a genius to figure out who had whacked him hard enough to turn him into an eight-legged break dancer. In fact, she was surprised the glare Andy was giving the poor critter didn't strip the paint off of him.

Andy's jaw was clenched so hard, the tendons in his neck stood out. A vein throbbed in the center of his forehead. His cheeks and ears were flushed, and if he curled his fists any tighter, his knuckles were going to shatter.

"See if I ever tell *you* anything again, Dawson," she muttered, giving Sam a dirty look.

"He was bound to find out sooner or later," Sam replied. He picked up Andy's coat and handed it to her.

"Well, he didn't have to find out like this. And since you blabbed your big mouth, you can stay and supervise the cleanup. I've got to go talk to him."

Sam nodded. "Yeah. Good luck, Gin."

Ginny sighed. Then she straightened her shoulders, gulped in a deep breath and slowly crossed the room. Andy turned and looked at her, his blue eyes as frosty as Charlie's used to get whenever she displeased him.

Her stomach knotted. Her mouth went dry. Her heart raced.

Nuts. She had thought she'd gotten over being intimidated by a man's anger, but the sick feeling of dread was awfully familiar. She despised being such a ninny. Charlie had never abused her physically. She knew Andy wouldn't do that, either. So why was she so damn scared of him? Well, she'd die before she'd let him see it. Andy accepted his coat from her and put it on.

"It's not far to my apartment," she said. "We can talk there."

"Fine. Where's your car?"

"I walked."

"I'll drive you, then. Meet me at the front door."

With that, Andy left. After taking one last loving glance at the room, Ginny made her way to the entrance, barely noticing the thanks and congratulations she received from a group of parents waiting for their kids. All too soon, a patrol car pulled up in front of the building.

She hurried outside, slid into the passenger seat and gave Andy directions. Neither spoke while he drove the five blocks to her apartment, the tension building between them like lava getting ready to blow the top off a volcano.

Ginny led the way into the building, bracing herself for the coming explosion. Andy slammed the door behind him and followed her into the small living room.

"Would you like some coffee?" she asked.

Scowling at her, he yanked off his Stetson and dropped it onto an end table. "I want answers, Ginny. *Now.*"

Ignoring the quaking in her knees, she faced him squarely. "I can hear fine, Andy. You don't need to yell."

"I'm not yelling, dammit. But I will be if you don't start talking. What the hell is going on?"

"If you'll sit down, I'll tell you."

Andy opened his mouth as if he would argue. Ginny straightened her spine, put her hands on her hips and glanced pointedly at the sofa. Muttering under his breath, he stomped across the carpet and plunked himself down at one end. Exhaling a silent sigh of relief, she sat in the big old rocker she'd found at a garage sale in Laramie.

"Okay, I'm sitting," he said. "Are you pregnant?"

"It's a good possibility."

"And I'm the father?"

"*If* I'm pregnant, yes, you are. There's no doubt about that, Andy."

He shot up off the sofa as if he'd been goosed with a hot poker. "Why the hell didn't you tell me?"

"Because I'm not sure I'm pregnant yet."

He scowled at her again. "You told *Sam.*"

She shrugged. "Sam's my best friend. I knew he'd listen without judging me or telling anyone, except maybe Dani. Nobody else knows."

"Dammit, you should have told me first. Or maybe you weren't planning to tell me at all?"

"Yes, I was. *If* there was anything to tell you."

"It's been two months. Seems like you oughtta be pretty damn sure by now."

"I have a doctor's appointment in Jackson next Monday. I'll know for sure then."

Andy sat down again, propped his elbows on his knees and rubbed the back of his neck with one hand. Ginny felt a flash of sympathy for him until he raised his head and studied her with a suspicious glint in his eyes.

"You told me you couldn't get pregnant."

She didn't really blame Andy for pointing that out, but his attitude stung her pride. For heaven's sake, did he think she wanted a husband so much, she'd go to these lengths to get one? Not hardly!

"I didn't think I could," she said, as calmly as possible under the circumstances.

"Would you mind explaining that?" he asked.

Hell, yes, she minded, especially when every syllable of his question dripped with impatience. Still, she supposed if anyone deserved to know, it was Andy.

"It's kind of a long story," she said.

"Then you'd better get started."

"Do you always interrogate suspects like this?" she asked. "Because if you do, I'm surprised they tell you anything at all, and—"

"Ginny!"

"All right, already." Ginny flipped her hair behind her shoulders to buy a little more time, then started talking. "I was in a car wreck when I was a junior in high school. I had some internal injuries, and the doctor told me there was a good chance I'd never be able to conceive."

"You call that a long story?"

"That's not all of it. If you'll stop interrupting—"

Andy held up one hand like a traffic cop. "Fine. I'll shut up. Just get on with it, will ya?"

"Okay. I married Charlie just before he and Sam went to Vietnam. We never used birth control, but I never got pregnant, so I figured the doctor must have been right. But the morning after you and I, um, spent the night out at the Circle D, I stopped in to tell Sam I was going back to town. He mentioned that he'd seen you leaving, and he was curious about what happened after I left the party."

"Yeah, I'll bet," Andy muttered. "He damn near bashed my face in when you ran out of the house like that. I don't know what he thought I'd done to you, but—"

"Look, Andy, I'm sorry about that. When Charlie died, Sam appointed himself as my protector. They were buddies during the war, you know?"

Andy nodded. "Yeah. So what does all this have to do with your not being able to get pregnant?"

"See, I, uh, told Sam what happened, and he said he hoped we'd had the brains to use protection. When I told him I couldn't get pregnant and why, he got this funny look on his face and said, 'Charlie never told you?'"

"For God's sake, cut to the chase. Told you *what?*"

"That Charlie had the mumps when he was thirteen. Sam said Charlie told him about it when they were in the army. And, that Charlie was worried that he was, well...shooting blanks was the way Sam put it."

Andy's mouth dropped open and he stared at her, his expression incredulous. "And your husband *never* mentioned that to you at all?"

"Nope. He always made it absolutely clear that it was my fault we couldn't have kids. I'm sorry, Andy, but I honestly didn't know, and—"

He cut her off with a disgruntled sigh. "Damn, what a mess."

"Hey, I don't expect you to marry me," she said, giving him a rueful smile.

His face blanched as if marrying her were the most hideous idea he'd ever had to contemplate. Then he leaned back against the sofa cushion and crossed one leg over the other. His gaze never straying from her face, he studied her for what seemed like an eternity.

"That's a pretty weird story," he finally said. "And it's mighty convenient. Really lets you off the hook."

"It's not a story," Ginny protested, jumping to her feet. "It's the truth. Why would I lie about it?"

"I don't know," he admitted. "But since you've already lied to me once—"

"I did *not!*"

Andy unfolded himself from the sofa and faced her toe to toe, the anger in his eyes hot enough to leave blisters. "When you didn't tell me the second you suspected you might be pregnant, you lied by omission. Dammit, Ginny, I had a right to know."

"I would have told you next week. You can ask Sam about Charlie if you don't believe me."

"I will. And you'd better not try to hide anything else from me, Bradford, or so help me, you'll regret it."

A shiver raced from her tailbone to the top of her neck at the quiet threat in his voice. Barely resisting the urge to back up a step, she lifted her chin.

"What difference does it make? It was my mistake. I'll take care of it."

Grabbing her shoulders, Andy gave her one hard shake. "What's that supposed to mean? You want an abortion?"

"No!" She batted his hands aside, then crossed her arms under her breasts, feeling sick that he thought so little of her. "I'm excited about being a mother. After all these years, I never thought I'd have the chance. But you're not going to be involved, so leave me alone."

"Who says I'm not gonna be involved?"

"I do. This is *my* baby," she said, thumping her sternum with one finger. "And I'll raise it myself."

"Hold on just a damn minute," he shouted. "That baby's as much mine as it is yours."

"Are you sure you believe me about that?" she asked, lowering her voice. "I mean, I was a pretty easy lay, Andy. Maybe you'd better wait until the baby's born so you can have a blood test done."

He reared back as if she'd slapped him. When he spoke again, his voice was low and utterly controlled. "I never thought of you as an easy lay, Ginny."

"Oh, right." She turned away so he wouldn't see her blinking back tears.

"No, I mean it. I know you were hurting that night—"

"It doesn't matter. You made it obvious you didn't want anything more to do with me. Let's leave it that way."

She heard him inhale a deep, ragged breath.

"Don't be stupid," he said. "Do you have insurance?"

"I canceled it before I found out my teaching job had fallen through."

"Then how are you planning to pay the doctor? And the hospital? Not to mention buying all the stuff a baby needs. You can't be making that much as a substitute."

"I'll manage."

"How? Have you got a savings account? Or have you already spent everything Charlie left you?"

Ginny considered her finances to be none of Andy's business. Still, she gritted her teeth to prevent herself from informing him that Charlie hadn't left her a nickel. His battle with cancer had taken care of that. If it hadn't been for Sam's generous loans, she'd still be working her way through college.

"I said, I'll manage," she said, glaring at him over her shoulder. "You're the one who's off the hook, Johnson. Just go away and leave me alone."

"I'm not going anywhere."

Suddenly feeling drained and exhausted, Ginny turned back around to face him. "Please, Andy. I'm tired and I don't want to fight with you anymore. I promise I'll take good care of the baby."

He glanced away from her and studied the living room. Certain she knew what he was thinking from the expression of distaste that crossed his face, Ginny winced inwardly. Oh, nuts, she thought, another Mr. Clean.

Frustrated to her toenails, she jerked her gaze away from Andy and surveyed the apartment. Books, magazines and dirty mugs littered the coffee table. Sock fuzzies and shreds of paper from an art project dotted the green carpet she hadn't vacuumed for three weeks. Two blouses that needed buttons sewn on were wadded up on the bookcase.

Through the open door of her bedroom, she could see her rumpled bed and four pair of shoes strewn across the floor. A glance at the kitchen revealed a sink piled high with dishes and a garbage can that desperately needed emptying. Sighing, she turned her attention back to Andy.

He stuck his thumbs in his pants pockets, then shook his head at her. "I'm not sure you're even capable of taking care of yourself."

"Look, I know it's a little messy, but—"

"A little messy? Hell, you'd better pray a health inspector doesn't decide to drop in."

How many times had she listened to remarks like that from Charlie? A hundred? A thousand? A hundred thousand?

"I've been busy all week with the haunted house. I'll clean it up tomorrow. Give me a break and go home, Andy."

"All right. I'll leave for now." He leaned down, picked up his hat and settled it on his head. "But I'm gonna drive you to Jackson on Monday."

"That's not necessary."

"I think it is. Whether you like it or not, I *am* gonna be involved in your pregnancy, Ginny. I want to know everything the doctor says, and I figure that's the only way I'll find out. What time is your appointment?"

Damn him, he wasn't going to relent. She could see it in his eyes. She rubbed her own grainy eyes with her fingertips. "Three o'clock."

"I'll be here around one-thirty, then." He turned and walked to her front door. Ginny accompanied him.

"Get one thing straight, Johnson. You're *not* coming into the examination room with me. I don't allow spectators at my pelvic exams."

His mouth quirked at one corner as if he wanted to smile. He must have resisted the urge, because his eyes narrowed to mere slits. "Fine. But I *will* talk to the doctor myself, so don't try to get sneaky. Remember, it's *my* baby, too."

Before she could reply, he was gone. Ginny collapsed into her rocker, pulled her heels up onto the seat and hugged her knees to her chest. She inhaled a shaky breath, then leaned back and set the chair in motion. The rhythmic creaks gradually soothed her nerves. Straightening her legs out in front of her, she laced her fingers together and rested them on her stomach.

"You've got a real dope for a mom, kid," she told the tiny life growing inside her. "When it comes to men, she has no judgment at all."

Resting her head against the back of the chair, she closed her eyes and gulped at the lump in her throat. Nuts. Of all the men in the world she could have had a fling with, why had she chosen Andy Johnson? He'd seemed like such a nice guy at Sam's party, but she should have known better than to let her emotions run away with her good sense.

Was she one of those pathetic women who were doomed to be attracted to men who were all wrong for them, over and over again? Why hadn't she seen that underneath Andy's nice-guy facade, there lurked a man who could be every bit as domineering and critical as Charlie had been? Or were all men really like that way down deep?

Ginny sighed, then opened her eyes and lifted her chin. She'd pretty much let Charlie have his own way because it had been easier to get along with him when she did. But she'd be damned if she'd let Andy push her around. It would be a mighty cold day in Hades before she gave any man the idea that he could tell her what to do.

Feeling a whole lot less confident than he'd tried to sound while he'd been talking to Ginny, Andy drove back to the office. Since Barb didn't have any problems to report, he decided to go home. Maybe if he had some peace and quiet, he could figure out what to do about Ginny.

When he pulled up in his driveway on the southern outskirts of town, he spotted his neighbor, Bill McNeil, taking his dog, Jake, for a walk. Andy detested Jake. The dog was ugly as hell, having some hound, some spaniel and God only knew what else in his background. Besides that, he thought Andy's yard was his personal outhouse.

Andy put up with Jake, however, because he enjoyed visiting with Bill, who was a retired railroader from Rock Springs. Though he had to be pushing eighty, Bill still mowed his own lawn and shoveled his own walks. Sometimes he even shoveled Andy's. He was a cheerful old soul, and Andy appreciated Bill's down-to-earth view of the world.

After stepping out of the car and locking it, Andy waved at Bill. "Isn't it a little late for you to be out?"

Bill's hearty chuckle carried across the yard. He approached Andy at a brisk clip. "Ol' Jake got all riled up by the trick-or-treaters ringin' the doorbell. I figured a little exercise'd settle him down. How's it goin'?"

"Not bad. Town's pretty quiet tonight."

"I'm glad to hear it." The old man tipped his head to one side and studied Andy's face for a moment. "You look kinda down in the mouth, though. Somethin' wrong?"

"Nah, nothing serious anyhow."

A knowing grin spread across Bill's face. "When a fella says that, I always figure he's got woman trouble."

Fighting back an answering grin, Andy shrugged. "You might say that."

Bill elbowed Andy in the ribs, coaxing a full-fledged smile out of him.

"Yeah, I knew it," Bill said. "I'll put Jake in the backyard and be right back so you can tell this old duffer all about it. Whaddaya say?"

Knowing he'd never hear the end of it otherwise, Andy agreed and went inside. With all of his years of experience, Bill just might have some valuable advice. Andy figured any man would need all the help he could get when it came to dealing with Ginny Bradford.

Bill let himself in through the back door and accepted a beer from Andy. They both sat down at the kitchen table. Then the old man cracked his knuckles and nodded at the Coke can Andy had fished out of the fridge for himself.

"Can't be too bad if she hasn't driven you to drink."

"I might get called out again tonight or believe me, I'd have a cold one with you," Andy said darkly. "Maybe three or four cold ones."

"Well, now, what's the problem?"

Sipping his beer and nodding occasionally in encouragement, Bill listened intently while Andy told him about Ginny. When Andy mentioned the baby, his eyes lighted up like a Las Vegas casino. He reached across the table and vigorously pumped Andy's hand.

"Congratulations, boy. You're gonna be a daddy!"

Bill's joy gave Andy a jolt. His heart started thumping and he knew the grin stretching across his face probably looked sappy as all get-out. Until this moment, it hadn't occurred to him that Ginny's pregnancy was something he could be happy about.

But now that he thought about it, he'd always wanted a son. Or a daughter. As long as the kid was healthy, it didn't matter which. He'd always thought he'd have a passel of kids by the time he was thirty. Now he was almost forty and he wasn't married or even dating anyone seriously. *Daddy.* The word made his throat and chest feel tight.

But why did it have to happen *now?* He liked his job okay, but he'd gotten a real taste of excitement when he'd worked that case with the DEA. He'd been flattered as hell when they'd sent him an application, and the thought of being something more than a small-town sheriff had started him dreaming in ways he hadn't dreamed for years.

Of course, the job was too dangerous for a guy with a family to worry about. He banged his pop can down, then smacked the table with his palm. Settling back in his chair, Bill studied Andy, his bushy white eyebrows drawn together in a frown.

"What's wrong? Don't you want to marry the girl?"

"*Marry* her?" Andy yelped. "Hell, no, I'm not gonna marry her."

Bill snorted. "In my day, if a gal was good enough to sleep with, she was good enough to marry."

Andy scraped back his chair and stood. Shoving his hands into his pockets, he paced to the window and back. "I didn't mean that, Bill. Ginny's a nice gal."

"What's wrong with her, then? Is she ugly?"

"Not so you'd notice," Andy replied, grinning in spite of his foul mood. "I'd say she's damned attractive."

"You're not makin' any sense. If she's nice and she's pretty, why don't you like her?"

"I *do* like her," Andy said, heading for the window again. "She's got plenty of spunk and she's a lot of fun."

"Was everything okay in bed?"

"You're gettin' awful damn nosy," Andy muttered, glaring at the old man. Jeez, he couldn't believe he was having this conversation twice in one night. He hadn't talked this much about his sex life since high school.

Bill chuckled. "Hey, if the sex part was lousy—"

"I didn't say that," Andy objected. "It was fine."

"Only *fine?*"

Feeling his neck and ears getting hot, Andy laughed. "All right, you old goat. It was fantastic. I couldn't think of much else for days afterward. Okay?"

"Now you've really got me confused. This gal sounds like prime wife material. Why don't you want to marry her?"

"She's a flake, Bill."

"You mean she's dumber than a fence post?"

"Nah. She's got a college degree. She's just not real down-to-earth, you know? She's an artist. Kind of a ditzy blond type."

"Oh, that's *terrible,*" Bill said, his eyes glinting with mirth.

"Knock it off," Andy said. He came back to the table and sat down again. "What I'm trying to say is that Ginny's not very practical and I'm not sure she's all that responsible in a lot of ways. She's a slob, too. God, you should've seen her apartment."

Bill laughed and glanced around the pristine kitchen. Andy's compulsive neatness had been a running joke between the two of them since the start of their friendship. "Now that could be a real problem. This place is so damn clean, it'd probably give her the willies."

"All right, go ahead and make fun of me," Andy grumbled. "But I'm serious, Bill. I've been married before, and I know Ginny and I would drive each other crazy in less than a week."

"What about the baby? Don't you want to be a part of his life?"

"Sure I do, but that doesn't mean I have to get married. We'll work out visitation rights and I'll give Ginny plenty of child support."

Bill snorted at that. "That's a cop-out, Andy, no pun intended. What kind of a life is that for a kid? Getting shuffled all over the place like a sack of spuds?"

"Plenty of kids have divorced parents and survive. It's not that big of a deal anymore."

"That doesn't make it right," Bill insisted. "What if Ginny marries some guy who doesn't like kids?"

"She wouldn't do that."

"How do you know? You won't have any say over how she lives. Hell, she could move to the other side of the country if she wanted and you'd never see your kid again."

"That won't happen, Bill."

"Hmmph! If Ginny's as flaky as you say she is, your kid just might need you. Have you thought about that?"

"I can make sure the kid's okay without marrying Ginny," Andy said. "Believe me, it just wouldn't work."

Bill polished off the rest of his beer, then pushed back his chair and climbed to his feet. Bracing both palms on the table, he leaned forward, his face more solemn than Andy had ever seen it before.

"You know what's wrong with too many kids today, Andy? Their parents are too damn spoiled and selfish to put their children's needs ahead of their own. You can justify what you're doin' all night, but that won't change one fact."

"What's that?" Andy asked.

"You owe that baby a helluva lot more than a child-support check once a month."

"I'll be there for him."

"Oh, yeah? When? On weekends? Every other holiday?" Bill jabbed his index finger in Andy's face. "Who's gonna give your kid the discipline he needs? A ditzy blond?"

"Ginny's not *that* ditzy," Andy protested. "She'll be a good mother."

"I don't doubt she'll try, but can she teach him how to bait a hook? Fix a car? Pound a nail in straight?"

"That's enough, Bill."

The old man sighed and shook his head. "It ain't even half of it, Andy. Every kid deserves to have a father and he sure as hell deserves to have his father's name. Your baby won't have either one unless you marry his mama."

With that, Bill stomped across the room and let himself out the back door. Andy walked into the living room, flopped into his favorite chair and propped his feet on the ottoman. God, he was tired, but he'd never be able to sleep with Bill's angry lecture still banging around in his head.

What had gotten into the old guy anyway? He was usually as even-tempered as a kid's saddle horse, but there for a few minutes, he'd looked mad enough to have a stroke. Well, he was a couple of generations older. He was bound to see things differently.

Besides, what did Bill know about modern relationships? As far as Andy knew, his neighbor had never been married or had any kids of his own. So where did he get off, telling him how to run his life?

But while he tried his best, Andy couldn't dismiss everything the old man had said. When his parents would find out about the baby, he knew damn well they'd feel the same way Bill did. And, Andy had been in law enforcement too long and had seen too many kids from broken homes get into trouble.

He'd seen kids from supposedly good, stable homes get into trouble, too. But statistically, a kid just plain had a better chance of turning out okay if he had both parents in there working with him. Hell.

Andy sighed and closed his eyes. What would his kid look like? Would he have the red hair and freckles that had plagued him when he was little? Would he call him Daddy?

"Daddy," he murmured, liking the sound of that so much he said it again a little louder. "Daddy."

After giving him a glimpse of a bald, squalling infant, his mind insisted on producing images of Ginny. In rapid succession, he saw her laughing, dancing, talking while her hands darted around every which way.

He recalled what she'd looked like with tears streaming
down her face in the moonlight when he'd finally caught up
with her at the old foreman's house, with her eyes all lonely
and sad and vulnerable, and tonight, with her eyes practically shooting sparks at him. Then he remembered how
she'd looked at him while they'd been making love.

Just thinking about the intense pleasure he'd experienced with her was enough to make him hard, but that
wasn't all he remembered about that night. Lord, he'd never
forget the awed, almost reverent wonder in her eyes when
he'd driven her to that first climax. She'd touched him way
down deep in some mighty private places. He'd never felt so
close, so connected to another human being in his life.

For that one short night, she'd filled up the holes in his
soul, and he wanted to share that connection with Ginny
again, baby or no baby.

But *marry* her? Live with her for the rest of his *life?* The
idea was enough to make him break out in hives.

Chapter Three

When the doorbell rang at nine o'clock the next morning, Ginny groaned and rolled onto her side. "Go away. Let me die in peace."

Although she'd already vomited twice, her stomach felt so queasy, she was going to have to make another run for the bathroom soon. If this was morning sickness, it was a wonder the human race hadn't become extinct centuries ago.

The doorbell rang again. Loudly. Insistently. As if whoever was out there didn't plan to leave. Ever.

Cursing under her breath, she pushed herself to a sitting position, then rose to her feet. Her head stopped spinning after a moment, but the doorbell went right on ringing. Telling herself it would serve whoever was out there right if she barfed all over him, Ginny cautiously made her way through the living room.

Then she opened the door. Sam Dawson stood on the other side, all six feet and four inches of him. He wore his usual jeans, boots and Stetson, along with a bulky jacket and a worried frown. Unfortunately she wasn't in any shape to chat with him or enjoy the sack of doughnuts he carried in his left hand. One whiff of that bakery-fresh aroma was all it took to make her bolt for the bathroom.

Sam followed hot on her heels, but she didn't have time to deal with him. She leaned over the toilet and heaved repeatedly, tears squirting out of her eyes from the force of her stomach's convulsions.

She thought she heard Sam murmur, "Good Lord, Ginny." Then he wrapped a strong arm around her back and brushed her hair out of her eyes with his other hand. When the spasms finally ended, he wiped her face with a cool, wet cloth, filled a glass with water so that she could rinse out her mouth and carried her into the bedroom.

"Thanks," she said as he tucked her under the covers.

He fluffed the extra pillow and stuffed it behind her head. "How long have you been sick?"

"Since I woke up. I've felt a little queasy every morning for the past week, but it's never been this bad before. I hope this kid is worth it."

"Aren't you taking that Reglan stuff Dani had for morning sickness? It worked great for her."

Ginny shook her head and instantly regretted it when her stomach lurched. "I haven't seen a doctor yet, remember? Besides, morning sickness only lasts a few weeks. I don't want to take any drugs that could hurt the baby."

"A few weeks?" Sam squawked. "Ginny, you're already skinny as a rail. You'll dry up and blow over to Utah if this goes on that long. I'm gonna call Pete."

Though she resented Sam's don't-give-me-any-argument tone, Ginny didn't try to stop him. For one thing, she didn't have the energy. For another, she suspected he might be right. He came back five minutes later, carrying a plate of saltines.

"Pete said you're supposed to just nibble on those. He's calling in a prescription that he swears won't hurt the kid. I'm gonna go pick it up. Need anything else?"

"No. Thank you."

The apartment seemed awfully empty after Sam left. She should have known the big lug would come into town and check on her after that scene at the haunted house last night. Ginny lay staring at the ceiling, grateful for his concern and wishing she could have fallen in love with him back when they were kids. Her life would have been so much simpler.

Oh, she'd dated him a time or two. The one time he'd tried to kiss her, however, they'd both started to giggle and that had been the end of that. There simply hadn't been and never would be any sexual chemistry between them, but they'd always been the best of friends.

She'd been delighted for Sam when he'd finally married Dani, but in a way, his marriage was responsible for the mess she now found herself in. The first time she'd seen the couple after their marriage had been the night of his birthday party. They'd looked so happy together, so content, so delighted with Dani's pregnancy, which had just started to show, Ginny had finally realized that her relationship with Sam was bound to change.

It wasn't that she'd wanted him for herself. It had been more a feeling that he'd found a new best friend, and she would inevitably be excluded from the most important parts of his life. Since then, she'd formed a close friendship with Dani, and no longer felt she had to worry about being left out. She was careful not to intrude on their marriage, but she was confident of her welcome at the Circle D.

That night back in September, however, she'd been in a world of hurt. Sam had been her rock during Charlie's illness and the three years since his death. The prospect of losing his support when she'd just found out she didn't have a job after all, had left her feeling scared, lonely and bereft, and she'd turned to Andy Johnson for comfort.

"Big mistake," she muttered, wincing at the memory of their argument in her apartment the previous night.

She'd tossed and turned for hours, wondering what she could have said that would have convinced Andy to trust her with the baby. Nuts. If only she'd told him in the beginning, they might have at least developed a friendship. But now... Vaguely hearing the front door open, she groaned and rolled onto her side again.

"You okay, Gin?" Sam called from the living room.

"Yeah."

He walked through her bedroom doorway a moment later, carrying a brown plastic bottle and a glass of water. "Here you go. As I remember, these things work pretty fast."

Ginny swallowed a pill, then flopped back against the pillows and grinned at Sam. "Does your wife know you walk into other women's bedrooms without bothering to knock?"

"She wouldn't worry about it if she did." Sam sat on the side of the bed, a self-satisfied smile on his face. "She keeps me too worn out to even look at other gals and she knows it."

"Smart lady."

"Yeah, she is." His smile slowly faded. "Well, I'm glad to see Andy didn't strangle you last night."

"There were a couple of moments when it was close," Ginny said with a rueful laugh. "You're not going to say I told you so, are you?"

"Not this time. So what happened?"

"Nothing much. He said I lied by omission when I didn't tell him about the baby right away. And he didn't believe me when I told him about Charlie and the mumps."

"I'll set him straight about that."

"I'd appreciate it, because now he's decided he can't trust me. He's planning to drive me to my doctor's appointment on Monday."

"I'm glad he's going with you," Sam said. "He's just as responsible for this as you are, Gin."

"He doesn't see it quite that way, Sam. I know he thinks I deliberately got pregnant to trap him into marriage. Isn't that the silliest thing you've ever heard?"

Sam studied her for a moment, then shook his head. "If you're pregnant, he damn well *better* marry you."

"I don't believe you said that," Ginny screeched, bolting upright to glare at him. "Read my lips, Dawson, I *don't* want to marry him. He's overbearing and sarcastic, and he thinks I'm lower than pond scum."

"Oh, come on, Ginny, give the guy a break. You gave Andy one hell of a shock last night. He had every right to be livid with you, but he'll calm down in a few days."

"Oh, *huh.*"

"Don't give me that," Sam scolded her. "Andy's a damn good man. You could do a heck of a lot worse."

"You're just saying that because he's one of your buddies. Dammit, Sam, you're supposed to be on *my* side."

"I *am* on your side. You're in a terrible position, here, Ginny, and I'll do everything I can to help you. But you're gonna need Andy's help, too. God knows your folks won't give you any support."

"They'll come around," Ginny said quietly.

"Like they did when you told them you wanted to leave Charlie? Let's see now, what was the line your mother used? Something about making your bed and lying in it?"

"Don't start with the sarcasm, Dawson."

"I'm just trying to get you to see reality, Ginny. I know you're an optimist, but it's damn rough being a single parent. Ask Dani about it sometime. And you'll never get a teaching job in this town if you're an unwed mother. Ask Hank and Emily about that."

"I can paint portraits. Everybody liked the one I did of Dani for your birthday present. Remember how many people wanted me to do one for them?"

"That might get you by for a while. But how many folks around here can really afford that? You've gotta get your feet on the ground, babe."

"I'll leave town. There *are* other school districts."

"Don't be dumb. You've wanted to come home for a long time."

"Not enough to marry Andy Johnson."

"You must have liked a few things about Andy or you wouldn't have slept with him," Sam said.

"It wouldn't matter if I did. The man hates me, Sam."

"No, he doesn't. He must have liked a few things about you, too, or he wouldn't have slept with you."

"Why don't you go home to your wife?"

Scowling at her, Sam got up and left the room, muttering something that sounded like, "Damn, stubborn, jugheaded female." Ginny called out to him. The only answer she received was the sound of her front door slamming.

After heaving her pillow at the wall in exasperation, she climbed out of bed and stomped into the bathroom for a shower. She wasn't a whole lot calmer when she finished, but her stomach had settled down and she realized she was hungry. She pulled on a pair of jeans and a sweatshirt and wandered out to the kitchen.

Well, at least Sam had left her the doughnuts. Fishing one out of the bag, she examined the room and reluctantly came to the conclusion that maybe it was time to clean up her act a little. She'd never been much of a housekeeper, mainly because she considered cleaning boring, repetitious and a royal waste of time.

Her attitude had driven Charlie berserk. She'd enjoyed not having to listen to his constant criticism so much during the past three years, she'd gone from mere messiness to total slobdom.

But this, she thought, glancing from countertops literally buried in clutter, to the art supplies covering the ironing board, to the three baskets of unfolded laundry, to the overflowing sink and the food-splattered stove, was a new low. Even for her. There was no telling what treasures she would find if she sorted out the whole apartment.

If she looked at it as an adventure, a quest of discovery, instead of a mind-numbing, disgusting job, it ought to keep her busy for the rest of the weekend. God knew she needed something to do to keep her mind off Andy and her trip to Jackson Hole with him on Monday.

By the time Monday afternoon finally arrived, Andy felt as impatient as a convict sweating out his last day in prison.

He wanted to know two things. Was Ginny pregnant? And if she was, what the hell were they gonna do about it?

Sam Dawson had called him on Saturday morning and confirmed Ginny's story about her husband's possible sterility. According to Sam, a man Andy liked and respected, Ginny was honest to a fault, and he'd hinted that Andy had damn well better be ready to do the right thing by her. In other words, marry the woman.

Andy was ready to admit that he was as responsible for Ginny's pregnancy as she was. He shouldn't have made love to her without protection; not having any with him at the time was no excuse. He was also willing to admit that maybe he'd judged Ginny a little too harshly on Friday night. He would even admit that he hadn't done a thing to encourage her to contact him.

But he just couldn't bring himself to forgive her for telling Sam, instead of him, that she might be pregnant. The big question in his mind was, *would* Ginny have told him about the baby if she hadn't passed out in front of him? Or would she have quietly left town and taken his baby with her? He'd never know for sure, but the thought of that happening was enough to keep his temper on simmer.

Still, he tried to be polite when he picked her up. He even told her how nice her apartment looked. She shrugged at his compliment, but didn't have much to say. She just followed him outside to his Blazer and fastened her seat belt, which was downright strange behavior for Ginny.

Well, fine, he thought, shifting into first gear. If she didn't want to be pleasant, neither did he. Her continued silence bugged the hell out of him. Then he glanced over and saw that she was sound asleep.

He remembered Sam laughing early in Dani's pregnancy, that she conked out at the least excuse as though she'd died. Ginny had just done the same thing. Add that to the nausea Sam had mentioned and her missed period, and it all added up. She was pregnant, all right.

Drumming his fingers on the steering wheel, he glanced at her again. There were dark circles under her eyes that hadn't been there on Friday. She must have worked for hours to get her apartment all slicked up, which probably wasn't good for a woman in her condition.

During the weekend, he hadn't been able to forget a single word Bill had said. He'd always seen himself as a guy who fulfilled his obligations, and his conscience had been giving him hell. But this situation wasn't as cut-and-dried as Bill had seemed to think it was.

If his divorce had taught him anything, it was that marriage was hard enough when the two people involved loved each other. When the love died, it was sheer torture. It sure hadn't taken Denise long to stop loving him.

Her list of complaints about his failures as a husband had been endless. He was never home. When he *was* home, he didn't talk enough. When he *did* talk to her, what he said was boring or, if it had to do with his job, too upsetting. He wasn't spontaneous enough. He wasn't any fun.

If Denise, who wasn't even half as lively and spunky as Ginny, had found living with him, "duller than dishwater," what would Ginny think, for God's sake? And even if *he* was willing to marry Ginny, would *she* be willing to marry him? Not likely. Thank God for small favors.

Of course, he *wasn't* willing to marry her. Despite the shortage of available women in the area, he'd had other opportunities to hook up with someone. He'd been interested in Becky Dawson before she'd married Pete Sinclair.

He'd been attracted to Dani and Emily too, before they'd married Sam and Hank. All of those gals were pretty, intelligent and fun, but he hadn't made a serious effort to court any of them. He hadn't been ready then, and he still wasn't. So why should he try to pretend that he was, just because Ginny was pregnant?

She awoke when they reached the Jackson city limits. Blinking rapidly, she sat up straight. Then she fished a piece of paper from her purse and gave Andy the address for the doctor's office. He parked in front of the small building with a fake log front designed to match the rest of the town's Old West architecture.

His heart contracted when he saw her inhale a deep breath, as if she were gathering courage to face an ordeal. He instinctively reached across the seat and touched her hand. She turned to him, both eyebrows raised in query.

"You don't have to go through this alone," he said. "Have the nurse call me in if you need a friend."

"I don't think you qualify, Andy," she said with a sad smile.

Then she climbed out of the Blazer and went inside. Muttering under his breath, Andy followed her. The young woman behind the reception desk handed Ginny a stack of forms to fill out. Women in a wide variety of shapes and sizes occupied all but two of the other chairs.

Andy stretched out his legs and tried not to stare at the red-haired woman seated across from him. Her abdomen jutted out from beneath her breasts, forming a handy shelf on which she'd propped a paperback novel. For her sake, he hoped she was close to delivery. He couldn't even imagine Ginny getting that big, although he supposed she might. They were both tall, and he'd weighed nine pounds at birth.

The redhead glanced up from her book. "Relax," she said, giving him a broad smile. "I'm having twins."

"Sorry," Andy replied, feeling a hot flush climb the back of his neck. "I, uh, didn't mean to be rude."

Chuckling, she patted her belly. "I'm used to it."

The woman went back to her reading, and Andy peeked over Ginny's shoulder. Damn. She was only halfway through the medical history, and he felt about as conspicuous as a black Angus bull surrounded by a herd of sheep.

He flipped through the stack of magazines on the end table beside him. *Redbook, American Baby, Working Mother. Ladies' Home Journal*, a year-old copy of *People*. He latched on to the issue of *People* and set the others aside. Nurses appeared periodically in a doorway to the left of the reception desk, calling patients to the examination rooms.

Ginny's turn finally came. Andy reminded her he wanted to talk with the doctor, then watched her walk away. He tried to get back into his magazine, but he really didn't give a rip about Madonna or Cher. The second hand on the wall clock behind the reception desk plodded around the dial as if it hated to give up even one blessed minute.

After twenty agonizing minutes of waiting, Andy tossed the magazine onto the table and drummed his fingertips on his chair's armrest. The woman across from him—a different one now, who wasn't nearly as friendly as the redhead with the twins—shot him a dirty look. He shoved his hands into his jeans pockets, crossed one leg over the other and jiggled his foot.

At thirty minutes, his imagination kicked into gear, tormenting him with pregnancy horror stories he'd heard over the years. Good Lord, was Ginny all right? What were they doing to her that took so much time?

When he was just about ready to get up and start pacing a trench in the carpet, the same nurse who had escorted Ginny came out to the waiting area and called his name.

"How's Ginny?" he asked, accompanying the nurse down the corridor.

"Pregnant," the petite brunette answered, giving him an impish grin. She opened a door on the left side of the hallway and ushered him into an office. "We need a complete family medical history from you while she's getting dressed. Have a seat and we'll get started."

Ginny entered the room five minutes later with a plump, gray-haired woman who wore a white coat. The older woman introduced herself as Dr. Washburn and shook Andy's hand. Then she walked behind her desk and settled into a high-backed swivel chair. Ginny sat in the armchair beside Andy's without giving him a glance. Man, she could really be a snot when she put her mind to it, Andy thought.

Dr. Washburn folded her hands together on top of the desk. "Everything about your pregnancy looks good so far, Ginny, but we're going to treat you as a high-risk patient."

Andy sat up straighter. "Why is that?"

"Primarily because of her age," the doctor replied. "I don't want to alarm you, but the chances of a number of complications increase when a pregnant woman is over thirty-five. It's important for Ginny to take extremely good care of herself for her own sake and the baby's."

"Can you be more specific about that?" Andy asked.

"It's basically a matter of common sense and not ignoring symptoms. I want her to get plenty of rest, moderate exercise and a nutritious diet." Dr. Washburn turned to Ginny, her expression stern. "I'll prescribe prenatal vitamins, but no more skipping meals. You're anemic and fifteen pounds underweight."

"All right, I'll try to eat more," Ginny said. "But what about my job? I can still substitute, can't I?"

Dr. Washburn leaned back and studied her patient with a thoughtful frown for a moment before slowly shaking her head. "If there's any alternative, I'd rather you didn't. If this was your second or third pregnancy, I might not worry about it. Now there's no reason you can't produce a healthy baby, but it's going to be harder on you physically than it would be on a younger woman."

"What do you mean?" Andy asked.

"She'll be more tired, have more aches and pains. We'll monitor her blood pressure and her blood sugar carefully. We want to eliminate every source of stress we can."

"But I love teaching," Ginny protested.

"Don't argue with the doc," Andy said, scowling at her. She shot him a mutinous glare, subsiding only when the doctor spoke again.

"It's a high-stress occupation. You'd be on your feet all day, dealing with excessive noise, exposed to every germ in town. I can't recommend it."

"I see," Ginny said, her voice so quiet, Andy could barely hear it.

"We'll work it out, Doc," he said. "I'll make sure she takes care of herself."

"I'll take care of my*self,* Andy," Ginny said with an angry huff. "Mind your own business."

"This baby's as much my business as it is yours," he retorted. "Get used to the idea."

Dr. Washburn glanced from Andy to Ginny and back to Andy again, her eyes narrowed in speculation. "Now, then," she said, after clearing her throat to gain their attention, "I want to have a test performed called chorionic villus sampling. Unfortunately the closest place we can have it done is in Salt Lake City."

"What's the test for?" Ginny asked.

"To check for genetic defects such as Down's syndrome. It's similar to amniocentesis, but it can be done earlier in the pregnancy and we'll get the results in a few days. I wouldn't suggest it if I didn't feel the information we'll get will be tremendously helpful."

The nurse opened the door and stuck her head inside the room. "Salt Lake can fit Ginny in tomorrow at one o'clock."

Dr. Washburn looked at Ginny. Ginny looked at her hands. "How much will it cost?"

Good Lord, what was the matter with the woman, Andy wondered. Cost wasn't an issue here. If the doctor said she needed to have a test, of course she would have it. And dammit, he didn't want the doctor worrying about whether or not *she* would get paid for her services, either.

Gritting his teeth, he silently counted to ten, then told the doctor, "I'll pay Ginny's medical expenses. Schedule the test and we'll fly down tomorrow."

"I didn't ask you to do that for me," Ginny said, her chin lifted to a proud, infinitely stubborn angle.

"I'm doing it for the baby," Andy snapped.

"Well, you don't have to come with me."

"We'll talk about it later, Ginny. Go ahead, Doc."

"Set it up, Betty," Dr. Washburn told the nurse. She then picked up a stack of pamphlets and handed them across the desk to Ginny. "Read these and call if you have questions. And I mean *any* questions or *any* concerns. If you can't reach me, call Dr. Sinclair in Pinedale. We've worked together several times and I have complete confidence in his abilities."

"Is there anything else I'm not supposed to do?" Ginny asked, warily eyeing the printed material.

"It's all in the literature," Dr. Washburn replied. "Just don't wear yourself out. When you feel tired, put your feet up and rest. Have your blood pressure checked at the Pinedale clinic once a week. I'll want to see you again in a month."

Ginny stood and shook the doctor's hand before leaving the office. Andy did the same, pausing when the older woman gave his hand an extra squeeze.

"May I speak with you for a moment, Mr. Johnson?" she asked quietly.

"Sure." At a gesture from the doctor, Andy shut the door and returned to his chair.

"I know this wasn't a planned pregnancy, Mr. Johnson. Do you want Ginny to have this baby?"

"I wouldn't be here if I didn't. What's wrong?"

"I'm concerned about your relationship with Ginny," she said. "Frankly, Mr. Johnson, the two of you don't appear to be getting along too well."

"We're not," Andy admitted, his tone suggesting that he didn't see what business it was of hers.

"That won't help either Ginny or the baby," she said.

"What's the bottom line, Doc? Are you trying to tell me I shouldn't go to Salt Lake with Ginny?"

Dr. Washburn shook her head. "Not necessarily, but I don't think you understand how much stress she's suffering. The CVS test will be difficult for her, and I don't want her to be unnecessarily upset."

"Hey, I don't try to upset her, you know."

"You don't have to try, Mr. Johnson. Understand what's happening to Ginny physically. Every hormonal system in her body is in an uproar, trying to adjust to the presence of the fetus. She would have every right to be extremely emotional under the best of circumstances. From what I've observed, Ginny's circumstances are far from ideal."

Andy frowned. "She's not in any danger, is she?"

"She could be if she doesn't take care of herself. My impression is that it won't be easy for her to slow down. She doesn't appear to be eager to accept anything from you."

"That's because she's so dang pigheaded."

"That may be true," Dr. Washburn said with a wry smile. "But if you can't offer her emotional support, I'm afraid I'll have to suggest that you allow her to go to Salt Lake City alone."

"She's not up to traveling by herself," Andy argued. "She looks like a strong wind'll knock her off her feet."

"I agree. And I'd hate to see her go alone because she'll have to stay in bed for twenty-four hours following the procedure. In her position, I would want someone to be there with me. But Ginny's not up to coping with hostility. If you can't get over your anger at her—"

"All right," Andy interrupted, his voice gruff with embarrassment that the doctor had thought it necessary to scold him. "I'll talk to her."

"Please, be as diplomatic as you possibly can."

"Yeah, I hear you, Doc. I'll do my best to take care of her, but it won't be easy."

Standing, Dr. Washburn smiled and extended her hand to him across the desk. "I suspect you're right about that, Mr. Johnson. Good luck."

Andy shook her hand and left the room. He found Ginny at the reception desk, already defying him by writing out a check for the doctor. He held back a sharp rebuke, shoved his hat onto his head and opened the street door for her. No, it wasn't gonna be easy to keep his temper with Ginny during the next couple of days. But he'd do it if he had to bite his tongue clean off.

Chapter Four

Wondering what was keeping Andy, Ginny looked over her shoulder and saw him coming out of Dr. Washburn's office, his expression dark as a thunderhead. Nuts. Now he would fuss at her for paying the bill.

Well, for all she cared, he could go ahead and make a big fat stink. She hated acting like such a shrew, but she was *not* going to let him push her around. Taking her sweet time, she finished signing her name on the check and handed it to the receptionist.

To her surprise, Andy simply frowned at her while she shoved the checkbook back into her purse. Then he walked over to the door and held it open for her. She stepped out into the chilly mountain air, pausing to catch her breath.

Though it was only four-thirty, the streetlights had already come on, and there was a definite threat of snow in the clouds overhead. Gazing off toward the west, she shivered, more with apprehension than with cold. There was something ominous about seeing the jagged peaks of the Tetons shrouded in mist and knowing that darkness was creeping down those massive slopes toward the town.

She felt small and insignificant. It seemed that her problems just kept stacking up and up, higher than those damn mountains. She didn't have the faintest idea where she would find the strength to start tackling all those problems, either. At the moment, getting to the car under her own steam looked downright daunting.

"Come on, you look dead on your feet," Andy said. "Let's get a motel room so you can rest."

Though his suggestion sounded wonderful, Ginny squared her shoulders and briskly walked beside him. She couldn't let him see how exhausted she felt, or anything else he might interpret as a weakness. His eyes searched hers for a moment when he helped her into the Blazer.

Too numb with anxiety and fatigue to even try to figure out what he'd been looking for, she collapsed against the seat and fastened her seat belt. He drove straight to the Snow King, a huge, chalet-style resort at the base of a mountain on the southeast side of town.

"That's a little expensive, isn't it?" she asked.

Andy waved her objection aside, and in ten minutes, she found herself installed in a spacious room on the third floor with two queen-size beds and a panoramic view of Jackson. He checked out the heater and the television, then headed toward the door.

"I'll be back in a couple of hours. After I get the plane tickets, I'll pick up a few things we'll need for the trip. What do you want besides a toothbrush?"

Ginny eyed the beds for a moment before realizing he intended to share the room with her. "How about my own room?" she asked.

He rolled his eyes in exasperation. "Relax, Bradford. I'm not planning to jump your bones. Shoot, we've already seen each other naked, so it's a little late for modesty."

Ginny couldn't come up with an argument that wouldn't make her sound like an idiot, but she still didn't like it. She glared at him for a moment, then shook her head and walked into the bathroom.

Andy was gone when she went back to the bedroom. Heaving a sigh of relief, she took Dr. Washburn's pamphlets, kicked off her shoes and curled up on the bed closest to the windows. She read until her eyelids started to droop. Flipping the bedspread over her legs, she snuggled into the pillows, but her brain wouldn't shut down.

How on earth was she going to survive being in such close contact with Andy over the next twenty-four hours? She was sick of his anger, sick of his impatience, sick of him! Other than the night of Sam's party, she couldn't remember the last time she'd cried more than a sentimental tear or two at a sad movie. But if Andy didn't back off or at least lighten up, she was afraid she would humiliate herself by dissolving into a puddle of tears.

At the moment, she couldn't believe she'd ever turned to him for solace. Or that he'd actually had it in him to provide it. But he *had,* dammit. What had happened to that nice guy who'd been so sweet to her?

But then, what did she know about Andy? She'd never really known him as an adult. If she'd thought of him at all, she'd remembered him as Sam's little brother's sidekick—a short, serious, red-haired kid who tagged along on Hank's escapades. But he sure hadn't come across as a kid at the party. Uh-*uh.*

He'd grown tall enough to look her in the eye without tilting his head back. His chest, arms and shoulders had filled out to impressive proportions, he'd developed one heck of a sexy smile and he'd carried himself with a quiet confidence that bordered on arrogance. And could he ever dance! Her attraction to him had been instantaneous.

When he wasn't glaring or yelling at her, the attraction hadn't diminished much. Not on her part, anyway, and that was why she felt so uncomfortable about sharing this room with him. Of course she was being silly. Andy certainly hadn't tried to hit on her. In fact, when he looked at her, she had the distinct impression that what he'd really like to do was throttle her.

Heaving a disgruntled sigh, she walked over to the windows and opened the drapes. Arms wrapped around her midriff, she gazed out at the lights of Jackson. The hollow, aching loneliness in the center of her chest was an old, familiar companion. She'd certainly felt it often enough during her marriage.

After Charlie had died and she'd started college, she'd been too busy to pay much attention to it. But it had always been there, waiting like an ugly little gremlin, ready to pop out and attack when she was least able to fight it off. Like the night of Sam's birthday party. Like now, when she was so worried about the baby. When managing on her own seemed impossible.

The enormity of the challenges this pregnancy would bring to her life were starting to sink in. A weak, craven part of her wanted to throw herself into Andy's arms and beg for the comfort he'd given her once before. But she couldn't do that when he so obviously disliked her.

Perhaps that was just as well. While she needed his financial support, she couldn't afford to start depending on him. Oh, he might help her get through the next seven months out of a sense of responsibility. He might even hang around for a while after the baby was born. But ultimately, she would be responsible for raising this child.

So what if she was scared? It wasn't the first time, and she'd always come out all right. She'd manage somehow because she had to—for the baby's sake as well as her own. She needed to develop her own strength and resources, and learn to stand on her own two feet.

Andy gathered up the packages he'd collected over the past two hours, locked the Blazer and ambled toward the lodge. During his shopping trip, he'd thought about his promise to the doctor. He knew he'd have to talk to Ginny tonight and try to clear the air between them, but he wasn't looking forward to it.

He figured he'd ticked her off so many times today, she wouldn't make it easy for him. Well, maybe some of the stuff he'd bought would sweeten her disposition a little. He quietly entered their room in case Ginny was sleeping, but found her sitting cross-legged on the bed on the far side of the room, watching the evening news.

She greeted him with a polite smile, then looked back at the television. He dumped the shopping bags on the bed closest to him, hung up his coat and stuck his Stetson on the shelf above the clothing rack.

"We've got reservations on a Delta flight," he said, smoothing down his hair. "It leaves here at twenty after nine and gets into Salt Lake about an hour later."

Ginny pursed her lips and studied him for a moment. Then she climbed off the bed and approached him, her arms folded across her chest. Oh, brother.

"I don't want you to come to Salt Lake with me, Andy."

"It's too late. I already bought my plane ticket."

"Then cash it in. There's no need for you to lose any more work time."

"Maybe not. But that's not really the issue, is it?" He stared at her, using the look that had intimidated more than one rough character.

She returned his gaze without any apparent discomfort. Man, she looked as if she could take on a grizzly, he thought with an inward smile. The woman had plenty of grit, he'd give her that much. And yet, there was a softness about her that made him want to hug her.

"No, it's not," she said. "I know you're angry, and I don't entirely blame you for it, but I can't cope with that right now. I've got more important things to worry about."

"I agree," Andy said quietly. "So stop wasting your energy trying to get rid of me and save it for tomorrow."

Her eyebrows swooped down into a scowling V and she propped her hands on her hips. "But, Andy, Dr. Washburn said I wasn't supposed to have a lot of stress, and—"

"Listen for a minute, will ya?" he said, cutting her off before she could build up a head of steam. He waited until she gave him a curt nod.

"I know this hasn't been easy for you." He shoved his hands into his jeans pockets while he groped for the right words. "It hasn't been easy for me, either. But I'll do my best to get over being mad if you will."

"Do you believe that I didn't get pregnant on purpose?"

"Yeah, Sam told me."

"I'm glad about that, Andy, but there's still no need for you to go to Salt Lake. I'm a big girl."

"I know that. But this sounds like a pretty rough test you're gonna have tomorrow. I'm coming along whether you want me to or not."

She clamped her jaws together for a moment, as if she wanted to grind her teeth to powder. Then she spoke her next words slowly and distinctly, as if she were struggling with her temper. "I hate it when you say that, Andy."

"When I say what?"

"That, 'whether you want me to or not,' stuff, like you're laying down the law. You don't have a right to boss me around."

Was she sensitive or *what?* Must be all those hormones the doctor had told him about. "I never thought I did."

"Hah!" She flung both hands up in the air. "You should listen to yourself sometime, Johnson. You make General Patton sound like a piker."

"Gimme a break, Bradford," he protested with a laugh. "I'm not *that* bad, am I?"

"Don't bet your badge on it."

"Okay, okay. I'll hold it down. But I think you're tough enough to handle me if you put your mind to it."

"You'd better believe it."

"Good. Then you won't mind when I come to Salt Lake with you tomorrow. Will you?"

She grinned at that. Just a little. "You're impossible. Dang it, Andy, we don't get along worth spit and fighting with you wears me out."

"So, we'll call a truce 'til after we get home."

"Well . . ."

She was weakening; he could see it in her eyes. "I'll be there to bring you stuff. Think how much fun you'll have ordering me around for a change."

Ginny laughed outright, as if the thought of anybody ordering him around tickled her no end. Andy suddenly found himself remembering how appealing her laughter had been the night of Sam's party. It had a rich, musical quality to it that warmed him from the inside out.

Giving in to an impulse, he reached out and tucked a strand of her long blond hair behind her ear. She went absolutely still for a moment, her gaze darting to meet his. Oh, man, there it was. The sweet, aching yearning in those big brown eyes of hers that had reached down into his heart and yanked on the strings.

He fought an urge to gulp, then a stronger urge to kiss the daylights out of her. Maybe sharing a room hadn't been such a good idea after all. Clearing his throat, he dropped his hand to his side and stepped back, accidentally knocking one of the paper sacks off the bed.

Ginny started at the crackling sound it made. Then she shook her head as if to clear it and focused her attention on the rest of the packages. "What's all that?"

"Some clothes and stuff." He picked up the biggest sack and handed it to her. "I had to guess at your size. Go on, take a look."

She shot him a wary glance before opening the bag and pulling out the purple ski sweater he'd chosen for her.

"Do you like it?" he asked. "The dress you wore to Sam's party is about the same color, isn't it?"

"Yes. It's gorgeous, but you shouldn't have—"

He waved her protest aside and handed her a smaller bag. "There's a T-shirt in this one. I thought you could use it for a nightshirt."

Ginny grabbed his arm and squeezed it. "Andy!"

"What?"

"It was thoughtful of you to buy all of this, but—"

"No 'buts,' Bradford," he said. "I was just being practical. The store owner gave me her phone number so we can get in early and exchange anything you don't like."

She raised her chin in that proud, stubborn way that always pushed his patience to the limit. "That's not the point. I can't accept any of this."

Why he'd expected her to appreciate his efforts, Andy didn't know. Cripes, did she have to make everything so damn difficult? Fight him over every little thing?

"Look, we're both going to need clean clothes tomorrow," he said, hanging on to his patience by a thread. "I got myself some, too. You're not under any obligation if you accept a sweater and a T-shirt, for God's sake. Now do you like them or not?"

Scowling at him, she muttered a few words under her breath. Andy figured they had something to do with denigrating either his parentage or his intelligence, but he bit back a retort.

"I like 'em fine," she grumbled.

"Well, good. There's a turtleneck and some slacks and underwear in there somewhere, too," he said, indicating the remaining sacks. He handed her another bag. "Your vitamins, toothbrush and deodorant are in that one. I can go out again if you need makeup."

"That won't be necessary. And I want you to keep track of every cent you spend. I'll pay you back when I can."

Her voice was frostier than the snowflakes pelting down outside. Andy rubbed the back of his neck. Then he looked at her again and saw that she was practically swaying with fatigue. She was probably hungry too. Inclining his head toward the bathroom door, he forced a more congenial tone into his voice.

"Fine. I don't know about you, but I'm starving. Why don't you go take a hot bath and relax? I'll order a couple of steaks from room service."

"All right." She hesitated for a second, then picked up the sack with the T-shirt, headed for the bathroom and paused in the doorway. "Thanks for the clothes, Andy. I didn't mean to sound ungrateful."

He shrugged. "No problem. Like I said, I'm just trying to be practical."

She closed the door. A moment later, he heard water gushing from the tap. After phoning in their dinner order, he called his office and told Barb not to expect him for a couple of days. He straightened up the room, throwing away the empty sacks and price tags and packing the things they wouldn't be using until morning into the black nylon tote bag he'd bought.

Then he plunked himself down in a chair, pulled off his boots and propped his feet on the end of Ginny's bed. Man, what a day, he thought. But it would soon be over. They'd eat, watch a little television and turn in early. Surely they could manage that much without another argument. The bathroom door opened a crack.

"Andy?" Ginny called. "My purse is on the desk. Would you mind bringing it to me?"

He found her shoulder bag and carried it across the room. She opened the door a little wider to take it from him, giving him a peek at a slender bare arm and equally bare shoulders. She held a white towel in front of her breasts and torso, but he caught a glimpse of her long, elegant legs.

"Thanks," she said. "I need to take some medicine Pete Sinclair gave me for nausea or I won't be able to eat."

Andy stood there for a long moment after she closed the door again, his heart banging against his rib cage and his groin heating up. He gulped when he heard the towel hit the floor inside with a soft plop. The next sounds were even more tantalizing. He had no trouble imagining Ginny sliding into the bathtub and leaning back with a sigh of pleasure.

Forcing himself to move, he paced the length of the room and back, silently calling himself a pervert. For God's sake, the woman was pregnant. She was tired, hungry and cranky. She was taking medication for nausea. The last thing in the world she would be interested in was sex.

He sucked in a deep breath, then let it out on a ragged sigh. He heard a little splash and immediately pictured Ginny in that damn tub, all wet and naked and beautiful. It didn't help much that two inviting beds stretched to the walls on either side of him.

"Get a grip," he muttered to himself, turning up the volume on the TV as he stomped back to his chair.

A woman who irritated him as much and as often as Ginny, shouldn't be able to turn him on without even trying. The two of them were about as compatible as a mouse and a hawk. Besides, he'd grown beyond casual encounters with women years ago—at least he had until that night with Ginny.

But that encounter hadn't *felt* casual to him at the time. It still didn't. Whenever he thought about it, his heart turned over, leaving him with an empty, aching sensation he didn't know what to make of. It was as if he'd held something precious for a second and then lost it.

Hell, now he was getting sappy. Or just plain crazy. Sleeping with Ginny again would be the dumbest move he could possibly make. He was already involved up to his neck with her because of the baby. Adding sex to their relationship would complicate it even more.

Well, he wasn't going to do it. He had plans that didn't include her or any other woman. He was gonna keep his hands to himself and his pants zipped, and maintain a sane physical and emotional distance from the woman.

A waiter arrived at that moment. Grateful for the distraction, Andy signed the check and tipped him. Ginny came out of the bathroom a few minutes later, looking refreshed and smelling like a bouquet of wildflowers.

Andy took one look at the T-shirt he'd bought her and knew he'd made a mistake. The shirt was baggy and had a picture of a mangy-looking bear on skis printed across the front, and it came down to within two inches of her knees. It shouldn't have looked sexy at all. But on Ginny it did.

The soft cloth draped around her body, hinting at the gentle curves it concealed, curves he remembered in graphic detail. Damn. Turning away, he unloaded the room service tray and sat at the table.

"That smells wonderful," Ginny said, sitting across from him.

He nodded in response and cut into his steak. She shot him a smile, then began to eat without any further attempts at conversation, which was a great blessing as far as Andy was concerned. After dinner, he stayed as far from Ginny as possible, occupying himself by reading the doctor's pamphlets while she watched a couple of sitcoms on the TV. At nine o'clock she crawled into her bed, said good-night and turned onto her side facing away from him.

Silently congratulating himself on his good sense and self-discipline, Andy turned off the lights, stripped down to his shorts and climbed into his own bed. At first he was so aware of the desirable woman lying only five feet away, every muscle in his body tensed. He forced himself to take slow, even breaths, however, and slowly began to relax.

He was just on the verge of sleep when he heard a muffled noise coming from the direction of Ginny's bed. Oh, cripes. She wasn't going to snore, was she? It would be just his luck...

There it was again, but it wasn't a snore. It sounded more like a sob.

Raising up on one elbow, he peered into the darkness. All he could see was the outline of a white pillowcase and a big bump under the blankets below it. Holding his breath, he listened intently until he heard the noise a third time and saw the bump give a little jerk.

Damn. He'd always been a sucker for tears. He lay back down, desperately trying to ignore her. But the sobs and jerks came faster, accompanied by an occasional sniffle. Each one assaulted his eardrums, ripped at his nerves, shredded more of his determination to keep his distance.

Gritting his teeth, he forced himself to stay put. Hearing her weep was killing him, but he couldn't let her get to him any more than she already had. Comforting Ginny was how he'd gotten into this mess in the first place.

He concentrated on the digital clock on the nightstand, hoping she would get it out of her system. A minute passed. Then a second and a third, but she didn't stop.

He sat up when he couldn't stand another second, swung his legs over the side of the bed and switched on the lamp. Oh, *jeez.* She was curled up in a fetal position, holding a pillow against her face to smother the sound of her sobbing. He hadn't been so mean to her she had to do *that.* Had he?

"What the hell's wrong?" he asked.

Ginny's whole body froze for an instant. She slowly lowered the pillow and looked over her shoulder at him. Then she turned away from him again and said in a voice thick with tears,

"Nothing."

"Right. You're just bawling your head off over there for the fun of it."

"I'm sorry," she muttered. "Go back to sleep."

"I would if I thought you'd be quiet."

He studied her rigid back for a moment, then raked both hands through his hair in frustration. If she kept this up, he'd be bald as Telly Savalas before morning.

"Come on, Ginny," he coaxed, deliberately softening his tone. "Turn over and let's talk about whatever it is that's bothering you, so we can both get some sleep."

"Leave me alone."

So much for the nice-guy approach. "You've got two options, Bradford. Roll over and talk to me or I'll come and get in bed with you. We won't get any sleep, but I'll guarantee you won't be crying, either."

She wiped her eyes with the backs of her hands before turning toward him. "Don't flatter yourself, Johnson."

"We'll talk about that one some other time," he promised her. "What's on your mind? The test tomorrow?"

Propping her head up on her palm, Ginny nodded with obvious reluctance. "I'm . . . scared."

"Of what? You're afraid it'll hurt?"

"No. I mean, I'm not afraid for me, really. But I'm scared to death for the baby."

"The pamphlet I read said it's pretty safe."

"There's a small chance it could cause a miscarriage, but that's not really what I'm afraid of." She sniffled, then shook her head, as if to deny the thoughts inside it. "But what if they *do* find some kind of genetic defect, Andy? What if they tell me I should have an abortion? I don't want to do that."

Andy's heart skipped a beat. "Wait a minute. I didn't hear Dr. Washburn say anything about an abortion."

"She didn't have to. But don't you see? She wanted me to have CVS instead of amniocentesis because they can find out if there's anything wrong with the baby before the end of the first trimester. That's when an abortion is safest for the mother."

"Nobody's gonna force you into anything, Gin," he said quietly. "We don't have to have this test done at all."

"Yes, we do," she argued, sitting up and hugging her knees to her chest. "They can fix some problems before the baby's born. You know, with microsurgery? What if the baby has something like that? If I don't have the test, we won't know until it's too late."

"Good Lord," Andy muttered. He drummed his fingers on his knee while he considered the problem.

Ginny heaved a sigh that sounded as if it had come up from the depths of her soul. "I want to make an informed decision, and I've been thinking about it and thinking about it, but I still don't know what to do."

He gave her a reassuring smile. "You're borrowing trouble, Ginny. The best thing we can do is assume the baby's fine and deal with the results when we get them."

"I guess there's not much else we *can* do, is there?"

"Nope." He lifted his legs back onto the bed and pulled up the blankets. After switching off the lamp, he turned onto his side facing her. "Whatever decision you have to make, I'll be there to support you."

"Thanks, Andy," she said after a moment, her voice wobbling at the end.

"Go to sleep, Gin. You need some rest and it'll be morning before you know it."

He rolled onto his back and stared at the ceiling, listening to the rustling of covers from the other bed as Ginny settled into sleep. Thinking back over everything she'd had to contend with today... well, he felt like a jerk for having been so rough on her. God, he hadn't even had enough sense to realize they could be in danger of losing the baby.

And what about the baby? Anxiety for the little guy rose up inside him, making his throat and chest hurt. The kid still didn't quite seem real to him, somehow, but the prospect of having to make a choice about whether he lived or died was enough to make him sick to his stomach.

Shoot, no wonder Ginny had been so freaked out and crabby. And no wonder the doctor had lectured him about his attitude. The situation was a lot more complicated than he'd thought. He'd have to do better by Ginny tomorrow, that was for damn sure. He turned his head toward her again and listened for a moment, but he didn't hear anything. Was she sleeping over there? Or crying into her pillow again?

Needing to know for sure, Andy got up and stepped across the narrow aisle between the beds. A faint shaft of moonlight streamed through a crack in the closed drapes, allowing him to see her face. Oh, yeah, she was down for the count. She looked exhausted and vulnerable, and a fierce surge of protectiveness rushed through him.

He pulled her covers up and tucked them securely around her neck and shoulders. Then he climbed back into his own bed and spent the next hour reminding himself that he was going to work for the DEA, and telling himself all the reasons he and Ginny were totally wrong for each other.

Chapter Five

When the Blazer entered the Pinedale city limits late on Wednesday afternoon, Ginny exhaled a sigh of relief.

"We'll be there in a few minutes, Gin," Andy said, turning his head to smile at her.

Resisting the urge to roll her eyes toward heaven, she gave him a quick grin, then looked out her window. For the past two days Andy had been amazingly supportive. There hadn't been a cross word spoken between them since they'd left for Salt Lake, and she didn't quite know what to make of the change in his attitude toward her.

He'd stayed with her during the CVS test, though he'd turned green around the gills at the sight of the needle. When the doctor had insisted, over her protests, that she stay in Salt Lake overnight, Andy had rented a motel room near the hospital with a minimum of hassle. He'd brought her meals and played poker with her, making the hours of forced bed rest bearable, if not downright pleasant.

Much as she'd appreciated his efforts, however, his unrelenting solicitude was starting to grate on her nerves. For one thing, she was pregnant, not an invalid. For another, she couldn't help wondering how long this latest nice-guy phase would last.

Oh, she didn't doubt the sincerity of his concern for her and the baby. After spending so much time with him, she could see why the people of Sublette County had elected him to be their sheriff. He had an inner strength and integrity that inspired trust and respect, and she couldn't deny that he'd come through for her when she'd needed a friend.

But now they were home again. She didn't have the faintest idea how he really felt about her, or what part he would expect to play in her life when the test results came back. Would he disappear again or stay in touch for the baby's sake? Could she hope to get along with him if he did? She had too many questions for which she had no answers, and she desperately wanted some time alone.

Andy pulled into the parking lot of her apartment house a moment later. She unfastened her seat belt and climbed out of the vehicle before he could turn off the ignition. If he tried one more time to take her arm as if she were a tottering granny, she was afraid she might deck him.

Frowning with disapproval, he reached into the back seat for the tote bag, then followed her up the steps to her front door. She had it unlocked and her coat tossed over a chair by the time he entered the living room.

"It's great to be home, isn't it?" she said, wondering how soon she could get him to leave.

"Yeah, it is." He set the tote bag on the coffee table, methodically took out everything that belonged to her and arranged the clothes and toiletries into neat stacks. "Tell me where you want this stuff and I'll put it away."

"Just leave it there. I'll take care of it later."

He gave her a knowing grin. "C'mon, Bradford, it won't take a minute and then you won't have to look at a mess."

Ginny gathered up the toiletries and hauled them into the bathroom. "You're a worse nag than my mother, Johnson," she called through the open door. "Just throw the clothes on my bed. They all need to be washed anyway."

When she returned to the living room, Andy had done as she'd asked and was zipping up the bag. Good, she thought, maybe he would leave now.

"Thanks for everything, Andy. I appreciate all your help. I'll call you as soon as I hear from Dr. Washburn."

"You wouldn't be trying to get rid of me, now would you, Ginny?" he asked, propping his hands on his hips.

"Well, I thought you probably have a lot to do. You know, check in at the office and that kind of thing."

"It'll keep. I think we'd better have a talk first. Mind if we sit down?"

After everything he'd done for her, how could she refuse? She shrugged, then pulled up her rocking chair while he took off his coat and settled on the sofa.

"All right. What's the matter? Is our truce over?" she asked, hoping to lighten the serious expression in his eyes. Nuts. He didn't crack a smile.

Leaning forward, he braced his elbows on his knees and drilled her with a steady gaze. "I've been thinking about your situation with the baby, and it's pretty complicated. You're going to need more help than I realized at first."

Ginny smiled. "I'll be fine, Andy. Honest. If you'll pay part of the medical expenses, I can manage."

"How do you figure that? The doctor said you can't teach, and you need plenty of rest. I'm not being nosy, Ginny. I need to know how you're going to pay your expenses. Do you have a savings account?"

"No, but I'll bet I can pick up some commercial art jobs, and I've already taken three orders for portraits like the one I did for Sam's birthday present. I don't need a lot to get by. That's why I didn't make a fuss when Mary Harper wanted her job back."

"Yeah, what happened there? I thought Jack got transferred."

"His company decided to reorganize and his position was cut. With three kids, they needed her full-time paycheck more than I did, so I let it go."

"That was pretty darn generous of you," Andy said, leaning back against the cushions.

"I figured Jack would find something else before long and I'd get the art teacher's job anyway," she said with a shrug. "The last time I talked to Mary, she said they were planning to move to Cheyenne next summer."

"But that doesn't help you in the meantime." He drummed his fingers on the armrest, his gaze focused on a point somewhere in the distance. Then he looked at her again, his expression grim. "Look, maybe we should get married. It would make things easier—"

Ginny lunged up out of the rocking chair. "No. Absolutely not. It was nice of you to offer, but don't even think about it."

Andy shook his head, a wry smile spreading across his face. "I don't want to get married any more than you do, so you don't have be insulting, Bradford. I'm not a monster."

"I didn't mean it that way, Andy," she said, sitting down again because her knees were too weak with relief to hold her up.

He glanced away for a moment. "I wouldn't blame you if you did," he said. "I know I acted like a jerk when I found out you were pregnant. I'm sorry for that, Ginny."

"Apology accepted."

"Thanks. I hope we can start over and be friends, whatever happens with the baby."

Her throat tightened at the sincere expression in his eyes. Lord, he really was a handsome man when he wasn't angry. And underneath that gruff, macho exterior of his, she suspected he just might be a pretty nice guy, after all. Still, she was curious about something.

"After the party, you didn't want anything to do with me. Why the change of heart? Is it because of the baby?"

"That's a big part of it," he admitted. "I've always wanted kids, but my ex couldn't stand the thought of having one. It hit me pretty hard to see how much you wanted this baby."

"I told you I was excited about being a mother."

"Yeah, but I never realized how much you were willing to go through. I admired how you handled yourself during that god-awful test. That had to be uncomfortable as hell, but you didn't whine and you kept your sense of humor."

"It wasn't that bad."

Andy leaned toward her, his eyes intense again. "So, whaddaya think? Want to be friends?"

"I'd like that, Andy."

"And you'll let me help you through this pregnancy? Financially and otherwise?"

"Maybe you'd better define your terms."

"I'll pay all of your expenses until the baby's born and you can go back to work. Rent, food—the works."

"That's too much," Ginny protested. "I'll be working some. I can't just sit around for the next seven months."

"Fine. Do whatever you feel up to. But it won't hurt for you to save whatever you earn for a nest egg. After the birth, I'll pay child support like a divorced dad would. Of course, I'll want visitation rights."

"Whoa, Johnson. You're getting way ahead of yourself, here. We don't even know if the baby's all right yet."

"I want to be a part of my kid's life, Ginny."

"I don't have any objection to that. But let's worry about getting the baby here safe and sound first, and work out these other things as we go along, Andy."

"I guess maybe you're right." Sighing, he rubbed the back of his neck. "But I intend to be involved in the whole pregnancy, Ginny. I want that understood right now."

"You want to be my labor coach?" she asked, unable to stop herself from smirking.

"Yeah. What's so funny about that?"

"Oh, I don't know. You seemed a little...squeamish in Salt Lake."

"I'm not squeamish."

"Uh-huh."

"I'm *not*," he insisted. "For God's sake, I've delivered calves since I was a kid, and I'm a cop and a trained paramedic. How could I be squeamish?"

"Beats me, but you were yesterday. Admit it."

"Knock it off, Bradford. I just don't like needles."

"Whatever you say, Johnson."

Andy eyed her wicked grin for a moment, then snorted with an exasperated laugh and pushed himself to his feet. "All right, be a snot. I'd better get over to the office and find out what's been going on."

He put on his coat and picked up his hat and the tote bag. Liking him more than she would have thought possible a few short days before, Ginny followed him to the front door. He put his hand on the knob, then turned back to face her.

"Have you told your folks anything?" he asked.

"Not yet. I don't want to upset them until I get the test results."

"I hear you," he said with a rueful smile. "I won't tell mine, either, then."

He hesitated for a moment, then muttered, "Aw, what the hell?" and pulled her into a bear hug. Ginny hugged him back, savoring his warmth and the reassurance she knew he was trying to offer her.

"Take care of yourself, Ginny."

"I will."

"You'll call me as soon as you get the report?"

"The very second, I promise. Cross my heart."

He pulled away, crammed his Stetson on his head and opened the door. With a gruff, "Be seein' ya," he left.

Suddenly feeling chilled, Ginny wrapped her arms around herself and walked over to the window facing the parking lot. She watched Andy climb into his big black Blazer and drive away, then shook her head. She generally accepted people at face value, granting them the benefit of the doubt unless they gave her a reason not to.

With Andy...well, she wanted to believe that they would become good friends and be able to work together for the sake of their child. She was painfully aware, however, that even though Andy's offer of financial support had been extremely generous just now, there were price tags attached.

Part of her wanted to tell him to forget about her medical bills, child support and visitation rights. This baby was *hers* and she didn't want to share it. She knew that attitude was neither fair nor mature. It wasn't even entirely rational.

After all, this *was* Andy's baby, too, and she didn't have any right to exclude him from his child's life. As stubborn as Andy could be, she'd be stupid to try. But she was *not* going to let him support her. No way.

She might feel differently about that if she knew he would continue to be the warm, pleasant, reasonable man who had just left. Unfortunately she remembered all too well the other Andy she'd seen—the one who barked out orders and expected to be obeyed, immediately and without question. She couldn't risk giving *him* that much control over her life or the baby's.

Borrowing a line from an old television game show, she murmured, "Will the real Andy Johnson please stand up?"

"Ring, dammit," Andy muttered the next Monday, glaring at the telephone on his desk.

He'd been patient all morning, but he'd had lunch over three hours ago and Ginny still hadn't called. His heart thumped with anticipation one minute, wrenched with anxiety the next. God, he didn't know if Ginny could handle it if the news about the baby was bad.

He couldn't stand to sit in his office one more second, but he was scared to leave long enough to go to the bathroom. He had a horrendous case of heartburn. His neck and shoulders hurt, and he felt as if he had ants crawling around under his skin. He'd have gone through four packs of cigarettes if he hadn't quit smoking five years ago.

"Ring, dammit," he said again, then damn near fell out of his chair when the phone obeyed.

He grabbed the handset and mashed the receiver against his ear. "Andy Johnson."

"Hi, it's Ginny."

Damn. He couldn't tell a thing from her voice. "Did you hear any—"

"Yes, and . . . Oh, Andy, the baby's . . ."

She sighed. The damn woman sighed! What the hell did *that* mean?

"What?" he demanded, struggling to keep his voice below a shout. "What did she say, Ginny?"

"The baby's fine. Everything's fine."

Now it was his turn to sigh. He shut his eyes against a sudden, funny, stinging sensation and sighed again. He had to clear his throat before he could talk.

"Did she tell you whether it's a boy or a girl?"

"She offered, but I wouldn't let her."

"You *what?*"

Ginny's laughter gurgled, but he thought he heard a sniffle, too. It was easy to picture her laughing and crying at the same time. Although he wouldn't admit it under torture, he wasn't far from doing that himself.

"I wanted it to be a surprise, Andy," she said. "Besides, it doesn't really matter, does it?"

"Well, it might be nice to know whether to buy pink stuff or blue," he drawled with a smile.

"Oh, don't be so practical."

"There's nothing wrong with being practical, Bradford."

"Yeah, but it's boring sometimes, Johnson."

He flinched at that word, but kept his tone even. "Are you feeling okay?"

"I'm fine. Actually, I feel like I'm drunk."

"Ginny, you haven't been drinking, have you?"

"After going through all this, do you think I'd do anything to hurt the baby?"

"I'm sorry. I've been a little uptight."

"You're not the only one. Well, uh, I guess I'd better let you get back to work."

"Wait a minute," Andy said. "Would you like to go out for dinner tonight? Celebrate a little?"

"That sounds like fun, but I'd better go tell my folks. If I put it off, I'll chicken out and they'll find out from somebody else. Then they'll *really* be upset."

Hearing the dread in her voice, Andy grimaced in sympathy. Ginny's parents were so straitlaced, he wouldn't want to be in her shoes. Maybe he shouldn't let her go out to their ranch alone.

"I'll be glad to come with you," he offered, though that was as big a lie as the one he'd told her earlier about being a "little" uptight.

"No," she said quickly. Too quickly.

"Hey, I know your folks, Ginny. I think you'd better have some reinforcements along."

"Please, Andy, don't fight me. It'll be easier if I handle this myself."

"If they have two of us to yell at—"

"Thanks, but no. I've got to go now, Andy."

Before he could argue further, she disconnected the line. Cursing under his breath, Andy replaced his own handset. Dang, stubborn, independent woman, he oughtta go with her whether she wanted him to or not.

Intending to do exactly that, he shoved back his chair, stomped across the room and put on his coat and hat. He dug his car keys out of his pocket and reached for the doorknob, then paused, remembering what Ginny had said to him about that particular attitude when they were in Jackson. Oh, boy. Maybe he'd better think about this.

While her folks were capable of being damn nasty, he didn't believe Ginny would be in any real danger if she went to their ranch alone. It might be more humiliating for Ginny if he was there to hear whatever they said. And, having a witness to their confrontation, especially the guy who'd gotten his daughter pregnant, just might enrage her dad to the point that he'd do something stupid. Like going for his shotgun and calling a preacher, for instance.

Shuddering at the thought, Andy decided he'd go tell his own folks about the baby first. Then he'd drive by Ginny's parents' place. If her car was there, he'd stop in and make sure she was all right.

He told the dispatcher where he was going and hurried out to his car. His mom would probably lecture him and his dad would grunt and scowl. But once they realized they were going to be grandparents, they'd both be thrilled.

Family had always been important to Marv and Donna Johnson. As an only child, Andy had grown up with plenty of love and attention, and he'd always gotten along well with his parents. His dad had never made him feel guilty about not wanting to take over the ranch, and they still hunted and fished together whenever they got the chance.

His mom had never crowded him, either. She'd taken a job as a secretary at the middle school when he'd gone off to college. The kids at the school all loved her, and Andy was grateful that he hadn't had to worry about her having an empty nest at home.

Of course, his folks had been disappointed that his marriage hadn't worked out. Though she didn't nag him, Andy had seen his mom fuss over his cousins' kids and heard a wistful note in her voice when she'd mentioned that one of her friends had a new grandchild.

This might not be exactly the way she might have wanted to become a grandmother, but Andy thought she wouldn't waste any time getting close to Ginny so she could baby-sit now and then. In his own gruff, quiet way, his dad would be just as crazy about the baby as his mom. Wouldn't it be something if the kid decided to be a rancher?

Smiling at the thought of his dad teaching another little red-haired boy to ride and rope, Andy turned in at the Lazy J sign. His dad's pickup sat in front of the barn, but there was no sign of his mom's Wagoneer. Parking at the side of the house, Andy climbed out and paused to pet Buster, his dad's old German shepherd.

"How're ya doin', boy? Where's Dad?"

Buster barked and wagged his tail, and a moment later Andy's father stepped out of the barn.

"Well, hi there, son," he said, crossing the ranch yard at a brisk clip. "This is a nice surprise."

"I've got some news for you and Mom."

Marv checked his watch. "She oughtta be rollin' in here in about five minutes. Want a beer while we wait?"

"Sounds good." Andy followed his father up the walk to the back door and stepped inside, enjoying the familiar smells of home for a moment. Then his dad handed him a can of Budweiser, and they went into the den.

"What've you been up to today?" Andy asked, settling into one of a pair of brown leather recliners facing a fireplace built from native rock.

"Not much. Gettin' ready for winter. You?"

Before Andy could reply, he heard the back door open, then his mother's voice. "Marv? Andy? Where are you?"

"In here, Donna," Marv called. "Grab a beer and join us. Andy says he's got some news."

Andy stood and kissed his mother's cheek when she breezed in a few minutes later. Insisting that she take his chair, he sat on the hearth.

"Well?" she said, giving him an affectionate smile, "What's up?"

Now that the moment had arrived, Andy couldn't think of a way to tell them without just blurting it out. He should have rehearsed an opening line or two, he told himself as the expressions on his parents' faces changed from expectant to concerned.

"I'm, uh..." He stopped and cleared his throat before trying again. "I'm going to be a father."

His mother's eyes widened in surprise, and for a second, Andy thought he detected a flash of joy. Then her eyebrows pulled together over the bridge of her nose. "But, Andy, you're not married," she said quietly.

"Who's the gal?" his father asked, his expression identical to his mother's.

"Ginny Bradford."

"John and Pat Tyler's girl?" Marv asked. "The one who was married to Charlie Bradford?"

"Yeah," Andy said. "That's the one."

"I didn't know you were dating her," Donna said.

The disappointment in his mother's tone jabbed at Andy's conscience. "I haven't been," he said. "It was just kinda one of those things, you know?"

"No, I *don't* know," Marv retorted. "For God's sake, I taught you about condoms over twenty years ago. With all the diseases out there these days, I figured you were smart enough to use 'em. What the hell were you thinkin' of?"

"Calm down, Marv," Donna said. "How far along is she, Andy?"

"A little over two months." Andy sighed, then rubbed the back of his neck. "Look, I know this is a shock, but Ginny and I are both adults. We're handling the situation."

His mother sighed and shook her head. "Well, I suppose it's not really a tragedy. I'll help her plan the wedding—"

"There's not going to be a wedding, Mom," Andy interrupted. "We talked about it and decided we didn't want to get married. I'll help her financially, but—"

Marv released the footrest and shot out of his chair as if he'd been sitting in a catapult instead of a recliner. His face flushed a dark red and his eyes held such fury, Andy instinctively leaned back.

"I don't believe I heard you right," Marv said. "I sure as hell better not have heard you right, boy."

Standing, Andy looked his father square in the eye. "I'm not a boy, Dad. I'm a grown man."

"Then you'd damn well better act like one."

"That's what I'm doing."

"A man accepts the consequences of his actions whether he wants to or not. You got the gal pregnant, you marry her."

"I offered. She refused."

"Change her mind, dammit. I won't have you dragging this family's name through the mud. Do you hear me?"

"Folks over in Idaho can hear you, Dad. But it isn't that big of a scandal anymore, so why are you gettin' so damn hot in the mouth?"

Donna stepped between the two men. "Stop it, both of you. Yelling isn't going to solve anything."

Marv turned on her with a ferocity Andy had never seen him show toward his mother before. "Dammit, Donna, you know I can't allow this and you know why, too."

"Andy doesn't, honey," she replied in a calm, gentle tone that still managed to brook no argument. "Now, sit down and tell him."

Marv's glare slowly faded. Anguish replaced the anger in his eyes and his shoulders slumped.

"Tell me what?" Andy asked, mystified by the nonverbal messages passing between his parents. "What don't I know?"

"It'll be all right, Marv," Donna said. "It's a miracle he hasn't heard it before now, anyway."

Andy's father gravely nodded, then returned to his chair. Donna and Andy resumed their seats, and a strained silence filled the room. Finally Marv heaved a deep sigh and began to speak.

"The reason I'm so damn hot in the mouth, Andy, is because..." He gulped and shook his head. "Well, hell, there's no pretty way to say it. I was illegitimate."

"What?" Andy yelped. "No way, Dad. I remember Grandpa Johnson."

"He wasn't my father, Andy. He married your grandma when I was ten and adopted me. He was the best friend I ever had, but he wasn't my real father."

"Who was your real father, then?" Andy asked.

"I don't know his name. He was a cowhand working for your grandma's folks. I don't know much more than that because she wouldn't talk about it. I've always figured he took off when he found out she was pregnant."

"I'm sorry, Dad. That must have been rough on you."

"Yeah, it was. The other kids called me a bastard every chance they got until I was old enough to defend myself." Rubbing the knuckles of his right hand, he uttered a quiet laugh. "I bloodied a hell of a lot of noses and blackened a lot of eyes before they quit, though. It was damn rough on your grandma, too.''

"I can imagine," Andy said.

"No, I don't think you really can, son. Her folks wanted to send her away and make her give me up for adoption 'cause that's what people did back then. But your grandma wouldn't let 'em. Threatened to kill herself, and they believed her. A lot of folks treated her like she was something you'd scrape off the bottom of your boots.''

"Things have changed since then," Andy said quietly. "Lots of women don't get married just because they're pregnant.''

"And maybe they can get away with it in some places. But Pinedale ain't Hollywood, Andy. Some folks are more open-minded, but there's a lot who aren't.''

"I understand that, but Ginny and I don't love each other. It seems to me that our getting married would create more problems than it would solve. As it is, we're starting to be good friends and I think we can do right by this kid.''

Marv shook his head vehemently. "You're wrong about that, Andy. Once you've been called a bastard, you don't ever forget. This baby deserves to have the protection of your name, and there's only one way he's gonna get it.''

"There's something else you need to think about," Andy's mother added.

"What's that, Mom?''

"From what I hear, Ginny's made an awfully good impression as a substitute this fall. The kids really like her and so do the other teachers. But she'll never get a teaching job here unless you marry her.''

"She could teach someplace else," Andy said.

"And take the baby with her. You might never see it again. Think about that, honey.''

"If you want to be a part of your kid's life, you're gonna be tied to Ginny anyway," Marv put in.

"The marriage won't last," Andy argued.

"It won't if you go into it with that attitude, Andy," Donna chided him. "I think if you and Ginny gave it your best, you might be surprised. But at least make it all legal and protect your rights to the baby.''

Anger, dread, desperation—all kinds of crazy emotions filled Andy's chest until he could barely breathe. Rubbing his hand down over his face, he racked his brain for a way out, but he couldn't refute the wisdom in his parents' words. Maybe he'd known all along that it would come to this, but damn, it was hard to swallow. Finally he lifted his head and looked from his dad to his mom, then back to his dad again.

"Well, then," he said, pausing to gulp at the lump in his throat, "I guess I'll have to marry Ginny. But I'm telling you both right now, it'll never work."

A sympathetic smile tugging at his mouth, Marv shrugged. "It's still the right thing to do, son. You won't regret it."

Andy doubted that. Given the way Ginny had reacted when he'd made his halfhearted offer before, he knew she'd pitch one helluva fit when he brought up the subject again. Only an hour or so ago, she'd even repeated two of Denise's complaints about him. Practical and boring. That was him—too practical and boring for a woman like Ginny.

Well, they could still be friends, but he sure as hell wasn't gonna fall in love with her. They'd have to keep up appearances in public, but she'd know from day one that this wasn't gonna be the forever kind of marriage. He'd give it a year. Eighteen months at the outside. That should satisfy the proprieties and legalities.

If he ever *did* fall in love with Ginny, well...he figured she could hurt him ten times more than Denise ever had.

Chapter Six

Her composure hanging by the skimpiest of threads after seeing her parents, Ginny stormed into her apartment, put an old Hank Williams album on the stereo and grabbed the box of tissues from her bedroom. Then she turned off all the lights, curled up in her rocker and let Hank's mournful voice wrap around her like one of her grandmother's quilts.

If she hadn't been pregnant, she would have had a good, stiff drink. This time, she'd have to settle for a crying jag. God knew she deserved to cry over the awful things her parents had said to her.

Resting her head against the high back of the chair, she waited for the tears to come. Her eyes remained disappointingly dry, however. The hurt and resentment she felt went so deep, not even "I'm So Lonesome I Could Cry" could coax more than a sniffle or two out of her.

"You're a sap, Bradford," she muttered, setting the rocker in motion. "You knew they were going to be upset."

Upset? Now *there* was the understatement of the decade. Maybe the whole damn century. Hell, upset would have been a quiet walk in the country compared to the way her father had frothed at the mouth. And her mother—Ginny had never gotten along with her very well, but she'd never dreamed that Pat Tyler could be so cold, so self-righteous, so completely...unforgiving.

Thank God Andy hadn't been there or she'd never be able to look him in the eye again. Well, it didn't matter that her parents had disowned her. If they could treat one of their own children that way, why, she was disowning *them*.

Her folks had never understood her, never once been there when she really needed them, never offered her anything more than condemnation and criticism. She'd been a fool to hope it would be different this time. But she *had* hoped. Oh, how she'd hoped.

She wished the baby had already been born so she could cuddle her, tell her how much she loved her, how she would never, *ever* let anyone hurt her like this. She wished Sam was here to reassure her as he had been so many times before, that she wasn't the awful person her parents always said she was.

She wished...dammit, she wished Andy was here to hold her and comfort her, the way he had the night of Sam's party. Lord, she hoped his meeting with his parents had gone better than hers had.

The record ended, but Ginny couldn't find the energy to get up and turn it over. She just kept rocking. Rocking and hurting. Rocking and hurting and wondering why she was always such a damned disappointment to the people she loved.

"Oh, stop feeling sorry for yourself," she whispered. "At least the baby's okay. That's something to celebrate."

The doorbell rang. Afraid that it might be her parents wanting to rage at her some more, or maybe one of her three brothers wanting to add his two cents' worth, Ginny didn't answer it. The ringing went on and on, then became a strident knocking, accompanied by Andy's voice.

"I know you're in there, Ginny. Open up or I'll break this door down. I've got to talk to you."

Fearing he would follow through on his threat before she could get to the door, Ginny lunged out of the chair and banged her shin on the coffee table.

"Keep your shirt on, Johnson," she shouted, hobbling across the room in the dark.

"Are you okay?" Andy asked when she opened the door.

"I'm fine. I'm just ducky."

She gestured for him to come inside. Turning away as he stepped across the threshold, she walked into the living room and turned on a lamp. Taking off his hat and coat, he followed her, glancing at the record on the turntable before choosing a spot on the sofa.

Returning to her chair, she crossed one leg over the other and rubbed her aching shin. "What do you want to talk about?"

"Us. The baby. Ginny, we've gotta get married."

She sat up straight and planted both feet flat on the floor, then shook her head to clear it. "Excuse me? I know I didn't hear that right. It sounded like you said—"

His expression grim, Andy interrupted her. "Yeah, I said it. We've gotta get married. The sooner the better."

Hysterical laughter bubbled up inside her while a cold, hard knot of apprehension formed in the pit of her stomach. "We already agreed that was *not* an option."

"I've changed my mind. You will too, once you've heard what my folks had to say."

"Oh, *that's* what this is all about. You went to see good old Mom and Dad, and they want you to make an honest woman of me? Well, tell them you did your duty and made the offer, but it's no dice."

"Knock off the sarcasm and be reasonable."

"Be reasonable? I *am* being reasonable. Why should I get married when I'm perfectly happy with the decision we already made?"

"Yeah, you look real happy, Bradford," Andy replied, his voice rough with anger. "Is that why you've been sitting in the dark listening to Hank Williams?"

"So I was a little depressed," she admitted. "I had my own family confrontation, but I'll get over it."

"What did your folks say?" he asked as she started rocking again.

"I'm not sure how to answer that," she said. "I told Pat and John Tyler the news, but I guess they're not my folks anymore. At least they don't want to be."

Andy winced. "Damn, Ginny. I'm sorry."

"Hey, it's not your fault. They're just not real liberal thinkers, you know?"

"They'd come around if we got married, wouldn't they?"

"I doubt it. And I don't give a rip if they would. I'm not about to wreck our lives just to satisfy their outraged morality."

"Come on, Ginny, it wouldn't have to wreck our lives."

"No, I mean it! I don't need them or my mealymouthed brothers. I have another family who likes me better than my own ever did."

"The Dawsons?"

Nodding, she braced her elbows on the arms of the chair. "I don't know what I'd do without them. They're the kind of folks who love you even when you screw up. Lord knows I've done enough of that in my life, and I'm not going to do it again by marrying you."

Andy studied her intently for a moment, then sighed and rubbed the back of his neck. "This isn't about you or me or what either of us wants, Ginny. It's about what's best for the baby. We've got a responsibility to him, and it's time we faced up to it."

Oh, nuts. This was exactly what she'd feared the day she'd taken the home pregnancy test. Forcing herself not to panic, she vehemently shook her head at him.

"We *have* faced up to it. Shoot, Andy, we don't love each other. We could never make a marriage work."

"I didn't say we were gonna make it work."

"So why mess with it in the first place?" Ginny demanded. "How could it possibly help the baby?"

Andy stood and shoved his hands into the pockets of his uniform trousers. "Nobody could call him a bastard."

"People don't do that kind of thing anymore. Who would care enough to make an issue out of it?"

He walked over to the window, snorting in disgust. "In a town this small? Where everybody knows everybody else's business and talks about it? Especially when it's got something to do with *sex?*"

"It'll be a nine-day wonder," Ginny argued. "By the time our baby starts school, nobody will even remember whether or not the parents were married."

"The Tylers aren't the only folks around here who aren't liberal thinkers." He shot her a hard look. "Do you want our kid to grow up feeling ashamed?"

"Of course not! But I don't understand where this is coming from, Andy. You weren't illegitimate."

He walked back to the sofa and sat down. "No," he said quietly, "but my dad was."

"You're kidding."

"Afraid not." He repeated the story his father had told him. "I didn't know any of this until tonight."

Ginny bit into her bottom lip, then sighed in sympathy. "Your dad must have been awfully upset."

"Yeah. He had it pretty rough, and he doesn't want to see his own grandchild go through the same thing."

"But that was a long time ago, Andy," Ginny said gently. "Things have changed since then."

"I wouldn't count on it. If even one other kid finds out, it'll be all over the school. That hasn't changed and you know it. And you know how hard it is for a kid who gets singled out like that to have any self-esteem."

Rubbing the bridge of her nose, Ginny sighed again. "Yeah, you're right, and I can see you really care about your dad's feelings. But marriage, Andy? *Forever?*"

"You make it sound like a prison sentence," he said with a wry grin. "Life without possibility of parole."

"That's what it would feel like."

"Well, that's not what I had in mind."

"I think you've *lost* your mind."

"Will you *please* just shut up and listen for a minute? Here's the deal. I don't want to do this any more than you do. But I can handle it if we agree up front to a no-hassle divorce after the baby's born."

"You'd really do that?" she asked.

"Why not?"

She bit her lower lip. "It just seems awfully dishonest."

"You want to stay married forever?"

"I don't want to get married at all."

He walked to the coffee table, sat on the side nearest Ginny, then took her right hand between his palms. "Look, I'll do my best not to crowd you. You can paint or teach after the baby's born, do whatever you want. You'll have me there to help with the baby, and nobody will hassle you about being an unwed mother. Does that sound so bad?"

"I don't know," she wailed. Yanking her hand away, she stood and stepped around him, pacing to the window and back as he had done earlier. "Can you really see us living together? Remember what this place looked like the first time you were here? And think about how you were always picking up after me when we stayed in those motels."

"But we got along all right, didn't we? We'd both have to make some adjustments, but—"

"I'm not interested in making adjustments. I *like* being a slob. I've always been one."

"Charlie didn't mind?"

"Are you kidding?" She snorted with laughter. "He hated it. We fought about housework all the time."

"And you never tried to change?"

Ginny rolled her eyes toward heaven, then looked at him again. "You'll never know how hard. But it didn't work, and I'm not going to try to be someone I'm not anymore."

"We'll get a housekeeper if we have to."

"No, you don't understand. I can demolish a clean house in half an hour without even trying. Messes just sort of follow me around. I guess I don't really feel at home unless they're there. Trust me, you'd hate living with me."

Clearly perplexed, Andy gazed at her for a long moment. Then he stood and walked over to her, grasping her arms with both hands.

"You're making a big deal out of nothing, Ginny. Our baby's more important than a messy house. We're gonna get married because it's the right thing to do. I know you're scared, but—"

"Yes, I'm scared," she said, knocking his hands aside. "And you're not going to bully me into this."

"It's for your benefit too, dammit! Can't you see that? It'll give you a legal claim to child support and protect your career."

"I don't care about my career anymore."

"Well, what about mine? I'm a public servant."

"Give me a break, Andy. It's always the woman's fault in this situation. Nobody's going to blame you."

Swearing under his breath, he raked both hands through his hair as if he were seriously thinking about ripping it all out by the roots. Then he lowered his arms and stuck his fists on his hips.

"You're the most irrational woman I've ever met," he said in a soft, deadly tone that made her shiver. "You're making up all these dumb excuses that don't have a damn thing to do with the baby. It makes me wonder just how much you care about him."

"That's not fair."

"Well, life's just not fair sometimes, Ginny. If you can't grow up and make a responsible decision here, I'll fight you for custody."

Fear seized her throat, forcing her to swallow before she could answer. "You wouldn't do that."

"Try me."

"That's blackmail."

"Call it whatever you want. But we're gonna get married one way or the other. As far as the custody thing goes, all I really want are some clearly defined legal rights to spend time with my own kid. You owe me that much."

In all honesty, Ginny believed she *did* owe Andy that much. As compromises went, it wasn't a bad offer. "How long do you want to stay married after the baby's born?"

"Hell, I don't know. Six months?"

"Three. And I swear I'm not gonna sweat the housework, Andy. I'm not much of a cook, either."

"I can live with that. There's one condition, though."

"Come on," she chided him. "You were doing fine, but you're going to wreck the whole deal if you're not careful."

Folding his arms across his chest, he just stood there and stared at her. Ginny stared right back, her nerves stretching along with the silence. Cripes, this was worse than when she'd played poker with him in Salt Lake.

"All right, all right," she finally said. "What's the condition?"

"I don't want anyone else to know we've talked about getting a divorce. To the rest of the world, we're like any other happily married couple."

"Don't you think that's a little hypocritical?"

Andy shrugged. "Maybe. But I don't see how it'll hurt anyone, and it might save us a whole lot of interference from my folks and a couple of friends I can think of."

"You mean Sam and Hank?"

Andy nodded. "Can you imagine what either of them would have to say if they knew?"

"I don't even want to think about it," Ginny said with a shudder. "All right, I'll agree to that. In public, we're Mr. and Mrs. Happy Couple. At home, we go our own ways. You have a guest room, don't you?"

His eyebrows crashed together in a fierce scowl. "Yeah, but you don't really expect us to live in the same house and not—"

"That's exactly what I expect," she said. "In fact, that's *my* one condition for going through with this farce. No sex."

"Now, why would you want to torture us both like that?" he demanded. "We were great in bed together before."

"Because I don't think we want to risk falling in love with each other if we're planning to split up."

Andy rolled his eyes. "That wouldn't happen just because we have sex."

"Maybe not for you," she conceded. "But I happen to think you could be a fairly lovable guy, and I've had enough heartbreak already. Now, do we have a deal or not?"

He studied her for a moment, his eyes narrowed as if he were trying to figure out just how serious she was about holding him to her no-sex condition. She returned his gaze without flinching. Finally he grumbled, "Oh, all right. You drive a mean bargain, lady. What do you say to a small, quiet wedding? Next Saturday."

"It's all right with me."

"Hank's father-in-law's a retired preacher. I'll ask him to perform the ceremony."

"Okay."

"Want to have it at the Lazy J? My folks won't mind."

"I'd rather have it at the Circle D. I'll ask Sam."

"Fine. I'll have my mom call you tomorrow, and you can hammer out the details. I'd better get out of here and let you get some rest," he said, retrieving his coat and hat from the sofa.

At the mention of his mother, Ginny's stomach did a swan dive. Great. Just what she needed. More people to disapprove of her. "Oh, Lord," she muttered, wrapping her arms around her waist.

"What is it?" Andy asked.

"Nothing. It's just, well…how angry are your folks about all of this?"

Coming back to her, Andy put one arm around her shoulders and brought her along with him to the door. "You don't have to worry about them. Now that we're getting married, I don't think they'll be angry at all. They'll welcome you into the family like we'd planned it all along."

"You really think so?"

"I know so. Call me if you need anything?"

She nodded. Andy brushed a quick kiss across her lips, then reached behind him and opened the door.

"You're already cheating, Johnson. No kissing, either."

He shot her a devilish grin that was entirely too appealing for her peace of mind. "I was just gettin' in a little practice for bein' Mr. and Mrs. Happy Couple."

"Get outta here," she said, giving him a playful push.

Then his smile faded and he gently squeezed her shoulder. "It'll be okay, Gin. I promise you won't regret this."

His words echoed in her ears long after he'd let himself out. She hoped and prayed that he was right. But deep in her heart lurked a nagging, insistent conviction, that they were both making the biggest mistake of their lives.

Still, she had only committed herself to spending a year with him. She could stand anything for that long. Couldn't she?

Chapter Seven

"Ready to take that little walk down the aisle?" Sam said, entering the upstairs bedroom Ginny had used to change into her wedding dress—such as it was.

Ginny shot him a mocking glance over her shoulder, then turned back to the mirror. Her bright blue dress was, no doubt, completely inappropriate for a wedding. It was the nicest one she owned, however, and even if she'd had the time to go buy something new in Jackson, which she hadn't, she wouldn't have spent good money on an outfit she'd probably never want to see again.

"I don't think I'll ever be ready," she said. "I don't know why I let Andy talk me into this."

Leaning his shoulder against the wall beside the dresser, Sam crossed one foot in front of the other. "Because it's the right thing to do and you know it. Was it really that bad with Charlie?"

"Not all the time, but it was bad enough, and Andy's so much like him—"

"No, he's not, Gin. Not really."

"Oh, come on. He's stubborn and bossy and a neat freak."

"Yeah, but he's a lot more flexible than Charlie ever was. I'd say he's more like me than Charlie," Sam said. "I think you'll be good for each other."

Inserting the second pearl earring into her earlobe, Ginny scowled at him. "How do you figure that, Dawson?"

"He'll give you the stability you need and you'll loosen him up. That's the way it's worked for Dani and me. It's not always bad to be different from your spouse."

"You're forgetting one important detail. You and Dani are crazy about each other."

"So, give it a little time. You're attracted to each other. It wouldn't surprise me a bit if you fell in love."

"Right. Dream on little dreamer."

Straightening away from the wall, Sam grasped her shoulders and turned her to face him. "It's not like you to be so negative, Ginny. You can still back out."

The idea was tempting. She'd thought about it more than once since Monday night. But the truth was, this marriage *would* solve a lot of problems, and if it would protect her child from future humiliation, well, she didn't see that she had much choice but to go through with it.

"No," she said, mustering up a smile for Sam. "I don't want to do that. I'm just having a few jitters."

Eyes narrowed, he studied her for a long moment. "You sure about that? I don't want you to be miserable."

"We'll make the best of the situation. I promise."

"All right. Let's get this show on the road, then. You'll feel better when it's a done deal."

Taking the arm he offered her, Ginny left the room with Sam. Her stomach clenched when they reached the top of the stairs and the familiar strains of "The Wedding March" floated up from the living room below. Fearing she'd bolt if she looked at anyone else, she focused on Andy.

Lord, but he looked handsome, standing next to Hank in front of the fireplace. He wore a dark gray suit with a white shirt and a maroon tie. The crackling flames behind him made his hair gleam with deep, reddish highlights. His eyes wrinkled attractively at the outer corners, and he smiled as if he were an eager, happy groom.

His gaze roamed over her with blatant admiration as she started down the stairs, clutching Sam's arm in a death grip. The wretch didn't even have the decency to look nervous. Well, she'd be dipped in chicken droppings if she'd let him see how terrified she felt. Squaring her shoulders, she raised her chin and smiled back at him.

Sam patted her hand in the crook of his elbow and gave her a wink of approval when they arrived at the front of the room. Rev. Marc Jackson started the ceremony. Repeating those sacred, beautiful vows when she knew they wouldn't be kept filled Ginny with such guilt, she half expected someone to stand up and denounce both of them.

Of course, no one did. Andy smiled encouragingly and squeezed her hand when she faltered over the "'til death do us part," line, and she managed to get through the rest of the ritual without disgracing herself. Looking into his intense blue eyes, she wished, for just a moment, that they'd meant the words they'd said. That this was going to be a real marriage with love and commitment. That they would bring their baby into a home filled with joy and laughter.

Rev. Marc Jackson interrupted her train of thought, saying, "You may kiss your bride."

Andy turned to Ginny, and she could tell by his expression the he was every bit as relieved as she was to have the wedding over and done with. Putting his arms around her, he gave her a quick, gentle smooch.

"Jeez, Johnson, can't you do any better than that?" Hank grumbled, loudly enough for everyone to hear.

Ignoring the chuckles and giggles behind him, Andy shot Hank a dirty look and pulled Ginny closer, his gaze trained on her mouth with obvious intent. Her heartbeat kicked into a frantic rhythm. Her lips tingled. Her breath caught in her throat. Had their one night of passion been a fluke? she wondered, instinctively meeting him halfway.

The tip of his tongue skated across her lower lip and ventured into her mouth, inciting a fierce yearning to have more of him. Inhaling deeply, she drank in the spicy scent of his after-shave. Her fingers explored the muscular contours of his back and shoulders; she could feel his heart pounding in time with hers.

Lord, it hadn't been a fluke. Kissing him again was like drinking the colors of a sunset. It filled her with warmth and light, sent excitement charging through her nerve endings, melted the cold ache of loneliness she'd carried around for so long.

It didn't matter that there were other people watching, or that she was shamelessly undermining her own rule about no kissing and no sex. The only thing that mattered at the moment, was that Andy was kissing her as if he'd been starving for the taste of her for months. Just as she'd been starving for the taste of him. She almost whimpered out loud when he finally raised his head.

"Was that good enough for you, Dawson?" he asked, obviously struggling to catch his breath.

"Yeah, you'd better quit for now, pard. You're steamin' up the Rev's glasses."

Certain her face must be scarlet, Ginny turned toward the minister, who immediately pronounced in a voice shaking with suppressed laughter, that they were husband and wife. Offering congratulatory hugs and kisses, the Dawsons and Andy's folks closed in on them. Ginny smiled and did her best to act like a happy bride, but she knew she was already in trouble. Big-time trouble.

She wasn't in love with Andy now, but she'd be smart to keep her distance from him. But how was she going to do that when she would be living in his house? And when she wanted to make love with him again so much, her whole body ached?

A painful lump formed in her throat as she looked around the room. Deep, nasty, gut-wrenching envy invaded her soul when she saw the three Dawson siblings standing together in front of the television.

She'd been closer to Sam, Hank and Becky than she'd ever been to her own brothers. And there they all were, head over heels in love with their mates, starting families that would stick together come hell or high water. Their wedding vows had been spoken without doubts or reservations, without an agreement to split up. Did any of them have the slightest idea how lucky they were?

She felt a warm, strong arm wrap around her waist and looked up to find her new husband gazing at her with concern clouding his eyes.

"You all right?" he murmured close to her ear.

"Yeah, I'm fine, Andy."

"This is a wedding, not an execution. Think you could try to look a little happier?"

Forcing a Miss America smile onto her mouth, she said, "Is this better, dear?"

A chuckle rumbled out of his chest and he squeezed her waist with his arm. "Not bad. Hang in there, Gin. Just a few more hours and we can go home."

Home? What home? The past week had been so hectic, and she'd been so blasted tired all the time, she hadn't even seen the inside of Andy's house or moved any of her things from her apartment. But since she didn't want to embarrass Andy, she would make an effort to act more cheerful.

The sun had already set by the time they drove back to his light blue ranch-style house. Ginny's feet throbbed from wearing high heels and her face ached from smiling so much. He parked in the driveway, helped her out and led her around to the front entrance. She shivered in the cold November wind while he unlocked the door.

Then he turned to her, and without a word of warning, he scooped her into his arms and carried her across the threshold. Yelping in surprise, she clung to his shoulders as he stepped inside.

"Put me down, you nut," she said, chuckling at the smug grin he gave her. "You'll hurt your back."

"Had to make it look good for the neighbors." He kicked the door shut behind him, leaned back against it and hitched her up a little higher on his chest. "Welcome home, Mrs. Johnson."

The husky note in his voice sent a shudder of anticipation up her spine and she suddenly felt as hot as if she were running a fever. Of course, she still had her coat on and it was warm in the house, but the lusty glint in his eyes would have made her feel hot in a blizzard. The man definitely wanted a traditional wedding night.

"We really did it, didn't we?" she murmured, a host of ambivalent emotions blossoming in her chest.

His smile became absolutely wicked, making her insides flutter. "Not yet, but I'm ready anytime you are."

"Andy, you promised."

"That was before you gave me that kiss. Don't try to tell me you didn't feel what I did. Holy smokes, Ginny, it was like spontaneous combustion or something."

"We made a deal and I expect you to honor it."

He searched her eyes for a long moment, then gradually lowered the arm he'd tucked under her knees, letting her slide slowly down the front of his body. When her feet finally touched the floor, he linked his hands at the back of her waist, holding her flush against him. Being this close to him, their bodies aligned, eyes on the same level, incited that fierce, sweet yearning all over again.

"All right," he said, heaving a disgruntled sigh. "But I reserve the right to at least try to change your mind."

Ignoring his challenging remark, she stepped back and unbuttoned her coat. "Where should I hang this up?"

Laughing softly, he took it from her and hung it beside his in the entryway closet. "Okay, I get the message. Come on in and I'll show you around."

She placed her hand in the one he held out to her and followed him into the living room. It was a nice room, she thought, although she would add a bit more color. Well, actually, a lot more color.

The sofa and a big, overstuffed chair with a matching ottoman were covered in a navy blue-and-pale gray print. The walls were painted white. The carpeting and drapes were a darker shade of gray. An oak entertainment center covered half of one wall, and a three-shelf bookcase was tucked into the corner beside the chair.

A framed photograph of Andy's parents sat on top of the bookcase. There was a clock to the right of a brick fireplace, and a stuffed elk head sporting a massive rack of antlers mounted to the left. Other than that, the walls were bare. Of course, everything was excruciatingly neat.

"We can redecorate if you want," he said, studying the room as if looking at it for the first time.

She grinned at him. "Somehow, I don't think our tastes would mesh real well."

Andy shrugged. "It's your home now, too, Ginny. I want you to feel comfortable here."

"Well, let's see the rest of it."

He led her down a hallway, pointing out two small bedrooms, only one of which had any furniture, a bath and a laundry room. They were all pretty much what Ginny had expected—tidy and functional, without a whole lot else that could be said about them. Then he opened the last door on the left, and her mouth dropped open in surprise.

The king-size bed's mirrored headboard and the massive armoire were stained a dark walnut, which she might have expected in a man's bedroom. In contrast to the subdued shades in the rest of the house, however, the curtains and comforter were made of a flowered, print material that was nothing short of wild. Vivid hues of pink, purple, blue, yellow, green and red leapt out at her.

"Like it?" Andy asked

"I love it," she said, tearing her gaze away to look at him. "But who bought it? You wouldn't have picked this out in a million years."

Obviously pleased with her reaction, he shrugged. "My dad did. Mom suggested it, though. She thought we should start out with new sheets and stuff, so Dad made a trip over to Idaho Falls."

"That was awfully nice of them."

"This is our wedding present. Mom ordered carpeting and a bed skirt to match, but they haven't come in yet."

"But how did they know what I'd like? They've never been to my apartment."

Andy chuckled. "No, but I have. I told Dad to buy the brightest, knock-your-socks-off stuff he could find and this is what he came home with. Wait'll you see the sheets."

Ginny raised an eyebrow at him. "I'm not going to be using this room, Andy. Can you live with this?"

"Well, what could I say?" he demanded. "'Don't bother, Mom. Ginny won't be sleeping with me?' You know, maybe you should stay in here with me. It's gonna look weird if anybody finds out we've got separate bedrooms."

"Nice try, but it won't work, Andy," she said with a wry smile. "If anyone notices and has the gall to say something, I'll just tell them you snore like a chain saw."

"Thanks a *lot*." He chuckled and shook his head, as if in resignation. "C'mon and see the bathroom. That might surprise you, too."

It did. The room was larger than she would have expected, and a greenhouse window made it light and airy. A profusion of plants gave it an outdoorsy atmosphere. But what really captured her attention was the oversize shower that filled at least half of the space. Through the smoked glass door, she could see twin shower heads on opposite walls and a tiled bench along the far wall. Oh, my, she thought, *that* certainly looked as if it might have some interesting possibilities.

"This is wonderful, Andy," she said. "Did you do it yourself?"

"Yeah, after the divorce. I've done some work in the kitchen, too. Want to see it?"

"Of course."

He guided her back through the bedroom and hallway, then on into the kitchen/dining room combination at the back of the house. The kitchen was a cook's dream, with tons of cupboards, plenty of counter space and shiny, almond-colored appliances. The work island in the center had a cook top and a small sink. While Ginny wasn't much of a cook, she could appreciate what Andy had created.

A lump rose in her throat when she saw the small round table set in the dining area with a lace tablecloth, china, silver and crystal. Tall white candles in silver candlesticks sat on either side of a centerpiece made with autumn leaves and dried flowers.

"Did your mother do this, too?" she asked, her voice wobbling on the last word.

"Yeah. She felt bad we're not going on a honeymoon, so she left a casserole and some other stuff in the fridge for us." He studied her face for a moment, his forehead creased with a frown. "Mom wasn't trying to be pushy, Gin."

"I know." Blinking hard, Ginny sniffled. "I just didn't expect your folks to be this nice. They were so sweet to me at the wedding."

"I told you they'd welcome you into the family." Smiling, he gestured toward the table. "If you think this is something, wait'll the baby's born. We'll be lucky to buy the kid anything."

"But they were so upset when you first told them."

"Only because we weren't planning to get married. My parents are practical folks and they've wanted to be grandparents for a long time. They're not going to hold anything against you."

A tear sneaked down her cheek, then another and another. She turned her head and wiped them away, but Andy must have seen them. Putting his hands on her shoulders, he sighed and pulled her into a hug.

"Aw, don't cry," he said, awkwardly patting her back. "Everything'll be okay, I promise. I know you must have wanted your family there today, but—"

"No, I didn't," she said, giving her head a fierce shake. "I don't want them anywhere near me or the baby."

"Then what is it? Do you really hate the thought of being married to me so much?"

"No. I just feel . . . guilty for deceiving everyone. Those vows are supposed to *mean* something, Andy."

"Like when you married Charlie? From what little you've said, it doesn't sound like you were all that happy with him."

She shrugged. "I wasn't. It didn't start out that way, though. The war did some ugly things to him and he wasn't ever the same man again. But we had so many hopes and dreams and plans. I don't know, it just seems like what we've done is so . . . cynical. Didn't it bother you?"

"Not really. We were doing the right thing for the baby. Don't you think you're being a little idealistic?"

"Maybe. But I can't help wondering how your parents and the Dawsons are going to react when we split up. I'm afraid they'll all feel betrayed."

Andy released her, then rubbed the back of his neck. "That's their problem, Ginny. They all wanted us to get married and we did. They've got no right to expect anything more from us."

Crossing her arms over her chest, she turned away from him. "Yeah, you're right. Forget I said anything."

She heard him sigh again, then felt his arms wrap around her from behind, pulling her back against him. "I understand what you mean, but I don't know what I can say to make you feel better."

"You don't have to say anything, Andy."

"Well, I'm a little frustrated here. I know you don't want to stay married to me any more than I want to stay married to you, so I don't see why either one of us should feel guilty. What bugs me is that whether it's right or wrong, we *are* married now, and it seems dumb that we can't have the one part of this marriage we'd both enjoy for as long as it lasts."

"How'd we get back to that subject?" she asked.

"That's what's behind all of this, isn't it? Do we have a real marriage or not? Is that what you want, Ginny?"

"No. And I don't think it's fair for anyone to expect you to pay for that night out at the Circle D for the rest of your life, Andy."

"I don't regret our night at the Circle D."

Ginny shot him a surprised glance over her shoulder. "You don't?"

"Nope. We were both lonely as hell, and we comforted each other. I refuse to believe that was so all-fired bad, whatever the consequences."

"You ended up with a wife and baby you didn't want," she said softly. "Those were pretty stiff consequences."

"Yeah, but I won't be lonely for a while, will I? I sure wasn't lonely when I was making love to you that night." He hugged her tightly for a moment, then turned her to face him. "Were you?"

"No." She sighed, resting her hands on his chest. "But that doesn't make it right. There should be love involved, Andy."

"Maybe. But if making love is as close to loving as we're ever going to get, Gin, it's still something special we can share with each other." He framed her face with his hands and gazed deep into her eyes. "It's something special I want to share with you."

"Oh, Andy—"

"Shhh," he said, kissing her forehead. "We both know it's gonna happen sooner or later. Why not now?"

Unable to breathe, much less think, when Andy looked at her with such naked hunger in his eyes, she closed her own eyes and rested her forehead against his. She could feel the want in him, tightly leashed, but so obviously there in the way his heart pounded beneath her palms, in his rigid muscles, in the husky timbre of his voice. She could feel it in herself, and she knew he was right—sooner or later, they probably *would* make love again.

But not tonight, a quiet little voice of wisdom said, deep inside her heart. *You're too vulnerable right now. Don't make the decision when your emotions are so riled up.*

Reluctantly, apologetically, she shook her head and stepped away from him. "I can't, Andy. I just can't."

Fearing he might feel that she had led him on, Ginny braced herself for a masculine temper tantrum, or, at the very least a major sulking fit. To his credit, however, Andy accepted her decision with a philosophical, can't-blame-a-guy-for-trying shrug.

"Whatever you say, Ginny." He cleared his throat and glanced around the room, obviously at a loss for what to do with her next. When his gaze landed on the table, he asked, "You hungry? I can heat the casserole in the microwave."

"No, thanks, I'm still full from Dani's buffet."

In truth, she hadn't been able to choke down anything but the traditional bite of wedding cake Andy had fed her when they'd cut it. But there was no way she could sit at that beautifully prepared table and eat without feeling more guilt than she already did. Nuts.

She didn't know what to do with Andy, either, and the atmosphere in the room nearly crackled with a lingering, almost painful awareness that they were alone. If his thoughts were even half as lusty as hers were at the moment, they'd never make it through the evening. Since she had nixed the activity they both wanted the most, she felt obligated to come up with a more suitable one.

Heaving yet another disgruntled sigh, Andy loosened his tie. Ginny gratefully grabbed onto that small action.

"I think I'll get my suitcase out of the car and change into something more comfortable," she said.

Andy's eyes glinted with mischief. "Oh, yeah? How comfortable?"

She gave him a playful swat on his shoulder, then turned toward the back door. "Give it a rest, Johnson. I'm talking about jeans and a sweatshirt."

"I'll get it for you," he said, crossing the room in long, purposeful strides, as if he craved a few minutes away from her.

Though she didn't blame him a bit, the thought stung, and she wondered if she had been wrong to deny him a real wedding night. After all, he had willingly shouldered the financial responsibility for her pregnancy and married her to protect her and their baby from scandal. Now he was losing his privacy, which, she suspected was extremely important to him.

And what was he getting out of this arrangement? Fatherhood and even more financial responsibility. Peace of mind for his parents. Compared to what he was giving, it didn't seem like much of a trade. If making love was the one thing he wanted from her, wasn't she being awfully selfish to refuse?

Perhaps. But perhaps this was just a convenient excuse cooked up by her libido to do what it really wanted to do. Andy wasn't the only one giving up precious privacy, and his body wasn't going to blow up to unwieldy proportions in the next seven months, either. Besides, she could live a whole lot easier with the guilt of being selfish now than she could live with a broken heart later.

Andy couldn't have made it any more clear that he wanted out of this marriage when the baby was born, so her original decision would have to stand. She would go on about her business, live the way she wanted to live and prepare herself for motherhood. That was really the right thing for her to do. For herself, for Andy and for the baby.

Later that night, long after Ginny had gone to bed in the guest room, Andy stood at the kitchen window, wearing only a pair of briefs and sipping a glass of the champagne his folks had left in the fridge along with the casserole. He had gone to bed over an hour ago, but he hadn't been able to sleep on those damn black satin sheets his dad had bought in Idaho Falls.

Of course, black satin sheets weren't meant for sleeping on, he thought, snorting in disgust. And who would have thought he'd be trying to really sleep on them—alone—or his wedding night? Especially after that soul-stealing kiss Ginny had given him at the wedding?

Damn, stubborn, irrational woman. Having her around all the time was gonna be pure, unrelenting torture. But, much as he hated to admit it, maybe she was right about having separate bedrooms.

The truth was, he'd been pretty darn cynical going into that wedding this afternoon. He'd told himself over and over, that he was simply fulfilling his responsibility to his kid and his folks, and he'd walk away without a backward glance in eleven months. Then Ginny had appeared at the top of the stairs, wearing a dress that was brighter than a Wyoming sky in the summertime, her hair falling in smooth, shining curves to her shoulders.

She hadn't exactly looked like a conventional bride, but he'd thought she was mighty damn beautiful. His heart had pounded to beat hell, his tie had started to strangle him and he'd remembered in a hurry why grooms usually crossed their hands in front of their flies while they waited for their brides to walk down the aisle.

He'd *never* wanted a woman as much as he'd wanted Ginny at that moment. His libido had gone into overdrive on the spot, and it hadn't settled down yet.

And though he'd denied it, he *had* felt a little guilty about taking those vows, with Rev. Marc Jackson standing in front of him like that, and his folks and friends gathered behind him, wishing them well. And Ginny...well, he couldn't help liking her.

In fact, the more he got to know her, the more he found to like about her. Oh, she could be ditzy, all right. And irritating and stubborn as hell. But she had a good heart and she was fun to be with, and he'd found out in Salt Lake that she could be pretty damn tough when she had to be.

He respected her and he cared about her. All right, he might as well get down and dirty and *really* be honest with himself. The fact was, he'd had one helluva crush on her back when he was a kid, and he wasn't entirely sure he'd ever gotten over it. Not completely, anyway.

Whenever he looked at her, he got these funny, tender, kind of...protective feelings in his gut that didn't have a damn thing to do with lust. And that worried him more than his desire for her did. If he made love with her again, got used to her sleeping in his bed every night, let her sink her hooks into him, he could find himself in a world of hurt when he had to let her go.

If he thought she could ever really be happy with him, he might be willing to take an honest shot at this marriage. But that was only wishful thinking. No, it was crazy thinking—brought on by the wedding and the champagne. The black satin sheets and the lateness of the hour. His hormones and his loneliness.

Dumping the rest of the champagne down the sink, he shoved the bottle into the garbage can and went back to the bedroom, stopping to get some plain cotton sheets out of the linen closet on the way. After remaking the bed, he tossed the satin sheets into the hallway, shut the bedroom door and crawled under the covers.

Yeah, that was better, he thought, heaving a tired sigh. Tomorrow he'd start moving Ginny's stuff out of her apartment and everything would get back to normal. He'd lay off the coaxing and innuendos, and consider himself lucky that Ginny had had the sense to demand her own room.

And if he repeated that sentence enough times, maybe he'd even start to believe it.

Chapter Eight

By the time Ginny crawled out of bed on Monday morning, Andy had already left for work. She showered and pulled on a pair of jeans, a purple sweatshirt and matching socks, then wandered out to the kitchen. Feeling like an intruder, she searched the cabinets for coffee and filters, her heart sinking another inch with every door and drawer she opened.

She'd known all along that she would have trouble with Andy over the issue of neatness. But *this,* she thought with growing dismay as she stared at the dishes and storage containers, lined up according to size with military precision, well, *this* was going to be impossible.

Andy owned every organizer that had ever been invented. His spices were arranged in alphabetical order. For cryin' out loud, he didn't even have a junk drawer! The only logical conclusion she could draw from such excessive fastidiousness, was that the man was truly demented.

"Nobody's really this neat," she muttered, banging the silverware drawer shut with a satisfying crash.

But Andy obviously was. After the way he'd behaved yesterday, she really shouldn't be at all surprised. He'd been such a pain in the rear end when they'd been packing her things, she'd actually threatened him with an annulment if he didn't back off. The funny thing was, he honestly hadn't understood why she'd become so hostile.

He'd watched her constantly and pitched a fit if she picked up anything he thought was too heavy for her. While she'd wanted to dump everything into boxes and be done with it, he'd wanted her to sort it all out and get rid of whatever she didn't need, which, as far as he was concerned, had included at least half of her most cherished stuff. He had no concept of what the term "sentimental value" meant.

Then he'd actually expected her to pack and label each box as if she were moving clear across the country. Except for her clothes and toiletries, all of her possessions were now stored—neatly of course—in a haystack of boxes at one end of Andy's unfinished basement. He was probably hoping she'd leave it all there until she moved out next summer.

"Fat chance, Johnson," she said, smiling wickedly to herself. "You won't know this place when I'm done with it."

She scrambled an egg and made a piece of toast while she waited for the coffee to finish dripping. Just as she was setting her breakfast on the table, a knock sounded on the back door. When she opened it, she found an elderly man with a weathered, friendly face standing on the steps.

"Morning," he said, giving her a thorough, but inoffensive once-over. "I'm Bill McNeil, your next-door neighbor. You must be Ginny."

Since Andy had already told her of his friendship with Bill, Ginny opened the door wider and stepped back to let him in. "I sure am. It's nice to meet you, Bill. Got time for a cup of coffee?"

His grin widened immediately, and he held up a white bakery sack. "I was hopin' you'd say that. I brought a little welcome-to-the-neighborhood present. You like cinnamon rolls?"

"If they're the ones Betty Collins makes down at the store, you've got a friend for life," Ginny said, her mouth already starting to water.

Chuckling, Bill crossed the room and draped his parka over the back of a chair. "Go ahead and eat," he said when he noticed Ginny's plate. "I'll get my own coffee."

He moved around the kitchen with the familiarity of a frequent visitor. That was fine with Ginny. Now that she couldn't substitute anymore, she'd wondered how she would handle being at home alone all day. It would be wonderful to have a friend next door.

They chatted about Pinedale and the weather, the usual nonthreatening topics people reached for when they were becoming acquainted with each other. Ginny enjoyed Bill's relaxed, jovial manner and his dry wit, and felt that he liked her as much as she liked him. When she'd finished her eggs and the cinnamon roll, he sat back in his chair and smoothed down the sparse white hairs on top of his head.

"I saw Andy cartin' in boxes yesterday," he said. "Need any help unpackin'?"

"It's sweet of you to offer, Bill, but I can manage."

He shrugged. "I haven't got anything better to do, and you shouldn't be carryin' heavy stuff in your condition."

Ginny raised an eyebrow at him. "You know about the baby?"

"I was here the night Andy found out about it. He needed somebody to talk to, that's all. And I don't judge other folks or gossip, so don't you worry about it."

Andy was so closemouthed about his feelings with her, it surprised her to find out he'd confided in anyone. Though she wanted to question Bill about what her husband had said that night, she resisted the urge. Bill had been Andy's friend first, and it wouldn't be fair to put him in an awkward situation.

"C'mon, Ginny," the old man coaxed. "I'm an old coot, but I'm in great shape. Never had a lick of trouble with my back. I can move furniture, hang pictures—anything you want. If you wait for Andy to find time, you won't have any of your own things around for weeks."

"You'll tell me when you're tired?" she asked.

He pushed back his chair and stood, his eyes alight with enthusiasm. "You bet. Let's get to work."

And work they did. Bill laughed when he saw the stack of boxes in the basement, and laughed again when he noticed the difference between the ones Ginny had packed and the ones Andy had packed. When she hesitated over rearranging the living room without Andy's input, Bill stuck his hands on his hips and rolled his eyes at the ceiling.

"I've lived next door to that boy for four years, now, and he hasn't changed a blessed thing once."

"Then maybe we'd better leave it alone," Ginny suggested, grimacing in distaste at the bland decor.

"Nah! If that rut he's in gets any deeper, it'll bury him alive. It'll do him good to shake him up a little."

"You don't think I've already done that with the baby and the wedding?" she asked in a dry tone.

Bill's eyes narrowed and a shrewd expression entered them. "You might have a point there, but this is your house too, now. Look around, gal. Is this any place for an artist to live?"

"Well, no, but this isn't exactly a love match, Bill."

"You're not chicken, are ya?"

"Why you sneaky devil," she said with a chuckle. "How did you know I could never resist a dare?"

"Takes one to know one," he answered. "C'mon, let's do it."

"All right, but if he throws me out, I'll have to come live with you."

By midafternoon, Ginny was exhausted, but extremely satisfied with what they had accomplished. It was amazing how comfortable and inviting the place looked with her knickknacks and art work livening it up. And adding her old rocking chair to the new living room arrangement made her feel much more at home.

Confident that Andy would immediately notice the improvement, she sent Bill home and stretched out on the sofa for a nap. Maybe tomorrow, he would help her set up a studio in the bedroom that didn't have any furniture.

Reluctant to go home because of the argument he'd had with Ginny yesterday, Andy finally left the office at seven o'clock. After the fiasco of moving her out of her apartment, he finally had his head on straight again. She'd had *some* nerve, screeching at him for making a few, helpful suggestions. How anyone could live with so much junk and all of it jumbled up the way she did was beyond him.

Man, he hoped she wouldn't spread it all over the house. Aw, what he worrying about? She'd never be able to find anything in that mess in the basement.

No matter what, though, he didn't want to fight with her anymore. He hadn't forgotten what the doctor had said about Ginny's avoiding stress, and God knew she'd had plenty of that in the past week. He had, too.

He hadn't been able to sleep on Saturday night because he'd wanted her in his bed; he hadn't been able to sleep last night because he'd wanted to strangle her. Word of their wedding had spread through the county like a forest fire in August, and he'd spent the whole damn day fielding congratulations, bawdy jokes and questions about why he wasn't on his honeymoon.

All he wanted at the moment, was a hot meal, some peace and quiet and the comfort of his living room. If Ginny still wasn't speaking to him when he got home, that was fine and dandy with him. The hair on the back of his neck prickled, however, when he turned into the driveway and saw that the house was completely dark.

He climbed out of his patrol car, checked to make sure her sedan was in the garage and hurried inside, concern for her safety increasing with every step. Maybe she'd passed out again and hit her head. Maybe she was miscarrying. Hemorrhaging.

"Ginny," he shouted as he opened the kitchen door.

No answer. He hit the light switch, glanced around the room and called her name again, already racing toward the living room.

"In here, Andy."

She sounded groggy. Damn, maybe she really *had* passed out. Barreling through the doorway, he flipped the switch that should have turned on his reading lamp, then banged his shins on something hard, tripped and fell flat on his belly before he realized the light hadn't come on. What the hell?

"Ginny, are you all right?" he demanded, straining to see her in the dark.

He heard a click from somewhere ahead of him and blinked at the sudden brightness before his eyes focused. Ginny was sitting on the couch with one foot on the floor, the other tucked under her. Her hair was tousled around her shoulders in an attractive disarray, and her eyes had a soft, sleepy, unconsciously sexy look that made him gulp.

"I'm fine, Andy. What are you doing on the floor?"

"I fell over something." Struggling into a sitting position, he looked behind him and cursed under his breath when he saw the ugly magazine rack he'd moved from Ginny's apartment yesterday. "What's that damn thing doing there? And where's my chair?"

"It's right over there," she said, inclining her head toward the opposite corner while she stifled a yawn with one hand. "I rearranged the furniture today so I could fit some of my things in."

"You *what?*"

"Don't worry. I was careful. Bill did all the heavy lifting. Gee, he's a nice guy." She yawned again. "What time is it?"

Andy scrambled to his feet and looked to his left, then to his right. Shutting his eyes for a moment, he prayed that he'd only imagined what he'd just seen. No such luck. If he didn't recognize the fireplace, the sofa and his chair, he'd swear he'd accidentally stumbled into the wrong house. After taking a better look, he wished he *had* stumbled into the wrong house.

The crazy woman must need glasses if she thought all this junk went with his furniture. A scarred, old mahogany cabinet covered with plants occupied the place where his chair *belonged*. He didn't even want to try to guess what that thing standing next to it was supposed to be. A metal sculpture, maybe?

For God's sake, she'd taken the sofa from in front of the picture window and angled it into the corner below his elk head. And what in the hell was the elk wearing? A floppy straw hat tied on with a red scarf? Gnashing his teeth, he turned to his left, noting her battered rocking chair, a trunk that must have come out of somebody's attic twenty years ago and on top of the trunk, a brass lamp shaped like a voluptuous naked woman. Oh, *jeez*.

Too dumbfounded and angry to speak, he turned away, but that didn't calm his temper any. A stack of big, paisley, tasseled—tasseled for God's sake—cushions lay on the floor in front of the fireplace. The damn woman had stuck a bunch of old plates and baskets on top of his entertainment center and filled the empty spaces on the shelves with tacky ceramic figurines. That three-foot-tall vase filled with mangy-looking peacock feathers in the corner to the right of the entertainment center didn't help anything, either.

The paintings she'd hung around the room weren't too bad, but for cryin' out loud, she'd stuck his chair in the corner, where he couldn't even see the TV! The absolute last straw was the bookcase built out of bricks and boards. Didn't she know that nobody but penniless college kids did that kind of thing?

"Well, what do you think?" she asked, reaching behind the sofa to turn on the floor lamp. "Doesn't it look better in here?"

"It was fine the way it was," Andy said, forcing the words out between his gritted teeth.

"Oh, come on, Andy. Bill told me you haven't changed anything in this room in years. After a few days, you'll get used to it."

"No, I won't." Folding his arms over his chest, he glared at her. "Because you're going to change it all back."

"You said we could redecorate."

"Not from a damned rummage sale. Change it back."

Her cheeks flushing a deep, vivid red, she climbed to her feet and rammed her hands onto her hips. "I agreed to this marriage to please *your* parents, and I'm not going to be miserable for the next ten or eleven months. I have just as much right to have my own stuff around me as you do."

"It's junk, Ginny. We can do better."

"Why, you...Andy Johnson, you're a snob."

"I am not. But at least my stuff matches."

"And it has all the personality of a pinecone. The only things of yours in here you couldn't find in a second-rate motel room are that picture of your folks and Elmer."

"Elmer?"

"I'll bet you didn't even name him, did you?" she asked, jerking one thumb at his elk.

"It's not a *pet,* for God's sake. It's *dead.*"

"Oh, hush," Ginny said, rolling her eyes in exasperation. "Have a little imagination. Have a little fun."

He let out an incredulous laugh. "You call this *fun?*"

"Why not? It's interesting. It's different. It's—"

"It's out of control, Ginny."

"Does everything always have to be controlled, Andy? Is that why you're so obsessively neat?"

Ready to fire back a furious denial, Andy sucked in a deep breath, then paused as he realized she might have a point. "Yeah," he said slowly, after considering the idea for a moment. "Yeah, maybe that's the reason."

The stiffness went out of her shoulders. Her eyebrows shot up under her bangs. "Really?" she asked, lowering her voice to a more conversational level.

Her interested expression encouraged him to share what he was thinking. "Could be. I've always been fairly neat, but I've gotten a lot more that way in the past four years."

"That's when you were divorced, wasn't it?"

He nodded. "I sure didn't have any control over that. It's the same way with my job. You know, handling accidents and family fights, stuff like that. Things just...happen sometimes. I can't prevent them or stop them. About all I can do is clean up afterward and try to help folks get on with their lives."

"So, home is the only place where you *can* control what happens," Ginny suggested, her eyes filled with such empathy, it made him feel embarrassed and exposed.

"I'd never thought about it that way before," he said, shrugging one shoulder. "But I guess it makes sense."

After giving him a lopsided smile, she glanced around the room. "Well, maybe we'd better change it all back the way it was. I didn't mean to destroy your comfort zone."

Andy smiled back at her, then shook his head. "Forget it. I'll try it this way for a week, and then maybe we can make some changes we'll both like better."

"Sounds like a deal to me." Her stomach rumbled. Putting one hand over it, she laughed. "Must be suppertime. Come on, Johnson. Let's go see what we can find to eat."

He followed her from the room, pausing at the doorway to take one last look over his shoulder. Funny thing was, with that silly hat on his head, the elk *did* sorta look like an Elmer.

"Oh, brother," he muttered under his breath, "flakiness must be contagious."

"Did you say something, Andy?"

"Not a thing, Ginny," he said, smiling to himself.

Later that night, Ginny propped her pillows against the headboard, leaned back and grabbed a sketch pad and a pencil from the drawer in the bedside table. Scooting her feet up close to her bottom, she balanced the pad on her knees and began to doodle while she mulled over the surprisingly pleasant evening she'd spent with Andy.

He hadn't said a word about the dirty dishes she'd left in the sink from breakfast and lunch. Though she would have cheerfully settled for a grilled-cheese sandwich and vegetable soup, he'd insisted on a more substantial meal and proceeded to cook most of it himself.

They'd chatted over the steaks he'd thawed in the microwave and barbecued on the gas grill on the deck. Afterward, they'd done the dishes together and gone back to the living room. He'd watched the second half of the Monday night football game and she'd read a book about childbirth Dani Dawson had loaned her.

Glancing down, she shook her head at the picture taking shape on the paper. Sketching in bed was an old habit, her own private method of working out problems the way some people wrote in journals. Her subconscious mind frequently took over, guiding her pencil to form images of things that bothered her.

It didn't surprise her that she'd drawn Andy's face tonight. But it *did* surprise her that she'd drawn him with the fierce glare he'd worn when he'd demanded that she change the living room back to its original arrangement. He'd actually gotten over his snit pretty darn fast, and hadn't referred to their disagreement again. Not once.

Charlie would have fussed and sulked all evening, if he hadn't rearranged the furniture on the spot, berating her the whole time. He would never have agreed to trying things her way or suggested a compromise the way Andy had. Charlie had *always* had to be right, and had never been able to leave a situation like that alone until he'd badgered her into admitting she was wrong, whether she believed it or not.

Interesting. Maybe Andy wasn't as much like her former husband as she'd thought. Maybe he really *was* more like Sam—only a zillion times more sexually attractive to her.

Well, they'd only been married for two days. She hadn't had much chance to *really* irritate him yet. Would he still be as reasonable in a month? Two months? Three?

Not likely, she thought, shaking her head. Charlie hadn't been a jerk at first, either, or she never would have fallen in love with him in the first place. Given enough time, this honeymoon period—if anyone would call it that since they weren't sharing a bed—would eventually end.

The real Andy Johnson would start to come out, and she'd probably find herself living with Charlie's soul mate.

But what if that doesn't happen? a quiet voice deep inside her asked. *What if you actually like living with him?*

Sighing, she studied the new picture of Andy she'd just finished. This time he was laughing. His hair was a little mussed and his eyes crinkled up at the outer corners the way she thought was so attractive. Funny. She'd never even noticed that little chip in his right front tooth before.

Her breasts tingled and she felt an empty, aching sensation low in her belly. Slamming the sketch pad shut, she tossed it and the pencil along with it into the drawer.

"Don't do it, Ginny," she whispered fiercely. "Don't even *think* about falling in love with him."

Yanking the extra pillow from behind her back, she hugged it against her breasts and slid down in the bed. She couldn't sleep, however, because one thought kept repeating itself in her poor, befuddled brain. Wouldn't it be just her luck to find out Andy was her one and only Mr. Right and then have to get a divorce after the baby was born?

Chapter Nine

One month to the day after the wedding, Andy drove home from work feeling cold, tired and cranky. Thanks to the weather, he'd had a miserable day dealing with jackknifed trucks all over the county. With only ten days left before Christmas and already a foot and a half of snow on the ground, the winter was shaping up to be a real killer.

Turning off Pine Street, he smiled as he wondered what the heck Ginny would be up to when he arrived. After a rocky start, the two of them had settled into a livable routine, as much of a routine as Ginny could tolerate, anyway. Never knowing what time they'd eat dinner or what weird thing she'd come up with on the nights when it was her turn to cook had bugged him at first. But now it was fun to try to second-guess her, even though he was usually wrong.

Another thing he was getting a real kick out of, was the game he'd started with Elmer. The morning after Ginny had rearranged the living room, he'd taken down the elk's dopey straw hat while she was still in bed, and stuck a baseball cap on him instead. When he'd come home that night, Ginny had added a pair of plastic Groucho Marx glasses with a big nose and bushy eyebrows.

Of course, he'd had to retaliate, and now he was really having to work to come up with something different every day. The game had seemed silly to him in the beginning, but it was fun, and he wasn't about to give up the competition. He could hardly wait until she got a load of the old hunter's cap, complete with earflaps and chin strap, he'd discovered in the Lost and Found at the office.

He was even getting used to her wacky decorating. He'd insisted on moving his chair back to its proper place, and he'd talked her out of the tasseled cushions and the mangy peacock feathers. He didn't worry too much about the rest anymore, because with Ginny around, nothing stayed the same for very long.

She hadn't been kidding when she'd told him that messes simply followed her around, but even that hadn't driven him as crazy as he'd thought it would. He could see she was making an effort not to let it get out of hand. She never did any lasting damage to anything, and she usually made her messes in the process of creating something interesting.

He'd figured out what her problem was during their second week together—her brain was filled with too many creative ideas. She'd start one project, like the Christmas ornaments she'd been making all week. She'd work on that for a while, and then she'd think of something else she could try, and she wouldn't be able to wait to finish the original task, much less clean up after herself, to see if her new idea would work.

One night he'd watched her go through the process four times in the space of an hour, and it had tickled him no end. He'd never realized marriage could be so entertaining. Considering how different their personalities were, it amazed him that they got along as well as they did.

The only real problem he had in living with Ginny, was that the more time he spent with her, the more he wanted her. She'd put on a little weight since the wedding, and she was starting to fill out her clothes in some mighty enticing places. She didn't flaunt herself, or anything like that, but he hadn't been able to help noticing the changes her pregnancy was making in her body.

He'd kept his hands to himself and behaved like a gentleman since their wedding, but doing that was getting harder every day. Shoot, he could get hard just thinking about her smile or hearing her laugh or coming across the underwear she'd forgotten in the bathroom after she'd taken a shower. Made him feel like a pervert or something.

It would help a lot if he knew she wasn't attracted to him, but he'd found out in Salt Lake that Ginny didn't have much of a poker face. No, everything she felt was right there in her big dark eyes for anyone to read. And, dammit, she wanted him every bit as much as he wanted her.

He figured at least half the arguments they had were more the result of sexual frustration than any real conflict between them. Who knew how long they'd be able to last before one of them couldn't take it anymore? He was determined however, that he wasn't gonna crumble first. Ginny had made the no-sex rule. She'd have to change it.

Turning onto his street, he sighed when he saw the line of cars and pickups parked in front of the house. Well, make that two real problems. After dealing with people all day, he liked to come home and hibernate, but Ginny collected friends the way other women collected recipes.

Not that he really blamed her. He'd been working hellishly long hours since the weather had turned bad, and he could hardly expect her to sit home alone all the time. At least she didn't whine about his job the way Denise had. But, good Lord, it looked as if she'd invited thirty people over. The least she could have done was warn him.

The rich aromas of popcorn, freshly baked bread and a kettle of chili simmering on the stove went a long way toward improving his mood. The cheerful round of greetings he received from his folks, half the Dawson clan and another couple who had been at Sam's party finished the job. Wiping his feet on the mat inside the kitchen door, he realized he hadn't entertained his friends since the divorce.

"What's going on?" he asked Sam and Hank, who were seated at the table with Emily, industriously stringing popcorn with needles and thread.

"Your wife decided it was time to decorate for Christmas and roped all of us into helping her," Sam said with a grin. "Don't ask how we got stuck with this job."

"Where is she?" Andy asked.

Hank pointed his needle at the sliding glass door to the deck. "Right over there."

Andy looked in the direction Hank had indicated, but didn't see anyone until he stepped closer to the table. Then he let out a startled laugh. Ginny was on her hands and knees between Sam's stepdaughter, Kim, and Hank's daughter, Tina, painting the outline of a pair of pudgy elves onto the glass. Both girls were watching her sure, easy strokes with the brush and listening to her explanation of how she wanted them to fill in the empty spaces as if she were imparting the secrets of the universe.

"Brace yourself, Johnson," Sam said. "When Ginny decorates for Christmas, she doesn't fool around."

"That's because she's still about ten years old in the brain department," Hank added.

Ginny glanced over her shoulder and stuck her tongue out at him. "I heard that, Hank. No Christmas cookies for you." She spotted Andy at that instant and sat back on her heels, giving him a thousand-watt smile that thawed out his frozen toes. "Hi, Andy. Do you want to do popcorn strings with these dodos, cook with your parents or help Pete and the other guys set up the tree?"

Her expression reminded him of the way she'd looked at the haunted house on Halloween—excited, delighted with the chaos, the joy of creating something stupendous glowing in her eyes. No wonder everyone jumped to do her bidding. All that enthusiasm was contagious.

"Let me think about it while I change my clothes," he said, shaking his head in bemusement.

"Okay, but hurry or you'll miss all the fun."

There didn't appear to be much danger of that happening, Andy thought, chuckling to himself as he entered the hallway off the kitchen and peeked into the living room. Elmer wore a Santa hat and a white beard. A red ornament dangled like an earring from his left ear, and a green ornament hung from the right one.

Becky and Pete Sinclair were engaged in a lively debate with Hal Baker, Eric Jordan and their wives, over where they should set up the tree. Bill, Johnny Conrad and Sam's stepson, Colin, were stringing lights across the mantel, the entertainment center and the picture window, receiving advice from Grandma D and Dani. Little Jonathan Sinclair was cruising around the coffee table with a cookie in each hand and a gooey chocolate ring circling his mouth.

Waving a greeting when they spotted him, Andy shook his head again and hurried into the bedroom.

The evening soon turned out to be one of the most enjoyable ones he could remember. Everyone laughed and talked and sang along with the Christmas carols playing on the stereo while they worked. When they stopped to eat dinner, Hal Baker teased Dani, who was expecting a baby in seven weeks, that she looked like the elves on the sliding glass door.

While she was still trying to come up with a suitable retort, Hank announced that he and Emily were expecting a baby around the beginning of June. Andy looked at Ginny, his eyebrows raised in query. She smiled and shrugged, as if to say, "Go ahead. They all suspect it anyway."

Andy waited until the congratulations for Hank and Emily died down, then made an identical announcement, which started up the hugging and backslapping all over again. After shooing everyone back to work, Ginny flitted from room to room, supervising, encouraging and absorbing the fun like a parched plant soaks up rain, her cheeks flushed with pleasure. Andy found himself automatically tracking her movements, smiling every time he spotted her in the crowd.

The party continued until the house looked like a band of crazed elves had decorated it. Hank and Emily were the last ones to leave. When the women became involved in a discussion of obstetricians, Hank pulled Andy aside.

"Heard from the DEA yet?" he asked quietly.

"Just a note saying they'd received my application."

"You're gonna withdraw it, though, right?"

"Why would I do that? I still want the job," Andy replied.

"Get real, Johnson," Hank said, frowning. "You've got a wife and a baby on the way now. What'll happen to them if you get yourself killed?"

"That's why life insurance was invented, Hank."

"Come on, you know they'll need more from you than money. That's why you married Ginny, wasn't it? So you could take care of her and the baby?"

Andy didn't want to lie to his friend, but he wasn't about to tell Hank that he and Ginny had agreed to get a divorce after the baby was born. The best response he could come up with was a noncommittal shrug. Hank's eyes narrowed and his eyebrows came together in a sharp V.

"Something smells fishy here, buddy. What's goin' on? You guys already havin' problems?"

"That's between Ginny and me," Andy said, growing more uncomfortable by the second. "You don't need to worry, Hank. I'll make sure Ginny and the baby are all right."

"Uh-huh. Then why do I get the impression you're not gonna be here to see to it yourself?"

"I didn't say that," Andy protested.

"Maybe not, but I can tell that's what you're thinkin' about. I can't believe you'd be that irresponsible."

"That's rich, Dawson," Andy said with a disgusted laugh. "*You're* calling *me* irresponsible?"

"Hey, I gave up rodeo and married Tina's mom for the same reason you married Ginny," Hank defended himself.

"Yeah, but you didn't stay married very long."

"She was the one who left, not me. If she'd stayed, I'd still be married to her."

"Oh, right," Andy muttered. "Tell me another one."

"Well, maybe not," Hank admitted. "Christine was always such a party animal, even I had a hard time keepin' up with her. But Ginny's not like that. You've got yourself one helluva fine wife there if you're not too stupid to see it."

Not for long, Andy thought, giving Hank another shrug. Emily interrupted them then, reminding her husband that she had to go to work early the next morning. After shooting Andy a perplexed frown, Hank turned away and joined her at the front door, thanking Ginny for her hospitality.

While Ginny waved them off, Andy glanced around the room, mentally comparing it to what his house had looked like last Christmas. On the front door he'd put a wreath he'd bought from the Boy Scouts, but he'd told himself he was too old and too busy to care about bothering with a tree or anything else. Since his divorce, holidays had become days to get through instead of special days to enjoy.

But looking at the tree and the lights, Elmer and the Nativity set Ginny had arranged on the entertainment center, the fake snow on the window and Ginny's glittering stocking hanging from the mantel...well, it brought back all the excitement and anticipation he'd always felt at Christmas when he was a kid. He couldn't help imagining what next Christmas would be like with a baby crawling around, getting into the packages, watching the lights blink on and off. Man, wouldn't that be something?

There was only one thing wrong with the picture forming in his mind—next Christmas, Ginny and the baby would be living somewhere else, and he'd be off God only knew where, chasing drug dealers. The thought held about as much appeal as getting a tooth drilled without novocaine. For the first time, he had to ask himself if he really wanted a divorce.

Anxiety filled his chest and closed around his heart like a clenched fist when he couldn't answer that question with any certainty at all. Dammit, that didn't make any sense. Of *course* he wanted a divorce.

It wasn't Ginny herself that was getting to him so much as the sentimentality of the season, which only lasted a few weeks at best. What about the rest of the year? Would he honestly want to be married to her then?

Sure, she was kinda fun to live with sometimes, but the novelty of their situation hadn't had a chance to wear off yet. In six months, he'd probably be counting the days until she moved out. And even if he wasn't doing that, would she want to stay married to him? Hell, she wouldn't even sleep with him.

"Fat chance, Johnson," he muttered, starting when Ginny closed the door with a loud snap.

"Wasn't that a great party?" she asked, turning to him with a grin that was wider than the fireplace.

"Yeah, it was," Andy said. "When did you decide to throw it?"

She crossed the room to her rocking chair and plunked herself into it. "I didn't actually decide," she said with a laugh. "I ran into Sam and Dani when I was downtown this morning and told them I was going to start decorating tonight. They offered to help and it just grew from there."

"Well, it was fun, and the house looks great," Andy said, taking a seat on the sofa.

Setting the chair in motion, she laughed again. "That's good, because everyone's coming back on New Year's Eve to help us put all this stuff away."

"Aw, jeez, Ginny," he protested. "Couldn't you at least ask me if I want a bunch of people in the house before you invite them? I always work New Year's Eve."

She stopped rocking and gazed at him for a moment, her smile rapidly fading away. "You don't have to be here, Andy. I can handle it myself."

"But you're supposed to be taking it easy," he argued. "Throwing a party's a lot of work."

"Maybe the way you do it, it is. But not the way I do it. Everyone will bring food, I'll provide the hats and noisemakers, and we'll call it good. What's the big deal?"

"You'll still wear yourself out."

"Oh, piffle. I'm feeling much better now. One late night isn't going to hurt me or the baby."

He couldn't think of another reason she shouldn't have the party—except that it stung his pride to know she considered his presence optional. Since he wasn't about to tell her that, he shrugged. "All right, Ginny. Do whatever you want."

"I'll check with you before I do it again," she offered quietly.

"That'll be fine," he answered, giving her a wry smile.

She returned it and they both fell silent. Andy felt the tension between them ease as he watched the lights blinking on the tree and heard the fire crackling in the fireplace, the rhythmic squeaks from Ginny's rocker. He snuck a glance at her, grinning to himself when he caught her sneaking one at him.

A new kind of tension gradually entered the room, the kind that had nothing to do with arguments. Turning his head, Andy admired the way the colored lights reflected off the diamond in Ginny's engagement ring, her smooth skin, her shining hair. Her eyes held a wistful, dreamy expression, and he would have given a lot to know what she was thinking about at that moment.

The baby? Their marriage? Him?

Damn, but he wanted her. Right here and now. On the carpet between the tree and the fireplace. Where he could watch the emotions play across her face, feel her heat and hear her excited little cries. Lose himself in the unbearable excitement of making love to her again.

As if she felt the touch of his gaze, she turned and looked at him. His heart jerked to a stop for an instant, then started again with a shaky, erratic beat. God, how could she stare at him like that—with all the same needs and desires in her eyes that were roaring through him—and not act on them?

He saw her throat contract, heard her swallow. Then, to his utter disappointment and disbelief, she stood and announced that it was time for her to turn in. Stubborn witch.

Gritting his teeth as she left the room, he hoped she suffered half as much as he knew he would.

Still, he had to admit, if only to himself, that even intense sexual frustration was better than the emptiness he'd felt before Ginny had come into his life. Whether she was tickling his funny bone or irritating the hell out of him, he felt more alive than he had in years. Did he *really* want a divorce after the baby was born?

Jerking her gaze away from Andy's and leaving him alone in the living room took every last speck of self-control Ginny possessed. She hurried through her bedtime routine, then went into her room, shut the door and leaned back against it. Closing her eyes, she willed her vivid imagination to stop remembering what it had been like to make love with him. But her body wasn't listening.

More sensitive than usual because of her pregnancy, her breasts swelled against the cups of her bra as if she could feel Andy's hands or his mouth touching them. Her skin felt hot and almost... itchy. Her arms ached to hold him, to press him against her in the most intimate ways possible.

Unfortunately, what she was feeling went a whole lot deeper than simple lust or loneliness. She could have handled either or both of those feelings, no sweat. But there were other feelings—warmer, deeper feelings—growing inside her that she didn't know what to do with. She had loved sharing those moments of quiet and the fire and the Christmas tree with him, but it had left her wanting more. So much more, she was terrified even to think about it.

Bill had pulled her aside about an hour after dinner and bluntly pointed out how much fun Andy appeared to be having—as if she hadn't already noticed. "You're good for that boy," he'd said. "Just look at him, will ya?"

She'd looked, all right, and some disturbing things had happened. Holding little Jonathan Sinclair, Andy had been talking to Susan Baker and Mary Jordan. It was all completely innocent, of course. Both women were married and their husbands had been within spitting distance.

But both women were also attractive and younger than Ginny by at least five years. The admiration in their eyes as they responded to Andy had made her want to march right over there, put her arm around his waist and remind Susan and Mary that he was already taken. She'd felt ridiculously jealous and incredibly vulnerable.

During the past month, she'd discovered her impression of Andy the night they'd fought over the living room arrangement hadn't been too far wrong. Yes, he had a strong, forceful personality, but he didn't run over her like a tank. While he was opinionated about a lot of things, he listened to her opinions, and more importantly, he didn't automatically try to change them to match his.

Yes, he had a temper, and he didn't hesitate to show it. But once an argument was over, that was it. He didn't hold a grudge. He was rarely sarcastic. And he stuck to the issue of whatever they were fighting about without resorting to personal attacks. He could admit he was wrong and apologize without acting as if it were killing him.

Yes, his neatness drove her batty sometimes, but the other side of that coin was that he was one self-sufficient man. He didn't expect her to do his laundry. He didn't complain when it was his turn to cook or do the dishes. And she certainly didn't need to clean up after him. In fact, with only her own messes to contend with, she thought she was doing pretty well in that department. At least, he hadn't yelled at her about it yet.

Their game with Elmer proved that though he was basically a serious kind of a guy, he *did* have a sense of humor. And he did little, thoughtful things for her sometimes that made her wonder if his ex-wife hadn't had a few screws loose when she'd left him—like changing the oil in her car when he changed the Blazer's or calling before he came home to see if she needed anything from the store.

Andy simply wasn't as harsh or as critical as Charlie had been. Maybe he was more sure of himself or he had a deeper, stronger character or he was simply more patient. Whatever the reason, she found herself liking him more every day. Looking forward to his coming home in the evening. Missing him when he was gone.

Tonight, for the first time, she'd felt possessive toward him. Afraid of losing him. Unless he changed drastically in the near future, she feared that he just might turn out to be everything she'd ever wanted in a man, a husband and a father for her baby.

It was too late to list all of his faults. Too late to remind herself they'd only been married a month, and that he could still change into a jerk. Too late to warn herself not to fall in love with him.

She'd already done it. In spades. And sleeping alone when he was right in the next room was about as appealing as cleaning a crusty oven.

Inhaling deeply, she forced herself to put on her nightgown and crawl into bed anyway. Making love with Andy would only deepen and reinforce the love she already felt for him. It would be hard enough to leave him after the baby was born, and there were two things she couldn't allow herself to forget no matter how much her own feelings had changed.

Andy had only married her because of the baby. He didn't love her, and he probably never would.

Chapter Ten

Since he'd gone into law enforcement, New Year's Eve had become Andy's least favorite holiday. Too many people left their brains and their common sense at home when they went out to celebrate. He rarely gave any of his deputies the night off, and he felt guilty about taking it off himself. Nevertheless, he decided it wouldn't be right for him to leave when his wife had planned a party. If anything really big came up, the dispatcher knew where to find him.

When Ginny stepped into the living room dressed in the hot pink-and-black maternity outfit he'd bought her for Christmas, he was glad he'd decided to stay home. Her face glowed with anticipation—or was that bloom the result of her pregnancy? He couldn't really say and it didn't really matter. She looked wonderful.

Seeing that excited sparkle in her eyes was worth any price he had to pay for not working tonight. Ever since the impromptu decorating party, she'd been pleasant, but subdued. He'd hated feeling responsible for squelching her naturally lively spirit. Especially at Christmas.

Andy suspected she feared the growing attraction between them might suddenly spark and burn out of control at the least provocation. It wasn't an irrational fear on her part. He'd taken so many cold showers lately, it was a wonder he hadn't caught pneumonia.

Her being subdued hadn't helped, of course. The more she withdrew, the more drawn to her he felt. He'd done his best to give her whatever space she needed, but it wasn't easy when he wanted her so much, his bones ached.

But tonight, the expression on her face told him that the real Ginny was back, ready to reach out and milk every last drop of fun out of this party. She glanced up at Elmer, and the delighted laughter that bubbled out of her throat sent a rush of desire straight through him.

"Oh, my," she said, admiring the black top hat and bow tie Andy had found for the elk. "Doesn't he look elegant?"

Andy winked at her. "He looks almost as nice as you do, Gin."

"Thank you," she murmured, shooting him a self-conscious smile. She brushed an imaginary speck of lint off her black trousers. "I'm not really showing that much yet, but the rest of my clothes are starting to get tight. You don't think this looks silly?"

"Not at all. You look beautiful," he said, his voice sounding husky to his own ears.

The doorbell rang at that moment. Andy bit back a disgruntled sigh when Ginny rushed to answer it, obviously relieved to escape the sudden tension that flared between them. For God's sake, did she think he was going to pounce on her without warning after he'd respected her no-sex rule all this time?

Then he didn't have time to think about it anymore as their guests began to arrive in what seemed to him like an endless stream. In minutes the house was filled with music and laughter. Platters of food appeared on the coffee table and on the work island in the kitchen as if by magic.

Andy passed out paper hats, noisemakers and soft drinks. Everyone appeared to be having as much fun taking down the Christmas decorations as they'd had putting them up, and he had to laugh at the thought that only Ginny would think to throw an *un*decorating party. His dad helped him cart the boxes to the storage room in the basement.

While Andy shoved the last one onto the shelf, Marv crossed his arms over his chest and leaned one shoulder against the door casing.

"Tell me something son," he said, gazing at Andy with a serious expression in his eyes. "How do you like living with Ginny?"

"Well, it's different, anyway," Andy said with a wry grin. "Never a dull moment."

"But are you happy?"

Andy shrugged. "Happy enough. What's the matter, Dad? You like her, don't you?"

Chuckling, Marv nodded. "What's not to like about Ginny? I think she's a real doll, but..."

"But what?" Andy asked, allowing a touch of impatience to enter his voice.

"Well, I'm just wondering if you two are getting along all right."

"We're doing fine, Dad. What's your point?"

"I've been watching both of you all night," Marv said. "You seem more like...well, roommates than newlyweds."

If he only knew, Andy thought, fighting the urge to roll his eyes in exasperation. "Give me a break. We've been busy tonight."

"Your mom noticed the same thing when you came out to the ranch for Christmas dinner."

"Come on, Dad. You know this wasn't the love match of the century. What did you expect?"

"Well, I hoped you'd be smart enough to try to turn it into the love match of the century," Marv retorted. "Any marriage takes a lot of work, Andy."

"Hey, we're not fighting or anything," Andy said. "I'm doing the best I can."

"Are you really? Or are you holding back because you're afraid Ginny'll leave you like Denise did?"

"Maybe," Andy grumbled. Then he sighed and rubbed the back of his neck. "But so is Ginny. It takes two people for what you're wanting to happen, Dad. She keeps to herself most of the time."

"Why do you suppose that is?"

"She hasn't said much about it, but I don't think her first marriage was all that happy."

"And maybe she feels that you don't really want this marriage," Marv said. "She's in a hell of a position, Andy. She knows you only married her because of the baby. Do you really think it's fair to expect her to stick her neck out first?"

"I'm in the same position," Andy argued. "She never would have married me in a million years if she hadn't been pregnant."

"Well, now, you don't know that for sure, son. Neither of you knows what mighta happened if you'd been able to date each other awhile. You must have been pretty attracted to each other once."

"Yeah, but that doesn't mean we would've ended up married."

"Doesn't mean you wouldn't, either."

"What is it you want me to do, Dad?" Andy demanded.

"Give it a fair chance. Be more affectionate with Ginny. Romance her a little. If you act like you've got a happy marriage, maybe you'll wind up having one."

"That's just wishful thinking."

"Could be. But you're gonna be living with her for a long time." Marv's steady gaze became even more piercing. "At least, I hope you will. What have you got to lose by making it the best marriage you can?"

Oh, not much, Andy thought, glaring resentfully at his father. *Only my pride. My freedom. Maybe my heart.* Marv glared right back at him.

Andy finally said, "Look, we got married like you wanted us to, Dad. The rest of it's our business."

Dropping his hands to his sides, Marv straightened to his full height. "You're right, son," he said quietly. "It isn't any of our business. We just wanted you and Ginny to be happy."

With that, he turned and left the room. Andy remained beside the shelves for a moment, trying to cool his temper. If he were honest with himself, he'd have to admit that part of the reason he'd been so testy with his dad was that deep down he had more doubts about his present and future relationship with Ginny than he wanted to think about. Before he could sort it all out, however, he heard her voice calling down the stairs to him.

"Telephone, Andy. It's your office."

"Be right there," he shouted.

He took the stairs three at a time and accepted the receiver from Ginny, his gut knotting as he listened to the dispatcher's description of a scene he'd dreaded, but expected for a long time.

"I'm on my way, Barb. Doc Sinclair's here, so I'll bring him along." Hanging up the phone, he turned to find Ginny still standing beside him.

"What is it, Andy?"

"There's been some trouble out at the Paxon place. I'm sorry, but I'll have to go."

"How long will you be gone?"

"I don't know. It sounds pretty bad."

"Be careful, Andy," she said, her eyes filled with worry.

Brushing the backs of his fingers across her cheek, he gave her a reassuring smile. "I will, Gin. Go back and enjoy your party and don't wait up for me."

"All right. I'll find Pete."

"Thanks."

Touched by her concern for his safety, he watched her disappear into the hallway. All Denise would have cared about was that he was wrecking her party. Was it possible that Ginny cared more about him than she was letting on?

But if she did, why was she still holding him at arm's length? Why wasn't she trying to get her hooks into him but good?

Unfortunately, he didn't have time to figure it out. Pete Sinclair rushed into the kitchen. After grabbing his medical bag from his car, they jumped into Andy's patrol car and roared out of the driveway.

Ginny stood at the living room window with Becky Sinclair, watching their husbands speed off down the icy street. When the taillights disappeared from sight, she exchanged a rueful smile with Becky.

"Don't you just love it when duty calls?" Becky asked.

"I thought you'd be used to it by now," Ginny said.

Becky shrugged. "I don't think I'll ever really get used to it. It's more a matter of accepting it when it happens. I always have to remind myself that somebody out there needs Pete even more than I do."

"That's the way I try to look at it, too," Ginny agreed. She linked her arm through Becky's and led her toward the kitchen. "Well, come on. You can have a glass of wine and I'll drown my sorrows in ginger ale."

Her eyes taking on an excited sparkle, Becky shook her head. "As of today, I'm back to ginger ale, too, for the next seven and a half months."

"Are you expecting again?"

Becky nodded eagerly. "I'm due in August."

"Oh, Becky, that's wonderful. I'll bet Pete's thrilled."

"That's an understatement." Becky laughed and rolled her eyes. "You wouldn't believe how nutsy he got while I was pregnant with Jonathan, though. I swear, he watched every bite I put in my mouth. How's Andy handling it?"

"He's been fine so far. He always comes to the doctor with me and as long as she's satisfied, he doesn't fuss too much. The only time he really nags is when he thinks I'm getting too tired."

"It's early days yet," Becky warned her. "Wait'll you really start to get big. I'm betting both Andy and Hank'll be even worse than Pete. And Sam's so protective of Dani now, he's just downright pathetic. She told me tonight that every time she rolls over in bed, he's on his feet and yanking on his pants.''

"I think that's kind of sweet," Ginny said, searching the room for Sam. She finally located him sitting at the table, visiting with Andy's dad and Bill. "Although now that you mention it, he does look a little haggard."

"Yeah, and he's still got another three or four weeks to go, Ginny. I'll be surprised if Dani doesn't brain him before it's over."

"No, she won't. She loves him too much," Ginny said, unable to keep a wistful note out of her voice. Suddenly, for no apparent reason, her throat closed up and her eyes filled with tears.

Becky took one look at her face, grabbed her by the elbow and hauled her down the hallway to the bathroom. Locking the door behind her, Becky firmly pushed on Ginny's shoulders until she sat on the side of the bathtub. Then she handed her the box of tissues from the counter.

"Okay, Ginny, what's going on?"

Ginny wiped her eyes and blew her nose. "Nothing, Becky," she said with a shaky laugh. "Just one of those hormonal surges, I guess."

"It looked like more than that to me," Becky said quietly. "I know you're really more Sam's friend than mine, but I can keep my mouth shut and I'm a pretty good listener if you need to talk. Are you and Andy having problems?"

"No. Not really." Ginny sniffled and stared down at the tissue wadded up in her fist. "I mean, we don't really fight much or anything, but . . . well, I'm sure you've figured out why we got married."

Becky lowered herself to the floor and leaned back against the locked door. "Yeah. I guess being around all of us Dawson lovebirds isn't too easy for you right now."

Ginny nodded, then reached for another tissue. "I don't mean to complain, Becky. Andy's been awfully good to me. He really has."

"I don't doubt that for a minute. I dated him for a while before I met Pete, and he's a good guy. But it'd be nice to know he really loves you, wouldn't it?"

Swallowing at the lump in her throat, Ginny nodded again. "Yeah. It would. But I'm afraid that's asking for too much, Becky."

"Well, it just might be a little too soon to expect him to say it. Andy's not real open about his feelings," Becky said with a sympathetic grin. "But you know something?"

"What?"

"I was watching you two the night of Sam's birthday party, and I'd never seen Andy really cut loose and have a good time like he did with you. And every time I've seen you together since then, I've thought you must be awfully good for him."

"Why on earth would you say that, Becky? If you want to know the truth, I drive him crazy half the time."

"That's just the point. Ever since he was elected sheriff and Denise left him, he's turned into a loner. It was like he turned his emotions off. He's needed somebody or something to shake him out of that."

"Bill said almost the same thing about him," Ginny said, snorting with laughter. "I can see what you both mean, but I don't see how my shaking him up is going to make him love me. Most people resent that sort of thing."

"Only at first," Becky said, smiling as if at a fond memory. "I was in a terrible rut when Pete came along. He almost had to use dynamite to blast me out of it and I hated him for it. But now, well, you'll never know how much I love him for having the guts to do it."

"You think Andy might feel that way about me someday?"

"I wouldn't be at all surprised, Ginny, if you can be patient. It takes time to get out of a rut as deep as the one Andy's been in. I think he's worth the effort."

"Thanks, Becky," Ginny said, smiling at the younger woman. "You're a good kid, you know that?"

Laughing, Becky climbed to her feet. "Oh, brother, you sound just like Sam when you say that. For heaven's sake, I'm not much of a kid anymore."

"No, you've turned into a wise, beautiful woman," Ginny said, accepting the hand up Becky offered her. "Your mom would be so proud of you."

"Thanks. You ready to face the troops out there?"

"I'm fine now, Becky. Thanks."

"Anytime, Ginny. Have you guys signed up for the childbirth classes yet?"

For the rest of the evening, Ginny laughed and talked with her friends and even instigated a game of charades. Unfortunately, it seemed as if all the zing had gone out of the party for her when Andy had left. Knowing where he'd gone, she couldn't help worrying about him.

It had long been common knowledge that Larry Paxon beat his wife, and Sam had told her about the trouble Emily had had with him during the past summer. Paxon had vandalized her car and nearly killed her dog, and even though he'd been ordered into psychiatric counseling by the judge, Ginny doubted the man was mentally stable.

What if he'd really gone over the edge this time? What if he turned all that rage on Andy? Those questions lurked in the back of her mind long after her guests had departed. She straightened the house and went to bed at one-thirty, but she knew she wouldn't sleep until Andy came home.

Heaving a sigh of relief when she heard the back door open at two o'clock, she snuggled down under the covers, expecting Andy to go directly to bed. The poor guy must be exhausted. She waited for the sound of his steps moving down the hall, but nothing happened.

After fifteen minutes, she couldn't stand wondering what he was doing any longer. Slipping a robe on over her nightgown, she quietly opened her door and tiptoed to the kitchen. She didn't want to bother him, but she needed to know he was all right.

Peeking through the doorway, she saw him standing motionless at the sliding glass door, staring out into the darkness. He still wore his Stetson and his coat. His hands were curled into fists, his broad shoulders slumped as if in defeat. Something truly awful must have happened to make him look so sad. So... lonely.

Not wanting to startle him, she softly cleared her throat and entered the room. He turned toward her and she gasped when the stove light she'd left on for him illuminated a huge bloodstain covering the front of his coat. Hurrying now, she crossed the space between them.

"Good Lord, Andy, are you okay?"

His throat worked down an audible swallow and one side of his mouth quirked up in a failed attempt at a grin. "Relax," he said, indicating the stain with a half-hearted gesture. "It's not mine."

"Whose is it?" she whispered, appalled at the bleak expression in his eyes.

"Larry or Janie Paxon's. I'm not sure which."

Taking his cold hand in hers, she led him over to the table, surprised when he offered no resistance. Moving like a robot, he surrendered his coat and hat, then collapsed onto one of the chairs. He braced his elbows on the table and rubbed his face with both hands while she laid his things on the work island and took the chair at a right angle to his.

"What happened, Andy?"

He raised his head and looked at her for a long moment. Then he exhaled a deep, ragged sigh. "You don't want to hear about it, Ginny. It'll only upset you."

"My imagination will go crazy whether you tell me or not," she said. "Did someone die out there tonight?"

"Not yet." He closed his eyes as if he wanted to shut out a gruesome memory and shuddered. "But I'll be surprised if either one of them pulls through."

"Come on, Andy, talk," she coaxed, folding his right hand between both of her own. "You'll feel better if you get it off your chest. I can handle it."

His fingers wrapped around hers in a forceful grip and his face contorted with a grimace. When he finally spoke, his voice sounded raw with pain.

"You know Larry Paxon?"

Ginny nodded. "I've heard some bad things about him."

"Yeah, well, every damned one of 'em is true. He's meaner than a rattler with a toothache, and crazy as hell. Why that judge thought a shrink could ever help him is beyond me. He should've been locked up a long time ago."

"What happened?"

"The son of a bitch celebrated New Year's with a bottle of Scotch. When he started yelling at his boy, Janie sent Ned to his room and made the mistake of telling Larry she'd finally had enough and she wanted a divorce."

"Oh, God," Ginny murmured, ignoring the pain he was unconsciously inflicting on her hand. "What did he do?"

"From the looks of their house, he went completely berserk, and beat the livin' hell out of that poor woman. If she lives, she's gonna need to have her face reconstructed, and Pete was pretty sure he broke both of her arms and four of her ribs. He couldn't tell too much about internal injuries."

"But you said you didn't know if either one of them would pull through, Andy. What happened to Larry?"

"Well, Ned..." Andy choked up and had to stop for a second. "That poor kid, he's only eleven years old. He, uh, came out of his room when he heard his mom screamin'. Anyway, he got hold of one of Larry's pistols and when his dad started comin' after him, Ned shot him in the belly."

"Is Ned all right?" Ginny asked.

"He's fine physically. Mentally and emotionally, the kid's a disaster. The only reason I hope Larry makes it is that I'm afraid for Ned's sanity if he doesn't. He was so damned upset, Pete had to sedate him. His grandparents are with him now."

"It's always the kids who suffer the most."

"That's for sure." Andy fell silent for a moment, then smacked the table with the palm of his free hand. "And, dammit, this one didn't have to happen."

"What do you mean?"

"Hell, everybody knew Larry was beating Janie. I've talked to that woman at least a dozen times in the past four years, trying to get her to press charges against him or at least leave him. But she wouldn't do it. I'll never understand why she put up with his abuse for so long."

"He probably had her convinced it was all her fault and she couldn't make it on her own," Ginny said quietly.

Andy shot her a surprised look. Then his eyes narrowed with suspicion. "How do you know that? Charlie didn't beat you, did he?"

"No, he never laid a finger on me." She sighed and shook her head. "But there are other kinds of abuse. Charlie specialized in verbal abuse."

He stared at her, his mouth clamped together in a thin, angry line. Then his temper suddenly exploded. "My God, Ginny, how could you let him do that to you?"

Ginny yanked her hand free and stood. "It wasn't my fault, dammit, any more than what happened to Janie was her fault. I survived it and that's all you need to know. I'm going to bed."

Andy lunged to his feet and grabbed her arm before she could leave. "Ginny, please, wait a minute. I'm sorry. I didn't mean to sound like I was blaming you."

"You wouldn't be the first one who did," she muttered, struggling to break his grip without success.

"No, really. I was just shocked, that's all." His expression softening, he grasped her other arm and pulled her closer. "I mean, you don't seem to have any problem standing up for yourself with me."

Unable to meet his gaze any longer, she looked away, that old, familiar feeling of humiliation burning in the pit of her stomach. "It's taken me a long time to learn how to do that. But you can bet your badge I'll never let anyone treat me that way again."

"Aw, Ginny." He put his arms around her and hugged her to him, sighing when she finally stopped resisting. "I really am sorry, babe. I see a lot of ugly things in this job, but that scene out there tonight was so bad, it made me sick. The thought of you going through anything even halfway like it . . . Well, I guess I'm just taking my guilt over Janie and Ned out on you."

"You tried to help them."

"Yeah, I did. But I felt so damn frustrated every time she wouldn't press charges, I gave up too soon. Instead of feeling sorry for her, I should've gotten tough with her."

Ginny pulled back far enough to look him straight in the eye, her anger dissipating when she saw the depth of his self-torment. Raising one hand to the side of his face, she slowly shook her head.

"That wouldn't have done any good. You can't help someone in a situation like that until they're ready to admit they need it. You're not responsible for what happened tonight, Andy."

He turned his head and planted a kiss on her palm, then hugged her tightly again. "I wish I could believe that."

Aching to comfort him, Ginny hugged him back. She lost track of how long they stood there holding each other. Gradually, however, she felt the tension ease out of his shoulders. His hands roamed slowly over her back as if he needed to warm them by touching another human being.

She instinctively pressed closer to him, letting out a surprised little gasp when she discovered he was fully aroused. She would have pulled away, but his arms tightened around her.

"It's okay," he murmured, gently kissing her forehead. "I can't help reacting to you, Gin, but I really don't want to be alone tonight. Will you sleep with me?"

"I don't know if that's such a good idea, Andy."

"I promise that's all we'll do," he coaxed. "I'll even wear pajamas."

"The supreme sacrifice, huh?" She grinned at the thought, then slowly nodded. "All right."

He studied her face for a moment, then released her and silently guided her down the dark hallway to his bedroom. After snapping on the bedside lamp, he turned down the bedspread, blankets and sheet.

"Go ahead and get in," he said, giving her a reassuring smile. "I'm gonna take a quick shower."

Folding her robe across the foot of the bed, Ginny glanced down and chuckled at her baggy flannel nightgown. It was old and faded, and it covered everything from her neck to her feet. Hardly the kind of lingerie to incite a man's lust.

That didn't stop her own thoughts from wandering down a decidedly carnal path as she lay in Andy's big, comfortable bed, however, listening to the sounds coming from the bathroom. She had an artist's eye for details, an excellent memory and a vivid imagination, and they all ganged up to conjure an incredibly erotic mental picture of him standing under the hot spray from the twin shower heads.

She squirmed deeper into the bedding, telling herself to knock it off. She trusted Andy to keep his word, but she was painfully aware that they'd both been celibate for months. She was probably a fool to believe that either one of them could resist the temptation to make love again.

And did she really want to resist it? If she loved the man, and she did, wasn't it natural to want to express that love physically? Especially since she didn't have the nerve to express it verbally? By denying them both the pleasures of a marriage bed, wasn't she passing up the one opportunity she might have to build a deeper bond of intimacy with Andy?

Wearing only a towel knotted around his hips, he came out of the bathroom then, and walked over to his dresser. His hair stood up in damp, unruly spikes, as if he'd run a towel over his head and decided to call it good. Her mouth went dry and her palms itched to touch his broad, muscular shoulders and chest, the patch of springy auburn curls that grew in the space between his nipples and narrowed to a thin line down the center of his flat belly.

He opened the bottom dresser drawer, glanced at her, then straightened abruptly, clutching a pair of black pajamas in his right hand.

"Don't look at me like that," he said, his voice quiet and husky.

"Why not?" she asked, whispering because she couldn't get enough air into her lungs to speak any louder. "I like looking at you."

Even across the room, she could see his chest expand as he inhaled a quick, harsh breath. "Don't start something you'll regret tomorrow, Ginny."

Raising up on one elbow, she flipped back the covers, inviting him to join her. "I won't regret anything. And I don't think you should bother with those pajamas."

He looked at the garments wadded up in his hand as if he were surprised to see them there. Then he flung them back into the drawer and approached the bed with two long, purposeful strides. Propping his hands on his hips, he stared down at her.

"Are you sure you want to do this, Gin? Really sure?"

She held his intense gaze without the slightest inclination to flinch. "I want you, Andy. Come to bed."

A slow, sensuous smile spread across his mouth and a low sound, somewhere between a laugh and a groan, rumbled out of his chest. He flicked one wrist and the towel hit the carpet with a soft plop. At the sight of his gorgeous body, the rampant evidence of his desire for her, she sighed in admiration and lifted the covers while he slid into the bed beside her.

Moving eagerly into his embrace, she squawked when her hands touched his bare skin. "What in the world? Andy, you're freezing!"

Roaring with laughter, he pulled her flush against him. "I took a cold shower."

She giggled at a vision of him shivering under the twin shower heads. "It doesn't feel like it did much good," she said, pressing her hips closer to his.

"It never does when I'm thinking about you."

"You've done this before?"

"Damn near every night since you moved in," he admitted with a lopsided grin that made her laugh. "Kiss me before my teeth start chattering again."

She obeyed willingly, eagerly, holding nothing back as she set about the pleasurable task of warming him. It didn't take long. Oh, how she loved the way he kissed, as if he had all the time in the world and her mouth was a luscious delicacy he couldn't get enough of. The taste of his tongue sliding over hers, the greedy little sounds he made deep in his throat, the firm, sure touch of his hands as they moved over her back and shoulders immediately took her back to that night in September.

Their first time together had been urgent, almost violent. She had never felt anything so powerfully, erotically exquisite. Wanting to experience all those sensations again, she put her arms around his waist and rubbed her pelvis over his aroused flesh. Need clawed at her insides as it had before—low in her belly, hot and fierce. More. She had to have more now.

She stroked his tongue with her own, trying to communicate her impatience. He moved his hands to her bottom and crushed her against him, planting sweet, fervent kisses on her nose, her eyelids, her forehead.

"God, woman, I want you so damn much," he murmured, his breath hitting her lips in warm, toothpaste-scented puffs.

Then he sat up and made quick work of undoing the buttons stretching from her neck to her waist. Sliding both hands under the voluminous folds of cloth, he tugged the nightgown off over her head and tossed it aside. Her heart climbed into her throat, setting up an anxious, erratic beat as he gazed at her breasts.

Charlie had always been disappointed that they weren't bigger. Andy hadn't said anything when they'd made love before, but they'd been in quite a hurry. Would he notice her breasts were fuller because of the baby? Would he like that?

Lord, she wanted him to touch her so badly, her skin tingled.

As if he could read her mind, he cupped her with both hands, gently massaging her nipples with his palms. They were so sensitive now from her pregnancy, she gasped. He jerked his hands away as if he'd been stuck with needles.

"Did I hurt you?" he demanded in a hoarse whisper. "One of those pamphlets the doc gave us said your breasts might be tender, but I was trying to be careful."

Smiling in reassurance, she took his hands and put them where they'd been before. "No, it felt wonderful. I'll tell you if anything hurts."

Heaving a ragged sigh, he increased the pressure of his palms, leaned down and claimed her mouth with a deep, searching kiss that sizzled her blood clear down to her toes. She flicked her thumbs over his flat nipples, smiling when they instantly responded to her touch. Then he trapped her hands flat against his chest.

"I like that darn near as much as you do," he said. "But we've gotta slow down, babe. I want to do this right for you and you're gettin' me too riled up."

"You're doing the same thing to me," she said, trying to tug her hands free.

Smiling, he grabbed them and spread her arms out away from her sides. "I've been imagining you lying there like that ever since the wedding."

Unbearably flattered by the lusty approval in his eyes, she smiled and whispered, "Shame on you."

He shook his head. "There's no shame between us," he said, lightly running his hand across her waist, then over her abdomen and up to her breasts. "That's what I couldn't forget about that night out at the Circle D. You were so honest and uninhibited, it was pure dynamite."

"I'd never been that uninhibited before," she told him. "Maybe I just had too much to drink, but you made me feel beautiful."

"You *are* beautiful. Don't you know that?"

"Oh, please. I'm too skinny and I hardly have any breasts and I'm too tall, and—"

Clapping a hand over her mouth, he silenced her. "I don't know where you got any of those harebrained ideas, but they're wrong. Every last one of 'em."

Then he swept his hand from her chin to her toes, lightly brushing the backs of his fingers over her skin.

"You're a tall gal, all right." The wolfish gleam in his eyes matched the smile on his lips as he retraced his previous path with a firmer touch. "But these legs of yours are sexy as hell."

"Oh, yeah?"

"Yeah. They're nice and slim, and they make a man wonder what it'd feel like to have them wrapped around him. And this tight little tush of yours," he continued, gently squeezing the appropriate area, "looks damn good in a pair of jeans."

"But don't most men like a little more in the way of curves?"

"Depends on the woman." His thumbs meeting an inch below her navel, he spanned her hips with both hands.

"You're built kind of like a racehorse," he said, slowly smoothing his palms over her stomach and torso, as if he truly enjoyed feeling her shape and the texture of her skin. "You've got these nice, long, lean flanks. It wouldn't hurt you to put on the rest of that fifteen pounds the doc said you were missing, but on you, I think fewer curves are better."

Chuckling, she reached up and ruffled his hair. "Why, you silver-tongued devil. I can hardly wait to hear what you come up with when I'm so pregnant I can't see my feet."

"You think I'm feedin' you a line so I can have my way with you?" he drawled, raising an offended eyebrow at her.

She glanced pointedly at his lap. "Now, why would I think that?"

"It's working, isn't it?"

His wicked grin and the unabashedly hopeful note in his voice made her laugh. "Come down here and find out," she said, holding up her arms to him.

His chest shaking with laughter, he stretched out beside her again and pulled her to him. Heads resting on the same pillow, they gazed into each other's eyes. His face gradu ally took on a more serious expression and he touched her cheek with fingertips that weren't quite steady.

"It feels good, being here with you like this," he mur mured. "I've thought about it a lot."

"Me, too," she admitted.

She snuggled closer, loving the way his body heated against hers, the way his arms tightened around her, the way his breathing roughened. Then he kissed her, delving deeply into her mouth, and she gave herself up to the pleasure of his lovemaking. He approached the task of arousing her with the care of a man who paid close attention to details.

He lavished caresses with his hands and his mouth, ask ing whether she liked this or that better, patiently rediscov ering all the sensitive spots he'd found before. He was so straightforward, so matter-of-fact, and yet, so obviously enjoying himself, what few inhibitions she had left where he was concerned floated away on the sighs and moans he coaxed from her.

Urgency filled her, and she found herself exploring his body with the delirious enthusiasm she had experienced only once before. With him. Lord, how she loved feeling the hard muscles in his arms and back and shoulders rippling under her fingertips. Tasting the salty sweat that gathered at the base of his neck. Hearing his voice grow as rough and rag ged as his breathing, his earthy words of approval, his hoarse cries when she got downright bold.

They romped over the bed, playful as puppies, eager to experiment, finding joy and excitement in their discoveries. She felt feminine and sexy and powerful, even as she parted her legs and begged him to take her. He slid a pillow under her bottom, then knelt between her thighs and entered her slowly, carefully.

"Oh, yes," she whispered, moving her hips in encour agement.

He leaned forward, bracing his palms on either side of her head. His biceps bulged and the tendons in his neck stood out in sharp relief. "Are you sure? I don't want to hurt you or the baby."

"You won't. It's wonderful. Please—"

With a grunt of satisfaction, he began to move, taking her back to that place of delight where thoughts fled and sensations ruled. It was drugging, addictive, full of life and bright colors and the wondrous sounds of two people finding the ultimate release together.

Then there was a moment of breathless silence. She gazed up into his face and found the same awed expression in his eyes that must surely be in her own. Raising her hands to the back of his head, she urged him down for a soul-shattering kiss, trying to show him how deeply he had touched her.

Cradling her in his arms, he rolled onto his side, holding her tightly against him. They sighed in unison, then smiled at each other while their heartbeats gradually slowed and their muscles became lax. Feeling safe and content in his embrace, she closed her eyes.

If this was as close to loving as they were ever going to get, she thought, drifting into the first stage of sleep, it wasn't half bad. And maybe, if she were very lucky... well, maybe it would be enough.

Chapter Eleven

The weather stayed rotten and the usual aggravations came up at work, but all in all, the month of January turned out to be a surprisingly pleasant time for Andy. Ginny moved into the master bedroom on New Year's Day, and without intense sexual frustration shortening their tempers, the atmosphere at home had brightened considerably.

Maybe his dad had been right when he'd said that if they acted like they had a happy marriage, they'd wind up having one. That was how Andy felt, anyhow. Happily married to Ginny Bradford. Go figure.

There were other changes in their relationship he enjoyed almost as much as having a regular sex life. Ginny had stopped giving him wary looks and started to touch him occasionally, with what he would describe as wifely affection. She didn't flinch when he returned the favor, and she didn't seem to mind a bit when affectionate gestures led to more passionate pursuits, as they often did.

Another thing he liked was that he and Ginny talked a lot more than they ever had before. He really looked forward

o hearing about her day, and she listened to him talk about
iis work with an interest he found flattering.

The woman continually amazed and delighted him with
ier capacity to enjoy life. It didn't take all that much to
·lease her, either. She could turn a trip to the grocery store
nto an adventure, and she'd made such a fuss over the
helves he'd hung in her studio, you'd think he'd built her a
astle or something.

Enjoying life didn't stop her from working hard, though.
he'd completed a portrait of Sam, had started another one
·f Hank's daughter, Tina, and was taking commercial art
obs for the local newspaper, as well. She'd already fin-
shed half the childbirth and baby books in the county li-
·rary and seemed incredibly pleased that he wanted to read
hem, too. She was teaching him things about friendship
vithout even realizing it.

No matter how long her to-do list might be, she was never
oo busy to have a cup of coffee with Bill or gab on the
·hone with anyone who needed a friendly ear. When Dani
lelivered a whopping, eight-and-a-half-pound boy on the
wentieth, Ginny couldn't wait to rush over to Jackson and
isit her in the hospital.

Her generosity spilled over onto Janie Paxon, who had
urvived the New Year's Eve ordeal. Larry Paxon had also
urvived, and Andy had feared that Janie would let him in-
imidate her again. One week after Ginny had started visit-
ng her every day, however, Janie filed for a divorce.

Andy would have given a lot to know what his wife had
aid to the woman. He was also curious as hell about Gin-
iy's first marriage. He sensed she hadn't told him half of
vhat Charlie Bradford had done to her, but he couldn't
juite bring himself to question her about it.

For one thing, Andy figured she'd tell him whatever she
vanted him to know. For another, Ginny seemed so cheer-
ul and content, he didn't want to rock the proverbial boat
r intrude on her privacy. Then, on the first of February, he
eceived two surprises.

The first one occurred at five o'clock in the morning and scared the bejesus out of him. He'd been sound asleep cuddled up to Ginny's back with his arm around her waist, enjoying an erotic dream about the first time they'd made love in the shower. All of a sudden, she'd bolted upright in bed and clapped both hands onto her abdomen.

"Oh my God...." she whispered, her mouth dropping open in astonishment.

Used to being wakened by emergencies, he'd jerked himself out of that dream and sat up so fast, he'd made his own head spin. "What is it, Ginny?" he demanded, switching on the lamp.

She turned to him, grabbed his right hand and laid his palm over the rounded little bump created by their baby. "Feel that?"

"Feel what?" he asked, relaxing when he realized she was smiling.

She increased the pressure on his hand. "A flutter. It's like a baby sparrow testing his wings."

Though Andy held his breath and left his hand on her belly, he couldn't feel a thing but the warmth of her skin through the flannel of her nightgown.

"There it goes again," Ginny whispered, her eyes shining with wonder. "Oh, Andy, the baby's really moving!"

"Sure it's not just indigestion?"

"No, silly. I've felt it before, but I wasn't sure what it was. I'm starting the fifth month, so it's about the right time. That's what the books say, anyway."

He slid his hand under the hem of her nightie and placed his palm directly on her bare stomach. He doubted it would help all that much, but he figured any excuse to touch her was a good one. The truth was, he loved being close to her like this, loved seeing her all soft and warm and rumpled from sleep, loved knowing that his baby was growing inside her.

Shoot, maybe he just plain loved Ginny.

The idea wasn't nearly as disturbing as it should have been. In fact, it seemed natural. Almost...inevitable.

And then he felt it. A delicate movement against the heel of his palm, so light he would have thought he'd imagined it if Ginny's delighted laugh hadn't confirmed it. She threw her arms around his neck and hugged him for all she was worth. In light of what he'd just been thinking, she was worth plenty.

Raising his free hand to her nape, he kissed her hair, her forehead, her eyelids with a gentleness he hadn't known he possessed. She slowly pulled away and looked at him, her big brown eyes misty with an emotion that reached down into his heart and gave it a hard squeeze.

Suddenly there was no maybe, no question about his feelings for this woman. He loved her, all right. Tenderly. Passionately. Completely.

For one wild, insane instant, he was tempted to just blurt it all out and see what happened. Then his heart started to pound and fear rose from the pit of his stomach, squelching the urge as quickly as it had come.

"Andy, what is it?" she asked, gazing at him with such sweet concern, he knew that if he didn't get himself under control but quick, he'd give himself away.

"Nothing, Gin," he said, giving her the best smile he could manage. "It's just, uh, really amazing. Feeling the baby move like that, I mean."

He lay back against the pillows, bringing her with him and realizing abruptly that his hand was still under her nightgown. He rubbed it slowly over her belly, then allowed the tips of his fingers to dip into the patch of golden curls below. He heard her breath catch, saw her eyes take on that sleepy, sexy look that never failed to make his blood rush to his groin.

One thing led to another, and he wound up getting to work an hour later than usual. Too satisfied from Ginny's lusty send-off to let his deputies' teasing about newlyweds irritate him, he grabbed a cup of coffee and walked into his office. And there, sitting on top of the stack of mail in the center of his desk, was his second surprise.

Carefully placing his mug on the blotter, he settled into his swivel chair, picked up the letter and examined the return address. He knew bureaucracies rarely moved fast, but the Drug Enforcement Administration had kept him dangling for so long, he'd pretty much convinced himself they weren't interested in him. After realizing that he loved Ginny this morning, he didn't care a whole lot.

But what if she doesn't love you back, Johnson? What if she only made love with you on New Year's Eve because she felt sorry for you? What if she's just making the best of a bad situation and can't wait to leave after the baby's born?

He didn't want to listen to that doubting little voice inside his head, but it was too insistent to allow him to ignore it. Ginny had never said or even hinted that she loved him. And she'd been so adamant about not getting married and not making love with him again, he couldn't afford to ignore it. Rubbing the back of his neck, he sighed, then reached for his letter opener.

He pulled the crisp sheet of stationery from the envelope, scanned the brief message and sighed again. So. The DEA *was* still interested. At least enough to offer him an interview in their Denver office next month.

Should he go? The thought of leaving Ginny and the baby, his parents and all the other folks who depended on him filled him with reluctance. Anxiety. Guilt.

But if Ginny left him, he didn't know if he'd be able to stand living in the same town with her. Especially a town as small as Pinedale. And if she started dating someone else who was more her type... He didn't even want to think about how he'd feel if she did that. Damn.

Drumming his fingers on the arm of his chair, he struggled to put his emotions aside. He finally decided that it wouldn't hurt to go through with the interview. Since the DEA was holding a conference in Denver for law-enforcement officers the same week, he wouldn't have to make up an excuse for leaving town or tell anyone why he was really going to Colorado. A job with the DEA would be like having an insurance policy in case his marriage didn't work out.

Ginny sent Andy out the door with a smile and a kiss, then glanced at the clock and hurried to put on a pot of coffee for Bill's daily visit. In the past two months she'd become extremely fond of the old geezer, as he cheerfully called himself. He treated her with a kind of gruff affection, as if she were a favorite granddaughter. Since her own family wouldn't have anything to do with her, she relished his attention.

Sure enough, his familiar knock sounded on the back door at exactly nine o'clock. "It's open, Bill," she shouted, fishing "his" mug out of the cupboard.

"Coffee ready?" he asked, stamping the snow from his boots onto the mat.

"You bet. Come on in and take a load off."

He met her at the table, rubbing his gnarled hands together. "Man, it's colder than a witch's ... uh, never mind. It's just really cold out there."

Ginny grinned at him. "You think I haven't heard worse language than what you almost said?"

"Well, you're not gonna hear it from me, Miss Smarty Pants." He sipped from his mug, then set it down and propped his elbows in front of him. "So, what're you gonna do today?"

"Nothing exciting," she said. "Make a pot of stew for supper and take some books back to the library. Work on Tina's portrait this afternoon. Why? Got something going you want help with?"

"Nah. I was hopin' you'd have something I could help you with. I'm so sick of this dang snow and ice, I'm gettin' cabin fever."

Ginny patted his hand. "I know what you mean. I'd forgotten how rough the weather could be up here. Want to come to the library with me?"

"I might, just to get out of the house."

"It wouldn't hurt you to read instead of watching all those soap operas," she chided him.

"My eyesight isn't good enough for that anymore."

"If you'd stop being so vain and wear your glasses—"

"Now, don't start naggin' me about that again."

"I'm just practicing for the baby, Bill. Mothers are supposed to nag, you know."

"Hmmph. Poor kid."

"I'll have you know, I'm going to be an excellent mother," she said, chuckling at his disgruntled expression.

He swallowed the rest of his coffee, then smiled and nodded at her. "Yeah, I reckon you will." He got up and poured himself a refill. "Mind if I take a look at that portrait you're workin' on?"

"Not at all."

She led the way into the bedroom she was using as a studio. Bill stepped into the small room and folded his arms over his chest. Ginny crossed to her easel and turned it around, displaying the portrait with a dramatic sweep of her arm. "Is she gorgeous, or what?"

Bill came closer, his head tipped to one side as he studied the painting. "That's a fine piece of work, Ginny."

"Emily wants to give it to Hank for his birthday. Think he'll like it?"

"He'd be crazy not to. That little gal looks so real, you almost expect her to talk. You did this from a snapshot?"

When Ginny nodded, Bill dug his wallet out of a hip pocket, dropping it in his haste to get it open. A trembling note of excitement entered his voice. "Will you paint one for me? I'll pay whatever you want."

She went down on one knee and picked it up for him. His hands shook so hard when he tried to take it from her, he dropped it again.

"Hey, take it easy," she said, handing it back to him. "Of course I'll do one for you. I'll even give you a senior-citizen discount."

"I don't want one." He inhaled a deep breath, let it out, then extracted a small, dog-eared, black-and-white photograph that had been laminated a long time ago. "I want your very best work and I'll damn well pay the going rate."

Intensely curious, Ginny accepted the picture and studied it. A beautiful young woman, probably still in her teens, gazed directly ahead, as if she were looking at an extremely dear friend. Though she had obviously tried to maintain a serious expression, her generous lips curved up slightly at the corners and her eyes shone with mischief and humor. Judging from the hairstyle, Ginny guessed the photograph had been taken during the late 1920s or early 1930s.

"Who is she, Bill?" she asked quietly.

"The only woman I ever loved."

"Was she your wife?"

The pain in his eyes brought a lump to Ginny's throat. "No. I've never been married." He shook his head and sniffed, his eyes avoiding hers. "She passed on a little over ten years ago."

"I'm sorry," Ginny said quietly. "It sounds like you loved her a lot."

"Yeah, well..." He gulped, then gave her a crooked smile. "It just didn't work out."

"What was her name?"

"Eleanor. I always called her Kitten, though 'cause she was about as playful as one. Can you paint her, Ginny?"

"I'll do my best. What color were her eyes and her hair? Do you remember?"

"I've never forgotten one blessed thing about my Kitten." Bill gazed off into the distance, his throat working down another gulp. "Her eyes were blue. A clear, palish blue like a mountain lake in the early morning."

"Kind of like Andy's?"

He answered without looking at her. "Yeah. Real close to Andy's."

"What about her hair? I can tell it was dark, but—"

"Dark brown. When she was out in the sun, you could see a little red in it sometimes. Lord, but she had beautiful hair."

"May I keep this, Bill?" Ginny asked, holding up the laminated square.

Starting as if he'd been jerked back from a faraway place, he looked at her. "How soon can you get started?"

"Probably not until April. I've already promised two other portraits. I can call and see if one of the others would be willing to wait."

"No. That's fine." He took the photograph out of her hand and studied it. "This is all I've had of her for sixty-five years. A couple more months won't make any difference. I'll give it to you when you're ready to start."

"Why don't you have a copy made?" Ginny suggested. "It wouldn't take more than a few days."

"'Cause it's the only one I got and I don't trust those photo places not to lose it, that's why." He tucked the picture into its compartment and shoved his wallet back into his pocket. "I'm gonna go home so you can get to work. Call me when you're ready to go to the library."

"You've got yourself a date."

Ginny kissed his cheek and saw him off at the kitchen door, watching to make sure he didn't slip on the icy steps. Then she set the Crock-Pot on the counter and assembled the stew ingredients. Her conversation with Bill broke into her thoughts as she peeled the carrots and potatoes.

When it did, her heart ached for him, for the young woman in his precious photograph, for herself. How would it feel, she wondered, to have a man love her so much that he would carry her likeness in his wallet for sixty-five years? Did anybody love like that anymore—for a whole lifetime?

During the past month, she'd hoped and prayed that Andy would come to love her—just the way Bill had loved Kitten, but it didn't look as if that were going to happen. Oh, she knew he enjoyed making love with her as much as she enjoyed making love with him. And, he'd certainly been more affectionate since they'd started sharing a bedroom.

She'd tried repeatedly to convince herself that what they shared together was enough to make her happy. After all, few if any marriages were perfect, so why be greedy? But it wasn't enough. It wasn't even close to being enough. Especially when she knew it would end in a few more months.

Romantic fool that she was, she wanted all of him—heart and mind, soul and body, and she knew herself well enough to know that she'd never be satisfied with less. Shaking her head, she sighed, sniffled a little, then forced herself to go back to work.

Hungry, tired and chilled to his bone marrow, Andy left the office at seven-thirty that night, hoping like hell that Ginny had figured out something for dinner. He wouldn't care what it was or how badly she'd burned it, as long as it was hot and there was plenty of it.

The snowplows hadn't been able to keep up with the storm that had settled in at lunchtime, and the roads were slick in every direction. He'd spent the past four hours coping with jackknifed semis and stalled cars and thinking about Ginny. The more he thought about her, the more irritated he felt, because he hadn't been able to figure out a way to convince her to stay with him for the rest of her life. Not without sticking his neck out farther than he wanted to, anyway.

Damn, but he wished he'd never made that bargain with her about getting a divorce after the baby was born. Of course, then she wouldn't have married him at all and he never would have gotten to know her well enough to fall in love with her in the first place. Which, after a day of wrestling with all sorts of conflicting emotions, was starting to sound like one helluva good idea.

He wasn't the kind of a man who wasted much time analyzing emotions. Oh, he had them, all right, but he'd rather deal with hard facts and tangible evidence any day, than sit around like a sissy, talking about his feelings.

Still, he couldn't deny that his flagging spirits perked right up when he turned onto his street and saw the porch light burning in welcome for him. It was just one of the thoughtful little things Ginny did every day that he'd never bothered—or maybe allowed himself—to notice before. After parking in the driveway, he hurried up the back steps and entered the house.

A rich, meaty aroma greeted him at the door. Telling himself he really oughtta let Ginny know how much he appreciated her efforts, Andy pried off his boots and set them on the mat. Before he could call out a greeting, however, he heard a splash, followed immediately by Ginny's voice hollering from the hallway.

"Come back here, you mangy little varmint!"

To Andy's surprise, a soggy, soapy animal no bigger than a jackrabbit charged into the kitchen, letting out high-pitched yapping noises with every step. It stopped directly in front of him and sniffed suspiciously at his socks. Then it planted all four feet and shook its scrawny body, spraying Andy and half the room with water and suds.

"What the hell?" he bellowed.

Wiping water off his face with one hand, Andy bent down and reached for the dog—at least he *thought* it was a dog—with the other. Needle-sharp teeth sank into his index finger, just below the second knuckle.

Carrying a towel, Ginny raced into the room. "No, no, no!" she shouted, flapping the cloth at the animal. "Bad girl! Shame on you!"

The dog rolled its eyes as if trying to spot Ginny, then sank its damn teeth another eighth of an inch into Andy's finger. Andy swatted its rump with his free hand. It released him with a surprised yelp, backed off two steps and shook itself again. Ears laid back against its head, the dog spewed out a series of fierce, ear-splitting barks that could have roused a whole cemetery.

Ginny tossed the towel over it and scooped it into her arms as if it were a baby. "Stop that, you silly thing," she scolded. "It's just Andy."

"Well, what the devil is *that*, Ginny?" Andy demanded, pointing his injured finger at the little black nose sticking out of the purple towel.

Cuddling the bundle closer to her breasts, she backed up a step and shot him a coaxing smile. "It's my new puppy. She didn't mean any harm."

"Like hell. She damn near ripped my finger off!"

"It wasn't *that* bad," Ginny chided him. "She was just defending her territory."

"Since when is my house her territory?"

"Since about eleven o'clock this morning. Bill and I found her wandering down the street in front of the library. We asked around, but nobody knew of anyone who'd lost a dog. I couldn't just leave her there, Andy."

The pup poked her head completely out of the towel and gave Andy a look that might well have said, "So there, you big jerk."

Gritting his teeth, he silently counted to fifteen. "Did it ever occur to you that there might be a reason I didn't have a dog?"

"You're not allergic, are you?" Ginny asked anxiously.

"No, but I sure as hell don't want one. Especially not one that bites," Andy replied.

"You probably just scared her, Andy. She won't do that again." Ginny dropped the towel over the back of a chair, turned the pup around and looked it square in the eye. "Will you, Schnoodle?"

The puppy slurped her tongue across the tip of Ginny's nose. When she laughed, the dog's stubby tail whipped back and forth in response. Andy wasn't at all sure he really wanted to hear the answer, but he *had* to ask the question.

"Did you say, 'Schnoodle'?"

Ginny cradled the pup in her arms again and wrinkled her nose at him. Oh, brother. That was a sure sign he was about to get one of her goofy explanations.

"Well, see, Bill and I think she's probably got some schnauzer and some poodle in her, so that makes her a schnoodle, doesn't it?"

"It makes her a damned mutt," Andy muttered.

Raising her chin, Ginny gave him a frosty stare. "That was a mean thing to say. As soon as she learns some manners, Schnoodle will be a wonderful pet."

"Come *on*, Ginny. The last thing you'll need in a few months is a dog to chase after, and I don't want a pet."

"She'll be *my* pet, Andy, and I'll take care of her. I'll enjoy having her company when you're working late."

Schnoodle sneezed. Ginny grabbed the towel and wrapped the dog up again. "Come on, sweetheart. Let's get you rinsed off and dried."

Unwilling to give in just yet, but fully aware that he'd already lost this particular battle, Andy followed her into the bathroom off the hallway. The place reeked of wet dog and it looked as if a tidal wave had swept through it. The instant Ginny tried to lower Schnoodle into the water, the dog went nuts, thrashing, clawing and yapping its fool head off. Andy shut the door to prevent another escape.

"It's okay, baby," Ginny coaxed, her voice suddenly carrying a note of exhaustion. "Please, don't fuss so much and we'll get done faster."

Arms full of the struggling animal, she went down on one knee. The foot she was using to brace herself slipped on the wet floor and she fell forward, banging her right elbow on the rim of the tub. Crying out with pain, she dropped Schnoodle into the water and all hell broke loose.

Andy had no choice but to jump into the fray before Ginny broke her neck or the damn dog completely destroyed the bathroom. He helped Ginny up and made her sit on the closed toilet seat, then turned back to the animal who was frantically trying to climb out of the tub.

Keeping a close eye on the pup's teeth, he grabbed her behind the ears, his temper abating abruptly when he felt her terrified trembling. Softening his voice, he spoke to her in the soothing tone he used with frightened people.

"Hey there, Schnoodle. Is that any way to act? If you're gonna live in my house, you can't be stinky. Nobody likes a smelly dog. Easy, girl, I won't hurt you."

Though her trembling continued, Schnoodle calmed down enough to allow Andy to finish the bath without further mayhem. Her eyes glowing with gratitude, Ginny handed him a fresh towel. He dried the squirming ball of fur as best he could, then sat back on his heels and let her shake herself.

While Ginny lifted the pup onto the counter beside the sink and used a hair dryer on her, Andy scrubbed out the tub and mopped up the puddles on the floor with the dirty towels. By the time they both finished, he decided Schnoodle wasn't a bad-looking dog if you liked the frou-frou, fur ball kind. And she was such a playful, inquisitive little thing, he couldn't help chuckling at her.

Ginny shot him a hopeful grin. "Bill loaned me a puppy crate she can sleep in at night. And I won't let her go in the living room alone until I'm sure she's housebroken. I'll even take her to an obedience class."

He glanced at Ginny, then at Schnoodle, struggling to keep a stern expression on his face. "If Jake comes calling with love in his heart, I'm not sure even a sliding glass door would stop him. You'll have to have her spayed."

"Oh, of course. I don't want a whole batch of puppies any more than you do. I'm planning to take her to Doc Shumaker tomorrow to get her shots and I'll talk to him about it then."

"All right," Andy said, chuckling again at the quizzical look the dog was giving him. "Unless somebody claims her, she's all yours, Ginny."

"You really don't mind?" she asked, her eyes anxiously searching his. "I couldn't just leave her out there, Andy."

"I know you couldn't." He shrugged. "She's kind of a cute little mutt, and with that god-awful bark of hers, she might even make a good watchdog."

Throwing her arms around his neck, Ginny hugged him as enthusiastically as she had that morning. Andy hugged her back, thoroughly enjoying his reward until his stomach's rumbling destroyed the moment.

"Sounds like I'd better get supper on the table," Ginny said, smiling as she released him.

They both changed into dry clothes. Then Ginny dished up the stew she'd made in the Crock-Pot. Seeing how tired she was, Andy insisted on doing the dishes and sent her into the living room with orders to put her feet up. He joined her ten minutes later. Sitting in her rocking chair with her feet on the coffee table, she held a dozing Schnoodle on her lap, stroking the dog's silver fur as she rocked.

"Guess what?" she asked as Andy squatted to light a fire. "Bill asked me to paint a portrait for him today, and I got another job drawing ads for the grocery store."

"There's no need for you to take on so much work," he said, frowning at her over his shoulder.

"I'm enjoying it, Andy. Don't worry about it."

He straightened up, then sat on the end of the sofa that was closest to her. "I can't help worrying about it. The doc said you were supposed to get lots of rest."

"I feel fine." She raised her chin and scowled at him. "The money will come in handy after the baby's born."

"You're my wife, Ginny," he said quietly. "I'm more than happy to support you and the baby."

Heaving an impatient sigh, she shook her head. "I don't want to be supported, Andy. Not by anyone."

"Why not? Have I been stingy?"

"No, of course not." She gave him a wry smile, then held out her palms to him. "It's just that having your own paycheck gives you dignity and independence. When you let somebody support you, they think they can tell you what to do, who to be and how to act."

"Is that what Charlie did to you?"

She shrugged, as if it didn't matter much, but deep in her eyes, he could see remembered pain. "Yeah. Kind of. You know the Vietnam vets took a lot of abuse after they came home. Charlie tried to act as if he'd never even been in the service. I guess he just wanted to blend in with everyone else and be 'normal'," she said, making quotation marks in the air with her fingers. "Whatever that is."

"He didn't think you were normal enough?" Andy asked incredulously.

"It wasn't too bad while he was still in college, but once he got his engineering degree and started climbing the corporate ladder, I don't think anyone could have been normal enough for Charlie." She shook her head and uttered a bitter little laugh that put an ache in the middle of Andy's chest.

"He didn't want me to work or go to school even though we didn't have any kids. None of that women's lib crud for *his* wife, by God. He wanted to be married to June Cleaver or Donna Reed—anybody but me. I couldn't please him no matter how hard I tried, so I finally gave up trying. It got pretty ugly after that."

The sad, hopeless expression in Ginny's eyes reminded Andy of Janie Paxon. Struggling to keep the fury he felt out of his voice, Andy asked, "Are you sure he didn't beat you, Gin?"

"No. He just yelled a lot."

"Can you tell me why you didn't leave him?"

She turned her head toward the window, but Andy didn't think she really saw it. Then she shrugged again. "It's hard to explain. We had some wonderful times together, you know? And he didn't wake up one day and start being a jerk. It was more of a gradual change. I loved him and I knew he hadn't completely recovered from the war, so I made a lot of excuses for him. I didn't even figure out what was going on for a long time."

Ginny hesitated, then shook her head and gave him a too-bright smile. "Dumb, huh? But, that's all history now. I must be boring you to tears."

"No, you're not." Leaning forward, he braced his elbows on his knees. "Janie Paxon's not the only abused woman in this county, Ginny. Maybe I can help the others more if I understand them better. Why didn't you leave after you realized what he was doing to you?"

"Well, for one thing, Charlie had complete control of our money. My family wouldn't believe I needed help and I didn't want to tell Sam what was going on because it was just too humiliating. I didn't have enough self-esteem to believe I could earn my own living. Charlie made sure of that, and he loved to tell me what a burden I was.''

''Didn't you have other friends?''

''Nobody I could confide in. It takes time to build friendships like that, and the company moved us so often, I hardly ever got to know the neighbors. If I did, Charlie always found an excuse to pick a fight with them and they wouldn't want anything to do with either one of us.''

''So he kept you isolated.''

''Yeah. It took me a while to figure that out, too. When I finally did, I decided it was time to leave him, come hell or high water. Before I could find a way to pull it off, Charlie found out he had cancer, and I couldn't bring myself to go then. He died eight months later. After paying off the doctors and the hospital, I hardly had enough money left to bury him.''

''How did you pay for college?''

''When Charlie realized he really was going to die, he told Sam I was going to need help. I had some part-time jobs, and Sam loaned me the rest. I still owe him money.''

''Damn, Ginny. I'm sorry you had to go through all that.''

Her chin came up and she glared at him. ''Don't you dare feel sorry for me. It's taken me a while, but I've put myself back together and believe you me, I'll never be that stupid or dependent on anyone else again. And I'll never be a burden to anyone else, either. Especially not you.''

''For God's sake, you're carrying my baby. You're not a burden and you never will be.''

She raised a doubtful eyebrow at him, then crossed her arms over her breasts. ''Uh-huh. Is that why you were so eager to marry me, Andy?''

It was Andy's turn to shrug. ''I don't always handle change real well, Ginny. It takes me a while to get used to things being different.''

''Well, you sure got 'different' with me, didn't you?''

"It hasn't been that bad," Andy protested, wishing to hell and back that he'd never asked about Charlie if *this* was the kind of mood talking about him put Ginny in. "And I don't think of you as a burden. Give it a rest, will ya?"

"Gladly. Just don't try to tell me how much work I can do. I need to be independent."

They settled into a mutually disgruntled silence then. Ginny used the remote control to turn on the television, effectively shutting Andy out. He returned the gesture by pretending to immerse himself in one of the books Ginny had brought home from the library.

Of course, he couldn't concentrate. Not when he could feel the tension radiating from her. Not when he was acutely aware of every stroke she gave the pup. Certainly not when he found himself feeling jealous of a damned dog.

After the way Charlie had treated her, could Ginny ever really learn to trust him? he wondered. Could she ever really love him? And how could he find a way to convince her to stay with him after the baby was born when she was so determined to be independent?

He didn't know the answers to any of those questions, but he figured he'd better start giving her some reasons to want to stay with him and he'd better be damned quick about it. Because, despite the heated words they'd just exchanged, despite the upheaval she continually caused in his life, despite everything she did that irritated him no end, he didn't know if he could ever stand to let her go.

Chapter Twelve

"Just put all the pieces over in the corner, Bill," Ginny said, opening the door to the bedroom she and Andy had cleared out for the baby's use. "The sanding and stripping will be easier if I don't put it together yet."

Scowling at her, the old man hauled in one side panel of the crib Ginny had just purchased at a neighbor's garage sale. "If you ask me, I still think you should have talked to Andy before you bought this stuff. He won't like it."

Ginny propped her hands on her hips and scowled right back at him. "I didn't ask you and I don't need to ask Andy, either."

"All I'm sayin', is that Andy wouldn't expect you to go to all the trouble of refinishing old junk. He can afford to buy his kid a new crib."

"Well, maybe he can, but I can't, and I'm buying the baby's furniture. There's nothing wrong with either the crib or the dresser that a little work won't fix."

Shaking his head, Bill huffed at her. "I've never seen a married couple handle their money the way you two do. Why don't you just put it all in one big pot?"

"Our system works just fine for us," Ginny said, struggling without much success to hold on to her patience. "I'll enjoy fixing this stuff up."

"Yeah, and I'll have to wait another damn month before you start on Kitten's portrait. Hell, Ginny, let *me* buy you a new crib."

Oh, so *that* was it, Ginny thought, smiling now that she understood Bill's attitude. "I can only work on a portrait so many hours a day, Bill. And I can't get started on it until you hand over that picture. I'll just keep it for an hour or two so I can make some preliminary sketches."

"You won't let that Schnoodle pup chew it up, will ya?"

"She hasn't chewed anything but a rawhide bone for a month now. What's the matter, don't you trust me?"

Bill gave her a sheepish grin, then pulled his wallet out of his hip pocket. "Okay, you can have it. But be careful. I feel naked without it."

Ginny accepted the laminated square and tucked it into the pocket of her maternity smock. "You'll have it back before suppertime, good as new."

"Mind if I ask you a nosy question?" Bill asked.

"Since when do you bother to ask permission?"

He gave her another sheepish grin. Then his smile faded and a worried expression entered his eyes. "I don't mean to pry, but I've been wondering about something. Is everything all right between you and Andy?"

"Of course. We've been getting along fine. Why?"

He hitched one shoulder halfway to his ear in a semi-shrug. "Well, you've been actin' kinda cranky ever since he came home from Colorado."

"Oh, *please,*" she said, rolling her eyes and placing both hands on her distended belly. "Women starting their seventh month of pregnancy are allowed to be cranky. It's in the rule book."

"I know you're not all that comfortable sometimes, hon, but it's more than that. You love Andy, right?"

Ginny nodded. "Yes, I do."

Eyes narrowed, he gave her a shrewd look. "And that scares the devil out of you, doesn't it?"

She hesitated, then nodded again.

"You've gotta know he's a good man by now. So why does it scare you to love him?"

"Because Andy doesn't love me, Bill," she said quietly. "You know why he married me—"

"Aw, horsefeathers! I've never seen that boy look or act any happier than he does right now." Taking her left hand between his palms, he softened his voice and continued earnestly. "Maybe he hasn't said the words, but Andy loves you, Ginny. Believe that."

"I'll try, but—"

"But nothing. And don't just try. *Do* it."

"Okay," she whispered, blinking back the tears brought on by his kindness and obvious affection.

"My days were pretty long and lonesome before you came along. I don't want to lose you because you're unhappy."

"I'm not unhappy, Bill. Not really."

"But you're not really happy, either."

Ginny gulped, then hugged him, forcing a smile onto her face before she pulled back. "Happiness is a relative thing, pal. Now, are you gonna stand there and jaw all day, or bring in the rest of my stuff so I can work on Kitten?"

"I'm goin', Miss Smarty Pants. I'm goin'."

While Bill retrieved the remaining pieces of furniture from the trunk of her car, Ginny walked into her studio and dug out a fresh sketch pad and three pencils. Deciding she'd rather work at the kitchen table, she retraced her steps and waved Bill off at the back door.

Then she poured herself a glass of milk, let Schnoodle out to romp in the sunshine and propped Kitten's photograph against the sugar bowl. Knowing Bill would pace until he got his beloved picture back, she gazed at the young woman's face for a minute before picking up a pencil. She made a few entative lines, but couldn't dredge up the concentration she needed because Bill's words kept bouncing around in her brain like a ricocheting bullet.

Maybe he hasn't said the words, but Andy loves you, Ginny. Believe that.

The problem was, she wanted to believe Bill. She had missed Andy desperately when he'd gone to Denver for the Drug Enforcement Administration's conference. Discovering how emotionally dependent on him she'd already become had scared her spitless. With good reason.

She hadn't told Bill anything but the truth. Ever since the day she'd brought Schnoodle home, she and Andy had been getting along incredibly well. Almost too well.

He'd been surprisingly patient with the puppy and had even started training her himself. He hadn't said another word about Ginny working too hard. He delighted in feeling the baby kick and even talked to her belly every night because he'd read that babies could hear voices while they were still in the womb. Though her stomach had long since turned into "Mount Baby," he still reacted to her as if she were the embodiment of all his sexual fantasies. He really *did* seem happy.

And yet, she couldn't shake the feeling that Andy was working too hard at getting along with her. It was almost as if he were trying to prove something, though what that something might be, she couldn't imagine. As far as she knew, he was still planning to get a divorce after the baby was born. For all she knew, he was counting the days until he'd be free again.

But what if he's not? her conscience demanded. *What if he's changed his mind about the divorce? Why don't you just lay your cards on the table and be honest about your feelings for him?*

"Because I'm a coward," she murmured. "I'd crawl in a hole and die if he rejected me."

Spoken out loud, the words sounded immature. If Marjorie, a friend who owned a library of self-help books had heard them, she'd have tossed her hands up in disgust.

"Stop being so melodramatic," Marjorie would have said. "Healthy relationships are honest. What good is your marriage if you can't even tell Andy how you feel? And since when did you become a mind reader? Doesn't it make more sense to let Andy tell you how he feels instead of trying to second-guess him? That's codependent behavior."

"And we can't have that, now, can we?" Ginny grumbled.

In truth, she really *couldn't* afford to allow herself to slip back into her old patterns of behavior. And it *did* make more sense to have a frank, open discussion about the future with Andy instead of torturing herself with fears and insecurities that might have no basis in reality.

They'd been married for over four months. That should be long enough for Andy to have formed a clear sense of his feelings toward her. If he didn't want to stay married, she might as well know it and plan accordingly. Maybe she would ask him tonight. No, not maybe. She *would* ask him tonight.

With that decision firmly settled in her mind, Ginny found her pencil zipping across page after page. After thirty-five minutes, she had several poses and moods for Kitten's portrait for Bill to choose from. She ran next door, returned his picture and got his approval for her own favorite sketch, then hurried home.

The phone was ringing when she walked through the back door. After taking a second to catch her breath, she picked up the receiver and heard the faint crackle of static on the line that sometimes accompanies a long-distance call.

"I'm trying to reach Sheriff Andrew T. Johnson, ma'am," a masculine voice with more than a hint of a southern drawl said. "Have I reached his home?"

"Yes, you have," Ginny answered. "He's not in at the moment. You might want to try his office."

"I've already done that, ma'am. Is this Mrs. Johnson?"

"Yes. I'll be happy to take a message for you."

"I'd appreciate that, Mrs. Johnson," the man said. "My name's Dan Black. I'm with the Drug Enforcement Administration in Washington."

"Is this an emergency, Mr. Black?" Ginny asked after copying down the number he rattled off. "I can try to track Andy down for you."

"That won't be necessary, ma'am. I have some good news for him about the job interview he had with us in Denver last month. If he can get back to me by tomorrow, that'll be fine. Y'all have a nice day, now."

"Thanks," Ginny murmured, then fumbled the handset back onto its hook.

Andy was going to leave town. He was going to take a dangerous job and leave town. He was already making plans to leave town, probably even the whole state. She might never see him again.

Feeling as if she'd been punched in the chest, she collapsed onto the chair she'd used while she was sketching. She stared out the sliding glass door until her heart and lungs began to function normally again.

"It's okay," she whispered. "Andy doesn't owe you any explanations. There's no reason to feel so betrayed."

But she *did* feel betrayed. Betrayed and disappointed and angry as hell. Well, at least she hadn't made a fool of herself by asking him if he wanted to stay married to her. She ought to call Dan Black and thank him for sparing her the humiliation of being rejected and Andy the discomfort of having to reject her.

Mentally thumbing her nose at Marjorie, Ginny went back to the phone, called Andy's office and repeated Mr. Black's message, then shredded the note she'd written and tossed it into the trash. If Andy couldn't be bothered to share his plans with her, let him think his damn secret was still safe. By God, he would never know how she really felt about him. When he finally got around to telling her he'd gotten himself a new job, she wouldn't even turn a hair.

Glancing at the calendar on her way back to the table, she released a bitter laugh. Now, wasn't that ironic? Today was April Fool's Day.

After tucking into his coat pocket the receipt the teller had given him, Andy headed back to work. Taking his messages from the dispatcher, he walked into his office, then settled in behind his desk. He flipped through the slips, pausing when he saw the one from Dan Black. Setting the others aside, he grabbed the phone and dialed the DEA's number.

"Thanks for getting back to me so soon," Black said when Andy identified himself. "I know you're a busy man, so I'll get right to the point. How soon can you come into Quantico for training? We'd like you to start right away."

"I can't do that," Andy said. "I told you on my application that I wanted to serve out my term of office, and the election's not until November."

"Damn," Black muttered. "We've got a situation brewing in Montana that would be perfect for you. Don't you have a deputy who could take over for a few months?"

Andy had two deputies who could probably take over today without a whole lot of trouble. But now that the offer had been made, he knew he didn't really want to accept it. Not if it meant leaving Ginny.

"Tell you the truth, Dan, I'm having second thoughts about changing jobs," he said. "I was single when I applied, but my wife's due to have a baby soon. I'm not sure this is the right move for me to make."

Black sighed, then fell silent for a long moment. "I can't say I'm not disappointed. Why don't you give it more thought before you decide?"

"I hate to take up any more of your time than I already have. I really don't think I'm gonna change my mind."

"Yeah, I hear you," Black replied. "Well, if you do, let me know. We can always use good men. Tell your wife hello for me. I enjoyed talking with her."

"When did you talk to Ginny?"

"This afternoon. I tried your office first, and called your house when you weren't in."

"Did you mention the job?"

"Yes. Is there a problem?"

"No, I was just, uh, surprised, that's all."

His gut roiling with an uneasy sensation, Andy replaced the handset and drummed his fingers on the desktop. Damn. He wished Ginny hadn't found out about the DEA job this way. Since he wasn't gonna take it, he wished she hadn't found out at all.

He spent the next two hours plowing through paperwork, but his mind repeatedly wandered to Ginny. He'd been doing his level best to make her happy, and for the most part, he thought he'd succeeded. But every now and then, when she thought he wasn't looking, she'd get this sad, almost hopeless look in her eyes—as if she wanted something so bad she could taste it, but she knew she'd never have it. And she'd been withdrawn ever since he'd come back from Colorado.

Dammit, he wished to hell and back that he'd never made that damn deal with her. He'd thought they'd at least become good friends by now, and it hurt that she wouldn't, or maybe couldn't, confide in him after almost four and a half months of marriage.

He hated being patient. Hated feeling as though he had to walk on eggshells around her, worrying that he'd say the wrong thing and ruin all the progress they'd made so far. Hated having this damn divorce hanging over his head.

Cursing under his breath, he cleaned off his desk. Then he grabbed his coat and hat, and told the dispatcher he was going home. He *had* to see Ginny.

Maybe it was just as well that she'd found out about the DEA job. If she was upset that he hadn't told her about it, he could use it as an opening to talk about their future. He arrived at the house ten minutes later and found her bending over the kitchen table, rubbing a piece of charcoal over a large sheet of paper. She glanced up and gave him a smile that was so brief, he couldn't tell if it was strained or not.

"Hi, there," she said. "You're home early."

He crouched down to pet Schnoodle, who was going through her tail-wagging, greet-the-master routine. "What're you doing there, Gin?"

She answered without looking up. "Turning this into carbon paper. Bill's sweetheart's on the other side. I'll tape it onto the canvas and trace over it in a second. Then I can start painting."

Straightening to his full height, he crossed the room and stood to the right of the table. Ginny was so intent on her work, he decided to wait until she'd finished before trying to talk to her. When she flipped the paper over and taped it to the canvas, he studied the sketch for a moment.

"That's Bill's sweetheart?"

"That's Kitten, all right. Wasn't she pretty?"

"Yeah." Leaning closer, he braced one hand on the table. "It's funny, but she looks kinda familiar to me."

"Didn't Bill ever show you her picture?"

"I didn't even know he'd had a girlfriend until he hired you to paint her. Have you got it here?"

Chuckling, Ginny shook her head. "He could hardly stand to let me keep it long enough to make sketches."

"You've been a good friend to him, Ginny."

"He's been a good friend to me. It seems so sad that he couldn't marry her."

"Why couldn't he?"

"I don't know. He said it just didn't work out. But he must have really loved her."

Andy nodded, then shoved his hands into his pockets. "I, uh, talked to Dan Black this afternoon. He said to tell you hello and that he'd enjoyed talking with you."

A mildly surprised look crossed her face, but if she was upset, she was doing a great job of hiding it.

"That's nice. You got the message then."

"Yeah. Thanks for passing it on. It could have waited until I got home."

Ginny shrugged. "I was afraid I'd either lose the note or forget to tell you. He told me he had good news?"

"He offered me a job with the DEA. I applied for it way back in September, Ginny. I didn't mention it because I wasn't sure anything would come of it."

"Well, congratulations. It sounds like a new challenge for you. When do you start?" she said, giving him a bright, interested smile.

Pulling out a chair, he sat down and motioned for her to join him. "I didn't accept the job."

Frowning, she seated herself at a right angle to him and propped her feet on the chair across from hers. "Why didn't you accept it?"

"Because drug runners are dangerous folks. I don't want to put you and the baby in jeopardy."

"They won't have any reason to bother the baby or me, Andy. We'll be divorced."

That thought sure didn't seem to upset her. Jeez, did she *want* him to leave town? "Well, uh..." He hesitated, then decided to take the plunge before he lost his nerve completely. "I've been, uh, rethinking the divorce, and I don't think it's such a good idea."

Her shoulders stiffened. "Wait a minute. We have a deal—"

"I know, but think about it," he said quickly. "It's as much my responsibility to raise our baby as it is yours. Every kid needs a dad sometimes, so I think we should stay married."

"Uh-uh," she said, giving her head an emphatic shake. "I stayed married to Charlie out of a sense of duty. I don't want you to do that, Andy. Trust me, it was the pits."

"Now, Ginny, don't be stubborn."

"No way, Johnson. You obviously wanted this job or you wouldn't have applied for it and gone through the interview. I never expected you to tie yourself down forever. You've more than fulfilled your responsibilities."

"It was just an ego thing," he argued. "I wanted to see if I could be something more than a small-town sheriff."

"And now you know that you can. So go do it before you wind up resenting both me and the baby."

"Dammit, be reasonable," Andy shouted, banging the table with his fist. "You can't raise this kid alone. This is real life, not some soap opera."

Her chin came up and her eyes flashed with pure temper. "Well, you're not God's gift! I can take care of myself and the baby just fine. We'll work out some kind of a custody agreement that will fit in with your job, and you can be a good dad without being married to me."

"Man, you really know how to go for a guy's throat." He shoved back his chair and stood. "Why don't you just spell it right out? You don't need or want me around."

"I didn't say that." She rolled her eyes in exasperation, then held out her palms to him. "I told you I didn't want to be a burden, and if you sacrifice your dreams this way, that's exactly what I'll be."

Andy walked to the sliding glass door and looked out at the yard. Was this where he was supposed to tell her he loved her? Risk humiliating himself by begging her to stay with him the way he'd begged Denise? Though Ginny wasn't cruel enough to laugh in his face the way Denise had, the thought still left a sour taste in his mouth.

But there was a lot more at stake this time. They couldn't go on circling around each other like a couple of wary dogs. One of them was gonna have to break down and be honest, and it looked as if he'd been elected.

Forcing himself to take steady, calming breaths, he imagined a swing set over by the blue spruce and a sandbox in the southwest corner by the fence. No matter how scared he was, he couldn't give up this easily.

Decision made, he walked back to the table, turned his chair around and straddled it, then folded his forearms across the top of the back. Meeting Ginny's guarded gaze, he groped for words that would save the situation without leaving him totally vulnerable.

"I haven't been completely honest with you, and I think maybe it's time I was," he finally said.

"What do you mean?"

"From where I'm sitting, giving up the DEA job isn't any big sacrifice. I've had second thoughts about it all along. I only applied for it because of that night we spent together at the Circle D."

"I don't understand."

"Well, I guess you'd need to know more about my ex-wife to do that. She was one of those gals who fell in love with the uniform and not the man inside it, you know?"

"What's that got to do with us, Andy?"

"I'm gettin' to that." He paused and cleared his throat, then forced himself to continue. "See, uh, once Denise found out what my job was really like, with the long hours and everything, she hated it. She wanted more of a social life and more money to spend."

"Did she have a job?"

"Yeah. She worked in one of the clothing stores downtown. She had a chance to buy it, but we couldn't raise the cash. My dad offered to mortgage the ranch, but I wouldn't let him. That really ticked her off."

"Why did you refuse?"

"My pride, partly. And I wasn't sure she could make a go of it. It didn't seem fair to let my dad risk everything when so many ranchers were going belly-up. Denise thought I was trying to force her to stay home and have kids."

"Were you?" Ginny asked.

"I don't know for sure. It wasn't a conscious thing, but it might have had something to do with it. Anyway, she decided I wasn't much of a husband. I came home one night and she'd moved out. Wouldn't even try counseling."

"That must have hurt."

"Yeah, it did."

"Where is she now?"

"Portland. Married a guy who owns a chain of clothing stores. Has a real glamorous life from what I hear."

"Does that bother you?"

"Well, it beat the hell out of my ego at first," he admitted. "But, you know, life goes on. I'm glad she's happy, and I've tried to learn from the whole thing."

"What have you learned, Andy?"

He grinned and gave his head a rueful shake. "I've done a lot of reading so I won't be so boring."

"She thought you were boring?" Ginny demanded with an incredulous laugh.

"Oh, yeah. She said I didn't talk enough, but I never could figure out what she wanted to talk about. But, see, that's what freaked me out so much after we made love the first time."

"Wait a minute. You've lost me."

"Well, shoot, Ginny, if I bored Denise to tears, I figured there wasn't a hope in hell that I could ever hang on to *you.*"

"Is that supposed to be a compliment?"

"Yeah. I guess it is. I've always liked lively, spunky gals, but after Denise laid that number on me, I lost my self-confidence with women."

"Oh, Andy—"

"Now, don't you go feeling sorry for me," he said, scowling at her. "That's not why I told you all this. I was trying to explain why I applied for that DEA job, and what it boils down to, was I thought if I had a more exciting job, maybe I'd be more interesting to a gal like you, Ginny. And that's the truth."

"But that's so—"

"Hey, I know it was a stupid idea, but after that night with you, I had to face how lonely I was, and...well, I knew I needed some kind of a change in my life."

"I wasn't going to say stupid," she chided him. "I was going to say unnecessary. Andy, you're not a boring person. I think that was Denise's problem, not yours."

He shrugged. "Well, forget her then. But, Ginny, there's something else you've got to know. I know we had a rough start together, and we haven't always gotten along too well, but I've, uh, enjoyed living with you."

She raised a skeptical eyebrow at him. "You have?"

"Sure, I have. I mean, the jokes with Elmer and the parties at Christmas and sleeping with you—it's all been great.

I know I'm not all that easy to live with, but have you really hated being married to me?''

"No," she said, slowly shaking her head. "Not at all, Andy. I've enjoyed a lot of things, too."

Releasing the breath he'd been holding while waiting for her answer, he smiled, then reached across the table and grabbed her hand. "Then why don't we forget about a divorce and do the best we can to make this marriage work, Gin?''

Her eyes widened with apprehension. "Do you really think that's possible?" she whispered.

"Why not? We both fought this marriage from the beginning. But when you consider everything we had going against us and how well it's actually worked out, it seems to me that what we started that night at the Circle D was meant to last."

"Are you trying to say I got pregnant because of fate?''

"Call it whatever you want, but that night was special, Ginny. It was a . . . forever kind of a night.''

"A forever night," she murmured, liking the sound of it even though she wasn't sure she wanted to believe it.

Biting her lower lip, she studied his face as if desperately seeking the truth about his sincerity. He returned her gaze without hesitation, holding his breath again until she spoke.

"Oh, Andy, I don't know. It scares me."

He laced his fingers with hers and rubbed their palms together. "It scares me, too. And there aren't any guarantees. But we've been able to work our problems out so far, and we've got something special going for us."

"What's that?"

"We're both gonna love that baby to pieces. Let's just close our eyes and ears to all our doubts and fight like hell to give him a stable home. Whaddaya say, Ginny?"

This time, she hesitated forever. That's what it felt like, anyway. If he didn't stop holding his breath every time she had to make a decision, he was going to black out from lack of oxygen. Then she nodded and a grin worked its way across her mouth.

"All right, Johnson. You're on."

Laughing in triumph, he abandoned his chair and raced around the table. Pulling her to her feet, he wrapped his arms around her and kissed her for all he was worth.

Ginny closed her eyes and gave herself up to the magic of Andy's kiss. God, but she loved him. The little voice inside her head tried to remind her that he hadn't said a word about loving her, but she silently told it to shut the hell up. She had hope now, and she wasn't going to let any negative thoughts tarnish it.

Maybe Andy didn't love her. But he liked her and he'd finally trusted her enough to tell her about his first marriage. Given enough time, love could grow out of that foundation. With any luck at all, perhaps it would.

Chapter Thirteen

"All right, this time, I want you to practice a pant-pant-blow sequence," Marie Strand, the childbirth instructor, said. "I'll time the contraction. Fathers get into the coaching spirit."

Ginny glanced over at Emily Dawson, who occupied the mat next to hers on the elementary school's gym floor. Emily grinned and rolled her eyes. Before Ginny could return the gesture, Andy tapped her shoulder.

"Pay attention, Ginny," he murmured.

"Ready?" Marie asked. "Contraction begins."

Ginny panted and blew, panted and blew, trying to block out the sound of Hank and Emily giggling like a couple of naughty kids. They always seemed to have so much fun at these classes, and she wished Andy would lighten up a little instead of taking it all so seriously. On the other hand, there wasn't a doubt in her mind that he would know exactly what to do when her labor started, and she found that thought extremely comforting.

"Let's practice pushing next," Marie said. "Fathers, sit behind your wives and let them lean back against your chest for support. Keep one hand on her abdomen so you can tell her when the contraction ends. Get into position."

"Got a crane up there, Marie?" Hank asked. "Emily's gettin' so dang big, I can hardly lift her."

Emily swatted his knee and laughed along with everyone else. Struggling to sit up with her own enormous belly in the way, Ginny couldn't resist sneaking another glance at the other couple. Though Hank teased Emily unmercifully, she never took offense. The reason was obvious—love and complete trust and an unself-conscious joy in being together shone out of their faces whenever they looked at each other.

Ginny tried not to envy them. It was dumb to compare her marriage to anyone else's, and she knew Andy was doing his best to be a good husband. Now that she was starting her eighth month of pregnancy, he was helping more around the house than ever, and he religiously nagged her into resting and practicing her breathing exercises. He was kind, considerate and even affectionate on occasion.

Her only real complaint, which she knew was probably silly and unreasonable, was that he'd never said he loved her. Charlie had said that he loved her, but it hadn't made their relationship any better. Andy showed that he cared about her in dozens of ways. She shouldn't need to hear the words from him so badly.

But she did. She needed to hear them soon. And she needed to know that he meant them.

No matter how many times she told herself to be patient, it didn't help. Listing all the good things in their marriage she was grateful for didn't help, either. There was a stubborn, selfish little part of her heart that absolutely refused to give up wanting everything Andy had to give—the love, trust and emotional intimacy that would only come when they both let down that final barrier and said the words out loud.

Hearing them even once would help her to get through the times when they irritated each other. When they didn't understand each other. When she woke up in the middle of the night, terrified that he'd change his mind again and demand a divorce.

During the six weeks since they had agreed to stay together, it had seemed as if she and Andy had been renegotiating all the terms of their relationship. She'd told herself that was only to be expected. After all, there were things she was willing to tolerate for a few months that she didn't want to put up with for the rest of her life. She couldn't fault Andy for feeling the same way.

Knowing that with the rational part of her mind was one thing. Living with it emotionally was another story. She hated any kind of conflict, and every time they argued over some dumb little thing, she worried that Andy must be regretting their decision to stay married. Though she constantly reminded herself that his feelings were his own responsibility—that she couldn't *make* him be happy—she still felt anxious whenever he was displeased with her.

"You're not concentrating, Ginny," he scolded a moment later. "Marie just said the contraction is starting."

Swallowing a sharp retort, Ginny dutifully put her hands behind her knees and did the pushing drill, then relaxed against Andy's chest. She'd like to see *him* try to do all these damn contortions if his belly stuck out as far as hers did.

Oh, quit it, her conscience demanded. *You're just tired and cranky and eight months pregnant. You're making a big deal out of nothing.*

But was she really? Was it really so unreasonable to want her husband to love her? Not because she was his wife or because she was the mother of his baby, but simply because she was Ginny?

Hank and Emily had obviously found what she so desperately wanted with Andy. So had Sam and Dani, Becky and Pete, and several other couples right in this room. So why couldn't she? Why couldn't someone love her, warts, insecurities and all?

Well, she always felt closer to Andy when they made love. Maybe after the baby was born and their sex life returned to normal their relationship would improve. Except to help haul her out of a chair or steady her going up and down steps, he hadn't touched her for almost two weeks. Considering how big and awkward she'd become, she couldn't honestly blame him.

Of course, that didn't stop her from missing him when he rolled over to his own side of the bed every night after a brief, almost brotherly good-night kiss. And he'd been acting so uptight lately. *Was* he regretting their decision to stay married?

"That's it for tonight," Marie said after running them through the pushing drill one more time. "Some of you are getting close to your due dates, so practice a lot."

"Hey, Johnson," Hank said, pulling Emily to her feet and into his arms for a hug. "We're gonna stop at the Sweet Tooth Saloon for an ice-cream cone. Want to come along?"

Andy raised an eyebrow at Ginny as he helped her up.

"Sounds okay to me," she said with a shrug.

"All right. We'll meet you there," Andy said.

Ginny's spirits lifted when he put his arm around her shoulders on their way outside. The warm May air and a vivid sunset gave her an added boost. Promising herself she would shake off the rest of her unusually dark mood and enjoy her ice-cream cone, she climbed into the Blazer and fastened her seat belt.

"Sure you're up for this, Gin?" Andy asked, driving out of the parking lot.

She nodded. "It feels good to be out of the house."

"You seemed awfully distracted at class tonight. I thought you might be too tired."

"I'm never too tired for ice cream," she told him with a rueful grin, "but I'm tired of a lot of other things."

"Like what, for instance?"

"Not being able to see my feet or get out of a chair without moving like a walrus. Backaches, swollen feet and heartburn. Going to the bathroom every five minutes."

Andy reached across the seat and gave her hand a sympathetic squeeze. "Well, hang in there. You've only got a few more weeks to go."

"Easy for you to say, Johnson," she grumbled. "That'll cost you another scoop of fudge ripple."

He laughed and shook his head at her. They completed the drive in a comfortable silence. Andy parked a block away from the restaurant and they ambled down the sidewalk holding hands. When they were no more than ten feet from their destination, the door opened. To Ginny's dismay, her parents walked out of the building.

John and Pat Tyler halted in unison the instant they spotted their daughter, their mouths automatically pursing with disapproval. Their expressions were so identical, so utterly... sour, Ginny would have laughed if it hadn't hurt so much. Andy put his arm around her shoulders and pulled her against his side in a protective gesture.

She shot him a grateful smile, then lifted her chin and gazed calmly at the two people who had brought her into the world. Her mother, with her gray hair scraped back from her face in a tight bun, looked from Ginny to Andy and back to Ginny again, her eyes showing not so much as a flicker of warmth.

"Evening, Pat. John," Andy said, his voice low and carrying a touch of steel.

Ginny's father gave him a grudging nod and shot a contemptuous glance at Ginny's abdomen. Then he grabbed her mother's elbow, steered her around the younger couple and marched her across the street.

Glaring after them, Andy cursed under his breath, released Ginny's shoulders and turned as if he would follow them. "Why, that son of a—"

"No." Ginny snagged one of his belt loops with her index finger and gave it a yank. "Nothing you can say will change their minds about me. Just... let it go."

"But that was insulting," he protested. "Where do they think they get off?"

"Please, Andy, it doesn't matter."

"Well, it matters to me. If you think I'm gonna stand by and let anybody treat my wife that way—"

"So, what're you gonna do, Johnson?" Ginny drawled, hiding her pain behind a sassy grin. "Arrest them for disapproving of me? And my brothers, too? Shoot, half of this town's disapproved of me at one time or another."

He tipped his head to one side, as if seriously considering the idea. She pulled the brim of his hat down over his eyes. He ruffled her hair in retaliation, then wrapped his arms around the area where she'd once had a waist and hugged her. Resting her cheek against his neck, she hugged him back, soaking in his silent comfort and fiercely resisting a powerful urge to weep.

"Merciful heavens, Emily," Hank said in a prissy falsetto from somewhere behind Andy, "is that our sheriff snuggling his wife right there in front of God and everybody? Why, that's just scandalous. We'd better get up a petition and have him run out of town."

Ginny smiled at him. "Shut up, Hank. Us fat pregnant ladies need all the snuggling we can get."

Hank waggled his eyebrows at her. "That's how you got to be fat pregnant ladies in the first place."

Emily clapped both hands on her cheeks and stared at him in feigned shock. "Why, Hank Dawson, you should have told me that. Well, that's it for you, buster. No more snuggling."

His eyes glinting with amusement, Andy interrupted. "All right, that's enough. Let's order some ice cream before these fat pregnant ladies get too tired to eat it."

"You've got a point, Johnson," Hank said. "But if you tip your hat a little to the left, nobody else'll see it."

The bantering lasted for the entire hour they spent with the Dawsons. Determined not to let her parents spoil everyone's fun, Ginny joined in, gleefully trading wisecracks with Hank. The effort sapped her strength, however, and by the time they returned to the Blazer, she climbed into the passenger seat and collapsed in an exhausted heap.

Someday, she told herself, her parents would regret their actions. Someday they would want to know this grandchild and wish they hadn't been so pigheaded. She would forgive them, because hating them would hurt her and her child more than it would ever hurt her folks.

But so help her God, she was done with trying to win their approval, or even yearning for it. And she would never, *ever*, allow near her child anyone who didn't have one heck of a lot more forgiveness in their hearts than John and Pat Tyler did.

Then another thought surfaced, a thought that had often worried her as a child. She'd repressed it successfully for years, but after the blatant rejection she'd suffered tonight, it raised its ugly head again. If her own parents couldn't love her, how could she expect anyone else to? Maybe she was simply... unlovable.

Andy shot worried glances at Ginny all the way home. Man, she had guts. After that vicious snub from her parents, he'd thought she'd want to go home and have a good cry and he wouldn't have thought any less of her for it.

But not his Ginny. No sir, she'd pulled herself together so well, Hank and Emily hadn't even suspected that anything unusual had happened. She must have been hurt a helluva lot of times to get so good at hiding her feelings.

The thought infuriated him all over again. During his years in law enforcement, he'd seen all kinds of folks hurt other people in all kinds of ways, but he still couldn't believe how cruel Ginny's parents had been to her. For God's sake, the woman was pregnant with their grandchild and getting damn close to delivery.

That alone should have stirred a little compassion in the Tylers' rotten, miserable hearts. Ginny had probably gotten married so young just to get the hell away from home. And then she'd wound up with a jerk like Charlie Bradford.

What amazed Andy, was that Ginny had come through all that without losing her own compassion for other people. Oh, he'd heard her make a bitter remark now and then, but ninety-nine percent of the time, she was pretty darn cheerful, and she was unfailingly kind and generous with everyone she met. It must take an incredible amount of inner strength for her to do that.

She didn't deserve the kind of treatment her folks had dished out. They'd better not dish out any more, or by God, they'd answer to him.

By the time they got home, Andy could see that she was fighting tears again, and he wasn't surprised when she announced she was going to take a shower and turn in for the night.

He let Schnoodle go outside for a few minutes, and wondered whether he should try to comfort Ginny or give her some space. Then he remembered her crying into her pillow the night they'd spent in Jackson. There was no way he could leave her alone. She was gonna have to learn that she didn't have to fight the world by herself anymore.

She was still in the shower when he entered the bedroom. He tugged off his boots and socks, emptied his pockets and rotated his shoulders, trying to get himself relaxed. She came out a moment later, pausing in the doorway to switch off the light. Breath caught in his throat, Andy stared at her, wondering why he'd never thought pregnant women were sexy.

Just the sight of her, standing there in her thin nightgown, her body ripe with his baby, sent a rush of blood to his groin, making him painfully aware just how long it had been since he'd made love to her. She froze when she saw him, as if she could see the lust rampaging through his body written all over his face.

"Don't look at me," she whispered, crossing her arms over her belly.

Andy couldn't have taken his gaze off her if she'd stuck a loaded .357 in his face. "I like looking at you. Why don't you want me to?"

She marched to the bed, jerked back the top sheet and crawled in, then covered herself with a snap of the blankets. "Because I look fat and dumpy and I don't need you to remind me."

"Fat and dumpy?" The description was so completely opposite of what he'd been thinking, Andy had to laugh.

Glaring at him, she yanked the covers higher. "Oh, shut up, Johnson."

"You don't look fat and dumpy." He walked over to the bed, sat down beside her and reached for her hand.

She shoved it under the bedclothes, still glaring at him. "Oh, huh! Do you think I haven't heard all the pregnant lady jokes everywhere I've gone for the past two weeks? There's the watermelon one, and the basketball one. And don't forget words like *whale* and *blimp*. And I've still got a month to go, so it's gonna get worse!"

Andy clamped his hands on either side of her head and kissed the daylights out of her. Her lips trembled when he pulled away, and her eyes filled with tears.

"Aw, honey, don't," he begged, wiping them away with his thumbs. "I didn't mean to be so rough."

"You weren't." She gulped. "I thought you were getting tired of me. Or maybe just turned off because I'm so huge."

"Turned off!" He grabbed her hand and held it against his fly. "Does that feel like I'm turned off?"

"Well, you haven't touched me for days."

Andy smacked his forehead with the heel of his hand, then shook his head. "I was trying to be considerate, Ginny. I know you don't always feel too great now. And you haven't given me much encouragement."

"Well, you've been moody and I felt too fat! And you *stared* at me like you couldn't believe how enormous I was."

"For God's sake, you're pregnant, not fat. When you came out of the bathroom, I wanted to throw you on the floor and jump your bones, lady. That's why I was staring."

The mutinous set of her chin told him words alone would never convince her. He peeled back the covers, then started undoing the buttons holding her bodice together. When she tried to stop him, he grabbed her hands and anchored them at her sides.

"I think you're beautiful, Ginny," he said, gazing straight into her eyes. "Let me show you. Please?"

He saw her throat work down a swallow before she nodded. Trailing his hands up her arms and shoulders, he leaned closer, teasing her lips with the tip of his tongue. Her breath struck his face in warm, sweet puffs as he stroked her collarbones and the base of her neck.

Deepening the kiss, he slid his left hand into her hair and put his right hand back to work on those buttons, separating the cloth, caressing the tops of her breasts and the enticing valley between them. Her skin was so smooth against his fingertips, so soft, he imagined even a light touch could bruise her. But he wouldn't bruise her.

Oh, no. He intended to love her so slowly, so tenderly, so thoroughly, the very last thing on her mind would be pain. Physical or emotional. This wasn't quite the way he'd imagined comforting her, but hey, he was willing to do whatever worked and the doctor hadn't forbidden them to make love. Not yet, anyway.

Unwilling to go through the rigmarole of getting her out of the nightgown, he grasped the bodice opening with both hands and ripped it down the middle. He swallowed her surprised gasp with another deep kiss, then her sigh of pleasure when he filled his palms with her breasts.

God, had there ever been such a delectable woman? he wondered, kissing her again and again, drinking in her husky little moans. She reached for him, her fingers spread wide across his chest, then fumbling at his shirt buttons. Needing to feel her hands on his skin, he took care of the shirt the same way he'd taken care of her nightgown. A button ricocheted off the headboard with a ping.

Chuckling deep in her throat, she caressed him, her dark eyes shining with enough admiration to make him glad he'd spent so many summers developing his muscles by stacking bales the old-fashioned way.

"If you keep ripping our clothes to pieces, we won't be able to afford to make love anymore," she said.

"Guess we'll just have to go to bed naked next time."

She ran a fingernail down the center of his chest, stopping at his belt buckle. "I think you should be naked right now."

His groin surged at the sultry note in her voice, the lusty, flirty look in her eyes. He tormented himself by letting her unfasten his belt, but stopped her when she reached for the button at the waistband of his jeans.

"Uh-*uh*, lady. If I let you do that, it'll all be over in about thirty seconds. And I'm not even close to being done with you yet."

"Maybe you'd better show me what you have in mind."

He raised her hand to his mouth and nibbled on her fingers, bathing them with his tongue, sucking the tips into his mouth until her eyelids fluttered shut. Then he cupped her breasts and kissed them, lavishing attention on her nipples. Shifting his weight, he moved slowly down her body, kissing and nipping, rubbing his cheeks and chin over her distended belly. A surprisingly strong thump from inside clipped his jaw.

"Hey, you, settle down in there," he said, laying his hand over the spot where he'd felt the foot or elbow or whatever the kid had hit him with. "It's Dad's turn to play with Mommy."

The baby whacked him again, and he looked up into Ginny's eyes with a delighted laugh. "How can you think this isn't beautiful? Every time I see it and realize there's a baby in there, I . . ."

"You what?" she asked softly.

"Well, I, uh, I don't know. It just makes me feel kinda . . . macho, you know? It's a hell of a turn-on."

Giggling, she pushed herself up on one elbow and ruffled his hair with her free hand. "Great. Now you won't want me unless I'm enormous. Pretty kinky if you ask me."

"It's not kinky, honey." He kissed her belly reverently. "It's wonderful. The most amazing thing that's ever happened to me. The only thing I'm sorry about is that you have to be so uncomfortable."

"It's the most amazing thing that's ever happened to me, too," she said, lying back on the pillow. "And it's not all *that* bad being pregnant."

He let his hand ride down the slope of her abdomen, then teased the patch of curls between her thighs with his fingertips. "Well, let's see if I can't make you feel *real* good for a little while."

Her neck arched back when he slid one finger deep inside her. God, but he loved touching her this way, watching the pink bloom on her cheeks, hearing her breathing get light and choppy, her excited little cries as he fondled her most sensitive spots.

Still touching her, he stood by the bed and shucked off the rest of his clothes. Then he stretched out beside her and kissed her, thrusting his tongue into her eager mouth, matching the cadence of his fingers below. She turned toward him, her hand smoothing down over his chest and belly until her fingers found his eager, aching flesh, coaxing a groan of sheer pleasure from him.

Unable to wait any longer, he pushed her onto her back, grasped her thigh and draped it over his hips. Then he entered her as slowly and carefully as he could.

"Is it okay?" he asked, his voice rough with the effort to restrain himself.

"Yes. Oh, yes, please."

She dug her heels into the mattress. Her buttock ground against his hip bone, forcing him deeper inside her. Then he lost track of everything but the rhythm they set together, thrusting, almost separating, thrusting again and again, creating the magical friction that sent them over the edge in a long, glorious free fall back to earth.

Gathering her into his arms, he pressed her face against his neck, stroking her back while their heartbeats gradually slowed and their breathing returned to normal. She snuggled into him like a child seeking warmth.

"Andy?"

"What, Gin?"

"Are you really sure you want to stay married to me?"

The hesitant, almost frightened note in her voice brought back the ugly scene with her parents. His heart aching for her, he tucked one finger under her chin and made her look at him.

"I'm positive. Why? Are you having second thoughts?"

"No, but you've been so moody lately, I thought maybe you were."

Her eyes searched his with an intense need for reassurance. Kissing the tip of her nose, he mentally damned the Tylers and Charlie Bradford for hurting this sweet, vulnerable woman.

"If I've been moody, it's because of the election, honey. Not you."

"Oh, come on. You won't have any problem getting reelected. We got wedding presents from all over the county. Everybody loves you."

"I know a few guys in prison who don't love me much," he said with a chuckle. "But I'm not afraid of losing. It's just been kind of tense at the office since Joe Redmond announced he was planning to run against me in the primary."

"Joe? He's one of your best deputies."

Andy nodded, smiling at her indignant expression. "Yup. He's got every right to run, Ginny. He hasn't realized I'm not taking his decision personally, so he's been pretty edgy."

"But he's just a kid. He's not even thirty yet."

"That's why I'm not worried about losing." Andy reached over and turned off the lamp, then settled Ginny's head back on his shoulder. "Give him ten years and he might just give me a real run for my money."

"Hah! That'll be the day."

"Hey, Ginny?"

"What?" she murmured, starting to sound sleepy now.

"We've gotta start communicating more. Denise never wanted to hear about what went on at the office, so I don't always think to tell you. Don't be afraid to ask if something's bothering me.''

"Okay, Andy."

Smiling, he continued to hold her while she drifted off to sleep, the mound of baby pressed against his hip. A moment later he felt the little varmint kick. Ginny frowned and sighed. Andy kissed her forehead and gently rubbed her belly.

"Knock it off, kid," he whispered. "Mommy needs some rest."

A deep sense of peace and contentment filled him. Now that he'd soothed Ginny's fears about her appearance and about him, everything would be all right. It just plain had to be.

"I love you, Gin," he added, kissing her forehead again and telling himself that one of these days, he'd have to get up the nerve to tell her that when she was awake.

Cuddled securely in Andy's strong arms, Ginny fought the pull of sleep, wanting to savor the closeness for a little while longer. The baby thrashed inside her, no doubt warming up for her nightly tap-dance practice, and Ginny smiled to herself when she heard Andy tell the kid to knock it off. His lips pressed against her forehead and his hand patted her belly as if he were trying to soothe the baby. He could be so sweet sometimes.

A burst of joy pierced her heart at the words he whispered next—"I love you, Gin." Lord, did he really mean that? Or was it just a result of the satisfying sexual release they'd shared together?

Too afraid to find out for sure, she lay absolutely still, listening to the sound of his breathing. When it became deep and regular, she raised up on one elbow and peered through the darkness, hoping to find a clue to his feelings in his face. She couldn't tell anything, of course.

He looked utterly relaxed, and a slight smile curved his mouth, but he always looked like that after they'd made love. God knew she'd watched him enough times to know.

Her heart still ached a little over her parents' rejection, and she'd never be able to forget all the put-downs Charlie had delivered over the years.

But maybe she'd finally grown up enough that she wasn't so unlovable anymore. Maybe Andy could learn to love her. Oh, God, *please*. He just *had* to.

Chapter Fourteen

"Hi, it's me."

Relaxing back in his swivel chair, Andy propped his feet on the corner of his desk four days later and smiled at the sound of Ginny's voice on the other end of the phone line. "Well, hi. What're you up to?"

"Oh, uh, not much. I'm sorry to bother you at work."

"No problem. I'm just doin' paperwork."

"That's good, because..." She paused, and he thought he heard a funny catch in her breath.

"Because why?" he asked, sitting up straighter.

"Because I think the baby might be coming."

"*What?*" Both of his feet crashed to the floor. He leaned forward, bracing one elbow on the desk. "Ginny, you're not due for another three weeks."

"I don't think anyone told the baby that."

"You're having contractions?"

"Yeah. They started about seven-thirty."

"Seven-thirty!" He glanced at his watch and felt his heart skip at least two beats. "Dammit, Ginny, it's almost noon! Why the hell didn't you call me sooner?"

"Because they haven't been regular. They're stronger than the ones I've had before, but I kept thinking they'd stop. I've already talked to Pete Sinclair, and he thinks it's a good idea to head on over to Jackson. But it's just a precaution. No reason to get excited."

"I'm not excited," Andy replied, though it was the biggest lie he'd ever told. "I'll be there in five minutes."

Without giving her a chance to reply, he hung up, grabbed his hat and left the office at a dead run, shouting his destination at the dispatcher on his way past her desk. Using the lights and siren on his patrol car, he made it home in just under four minutes. Ginny met him at the back door with a big smile on her face.

"Gracious, that was fast."

"Are you all right?" he demanded.

Regarding him with amused indulgence, she patted his cheek. "I'm *fine*. Take it easy. If this is the real thing, we'll have plenty of time."

He sighed, then smiled and shook his head at his own behavior. Unless he wanted to spend the rest of his life hearing about how he'd acted like one of those dumb sitcom dads on TV, he'd better calm down pronto.

"All right. I'm cool now. You sit down and relax, and I'll get everything together. Where's your suitcase?"

"In the bathroom. I was just putting in my makeup when I heard you coming."

"Anything else you want me to throw in?"

"The book of baby names and my toothbrush. I think I've got everything else. No, wait. Leave the baby book out and we can argue some more on the way. Don't forget the camera. And the baby's tote bag's in the nursery."

Before Andy could leave, Bill poked his head in the back door. "I saw Andy's patrol car out front. What's goin' on?"

"Come on in, Bill," Ginny called cheerfully. "I'm having a few contractions, so we're going to Jackson."

The old man paled at her announcement and hurried across the room. "You're not due yet."

Ginny chuckled. "That's what Andy said. Don't look so worried. It's probably a false alarm. Would you mind dog-sitting while we're gone?"

"Not at all. Jake and I'll take real good care of Schnoo-dle." Bill shot Andy a sympathetic smile.

Ginny clasped her belly with both hands and sucked in a deep breath. Bill shooed Andy toward the bedroom. "You'd better get a move on, boy. I'll stay with her."

Barely restraining himself from running, Andy left the room. Urgency clawed at his gut as he collected Ginny's things, but he forced himself to concentrate. He even threw in a change of clothes and a few toiletries for himself. When he returned to the kitchen, she started to get up.

"Sit still, honey," he said. "I need to move the baby's car seat into the patrol car, then I'll—"

"I don't want to go in the patrol car, Andy."

"Ginny, I've got a radio and emergency equipment in it," he said. "If we run into trouble—"

She shook her head. "We won't. My last two contractions were ten minutes apart."

"The Blazer doesn't have enough gas in it," Andy replied, forcing a calm, reasonable tone into his voice.

"It won't take that long to buy some," Ginny said with an irritated huff. "The Blazer will be more comfortable."

"For God's sake, it don't matter spit which car you take. Stop squabblin' and just get goin'," Bill said.

"Bill's right, Andy. Can't we *please* take the Blazer? I don't want to bring my baby home in a cop car."

Against his better judgment, Andy decided he might as well give in. Ginny looked as if she were willing to argue all day. And since this was her first baby, they probably did have plenty of time.

"All right. Whatever you say, Gin."

He hurried out of the house, moved the patrol car to the far side of the driveway and backed the Blazer out of the garage. After tossing the suitcase and infant car seat into the way-back, he ran back inside to get Ginny. Of course she was in the bathroom, and every second he had to wait cranked his anxiety up another notch.

Bill yammered away the entire five minutes she was in there, and it was all Andy could do not to bellow with impatience. Then she had to say goodbye to Bill and Schnoodle, and the way she carried on, a man would think she never planned to see either of them again. By the time he'd convinced her to let him carry her out to the car and stopped for gas, they'd lost another twenty minutes.

With an imaginary clock ticking inside his head, he sped out of town on Highway 191. Ginny had a contraction at the Cora junction. Andy pressed harder on the accelerator and told himself that was fine, perfectly natural, in fact—until she had another one only five miles later at Daniel.

"Those were pretty close together," he said. "Maybe we should go back to Pinedale and let Pete deliver—"

"Don't even think about it, Andy. First babies take forever."

"You sound awful cranky. What if you're already going into transition?"

Ginny rolled her eyes in exasperation. "I'm fine. The baby's fine. The sooner we get to the hospital, the sooner *you'll* be fine. Just drive, Johnson, will ya?"

She turned on the radio, then leaned back against the seat, folded her arms across the top of her belly and shut her eyes. Andy shut his mouth and drove, his gaze constantly shifting from the road, to his wife, to his watch. Which was why he didn't see the beer bottle that took out his right front tire ten miles northwest of Daniel.

Cursing under his breath, he wrestled the vehicle to the shoulder and set the emergency brake just as Ginny had another contraction. She had four more during the fifteen minutes it took him to change the flat and get ready to roll again. When he climbed back behind the steering wheel, she was leaning against the window, biting her lower lip, her face pinched with pain. Aw, hell. Another one.

He slid across the bench seat and took her left hand between both of his. "Breathe, Ginny," he said, fighting to keep the fear out of his voice. "Nice, deep breaths."

She nodded once and inhaled, then exhaled a sigh as the contraction ended. "They're getting stronger," she said, looking at him with apology in her eyes.

"Yeah, and they're coming faster, too. We're still closer to Pinedale than Jackson. What do you want to do?"

"Go on to Jackson, Andy. We can probably still make it, and if the baby needs any kind of special care, we'll be closer to Salt Lake."

He tucked a strand of hair behind her right ear and kissed her forehead. "All right. But from now on, we quit fighting each other and work as a team, okay?"

"Okay." She gave him a misty smile, then whispered, "I'm sorry I didn't let you bring the patrol car."

"Don't worry about it now. There's no sense fussing over something we can't change."

Sliding behind the wheel, he fired the ignition and drove back onto the road, keeping a sharp eye out for other tire hazards. The time between Ginny's contractions grew shorter and shorter, each one more intense and lasting longer than the previous one. He coached her through them as best he could, maintaining a stream of chitchat between contractions to keep her mind occupied.

Her water broke five miles west of Bondurant. She was in so much pain and distress by then, Andy knew they weren't going to make it. Sure enough, two minutes later, Ginny announced that she had to push. Unfortunately the road had already narrowed and started to follow the twisting, turning route of the Hoback River.

"Andy, *please*," she wailed, "pull over. I think I'm gonna barf."

"There's no shoulder. Hang on, I know there's a scenic overlook here somewhere. Pant, honey."

"I can't! I'm telling you, I have to *push*, dammit!"

The road narrowed even more, with a sheer drop-off to the river on the right side and a mountain on the left. One blind curve followed another. Sweat rolled down the sides of his face. Where the hell was that damn turnoff?

Somehow, he managed to keep the Blazer on the pavement, mentally review the procedures he'd learned in his EMT training and keep Ginny talking. By the time he finally saw the sign for the overlook, he wasn't far from out-and-out panic. He took the exit on two wheels, parked and yanked the key out of the ignition.

Then he shoved the seat back as far as it would go, jumped to the ground and raced to the rear end of the vehicle. Ginny's moans sent shivers up his spine as he pawed through the suitcase for the clean baby blankets she'd packed and the little bottle of rubbing alcohol from her makeup kit that she used to clean her earring posts. Grabbing the first-aid kit and a stadium blanket he always kept in the car, as well, he charged to the passenger door.

Ginny had already unfastened her seat belt and was struggling out of her soaked maternity slacks and panties. He helped her to raise her hips for a moment and spread the stadium blanket beneath her. She whimpered as she lay back, lifting her feet onto the seat.

Yanking his handkerchief out of his hip pocket, Andy plastered on a smile and wiped the perspiration from her face. "Relax, sweetheart. Everything's gonna be fine. I'm gonna clean my hands and then you can push, okay?"

She nodded, then begged, "Hurry," and resumed the quick panting drill she'd learned in class.

Andy laid the baby blankets over the top of the seat, then doused his hands with the rubbing alcohol.

"All right, honey," he said, standing between her knees, "take your cleansing breaths and let 'er rip."

"Great choice of words," she muttered, bracing herself on her palms. "Oh, Lord, here it comes."

Her face turned red as she grunted and strained with the contraction. Andy shoved his fears to a remote corner of his mind and went into his coaching mode.

"Come on. That's it, *push*. Okay, rest a minute. You're doing great, babe."

The afternoon sun beat down on his back and he could hear the river and an occasional passing car, but he was too engrossed in the drama taking place in the front seat of his Blazer to pay more than fleeting attention to anything else.

"That's it. *Big* push. You sound like you're lifting a piano, honey. I can see the head."

Gasping for air, Ginny flopped onto her back when the contraction ended and gave him a crooked grin. "You should've been head cheerleader in high school. Oh, jeez, here we go—"

She struggled up onto her elbows and bore down. Andy held his breath with her, watching that tiny head protrude a little farther, his hands ready to catch the baby.

"You're almost there, Gin," he said when she paused to rest again. "I think you'll have it on the next one, so really give it all you've got."

"Not much left."

"Don't talk. *Breathe*. That's my girl. Here it comes...." He carefully supported the baby's emerging head while Ginny gathered her strength for another push. "One more, babe. Just one more."

She sucked in a great lungful of air and bore down again, her face turning scarlet with the effort. A shoulder emerged, then the second one, and the rest of the slippery little body slid out an instant later.

"It's a *girl!*" Andy shouted.

He grabbed a clean blanket, wiped the blood and mucus from the baby's mouth. Then he realized she hadn't cried yet and his heart lurched. He lowered her head for a moment in case there was more mucus in her mouth.

"Andy, what's wrong?" Ginny demanded, struggling to sit up.

"Hold on."

He massaged the baby's chest and back, wiped her mouth out again and tapped the soles of her tiny feet. Much to his relief, she made a little mewling sound, then cut loose with a lusty cry that would have done an opera singer proud.

"Oh, God," Ginny murmured, her voice thick with emotion. "Let me see her, Andy."

Grabbing another blanket, he wrapped it around his new daughter and gently laid her on Ginny's abdomen. His eyes stung. His knees felt shaky. His hands started to tremble. Laughing at himself, he tucked his hands into his armpits, propped his shoulder against the side of the door opening and looked inside.

Her face glowing with happiness, Ginny was laughing and crying, counting fingers and toes and talking softly to the baby. The baby was still squalling to beat hell and thrashing her little arms and legs like a couple of eggbeaters. Andy wiped his eyes with the backs of his hands and exhaled a deep, thankful sigh.

"Oh, Andy, isn't she beautiful?" Ginny asked.

"Yeah."

"She's just perfect. Do you—" she inhaled a sharp breath and grimaced. "I think the afterbirth's coming."

Andy straightened away from the car and dug out his pocketknife. He poured rubbing alcohol over the blade and sliced a couple of strips from the last clean baby blanket. Then he tied the cord in two places, sterilized the knife's blade again and sliced between the strips of cloth.

"You're on your own now, kid," he said, grinning down at the infant.

He leaned into the Blazer and kissed Ginny's cheek. "You did a hell of a job, there, Mommy. How're you feeling?"

"I'm okay." She smiled, then winced a second later.

"Let me put the baby in the back seat until we get you taken care of. She'll be fine back there. It's nice and warm."

"I want to nurse her."

"I'll put you back there, too, when we're done, and you can nurse her before we go on to Jackson."

Ginny pouted, but allowed him to take the baby. Andy cuddled his daughter against his chest for a moment and felt an almost violent surge of love for this little person with the funny, scrunched up face and piercing cries. Right from the beginning, she'd been fiercely determined to be born, and God, he was glad she had. She was so tiny and perfect, he felt humbled and ecstatic and scared to death all at the same time.

He looked up and found Ginny watching him, tears streaming down her face, her chin quivering as if she were trying to hold in gut-wrenching sobs. The emotions in her eyes as she gazed at him were so stark, so...naked, it was more intimate than lovemaking, in a strange, wonderful kind of way.

Tears welled up in his own eyes. He blinked hard, but a few of them escaped and ran down his cheeks. He decided he didn't give a damn that Ginny saw them. If a man couldn't shed a few tears over his own kid, this was one sorry excuse for a world. She nodded ever so slightly, silently telling him she'd felt the same sense of connection he had.

Swallowing at the lump in his throat, he laid the baby down, wiped his cheeks and went back to Ginny.

Twenty minutes later he'd delivered the afterbirth, made sure Ginny wasn't bleeding too much and installed her and the baby in the back seat. The infant slurped at Ginny's breast for a few minutes, then curled her hands beside her face and went to sleep. Then it was all Andy could do to coax the baby out of Ginny's arms so he could strap her into the car seat and get back on the road.

Figuring they were about sixteen or seventeen miles from Jackson, he pulled onto the highway. Man, would he ever be glad to see that hospital. Other than a damn fast labor, the entire birth had been normal as far as he could tell. But he'd feel a whole lot better when Ginny and the baby had been checked out by a doctor.

With each passing mile, he thought of some new something that could have gone wrong and had to glance over his shoulder to make sure his wife and daughter were still all right. Ginny looked exhausted and pale, but he told himself that was typical. She'd lost some blood and they didn't call it labor for nothing, right?

Nevertheless, the second he passed the last switchback curve out of Hoback Canyon, he pressed harder on the accelerator and had one devil of a time limiting his speed to ten miles an hour over the posted maximum. By the time he stopped in front of the hospital's emergency entrance, his torso was drenched with a clammy sweat and his knuckles ached from gripping the wheel. He rushed inside and bellowed for a doctor, then ran back to the Blazer.

After they'd whisked Ginny and the baby off to an examination room, Andy filled out admission forms, answered at least a thousand questions and repeatedly demanded to see his wife and baby. A dark-haired nurse in her mid-forties kept trying to soothe him, saying that it wouldn't be much longer and the doctor would be out to talk with him shortly. It didn't help.

He snarled at her twice and she finally left him alone in the waiting room. His gut knotted with apprehension. His mouth felt parched. His hands started to tremble again. He shoved them into his pockets.

Ten minutes passed. Fifteen. Twenty-five. He could smell his own armpits and the blood smeared across the front of his uniform. Damn, why were they taking so long? Was something wrong with Ginny? With the baby? Had he made a mistake during the delivery?

It didn't seem to matter that he was a trained EMT. That he'd delivered hundreds of calves. That he was used to handling all kinds of emergencies. This was *different*.

That was *his* wife who'd had a baby out there in the middle of nowhere, under unsanitary conditions. Who was in another room somewhere with a damn doctor he'd never seen before. Who was the most wonderful, courageous woman he'd ever known. A lot of women would have screeched their heads off if they had to give birth the way Ginny had. But she'd just dug her heels into that seat, focused on what she had to do and got through it with no pain medication at all.

Damn, but he loved her. If anything happened to her or the baby...

He paced and sweated, sweated and paced. What if the doctor was incompetent? What if he was a jerk? What if—

"Mr. Johnson?"

Andy whirled around so fast, he had to wave his arms to keep his balance. The dark-haired nurse stood in the doorway. The doctor, who didn't even look like he was old enough to shave, for God's sake, walked into the room, his hand outstretched toward Andy. The nurse came in behind him, but kept her distance.

"I'm Dr. Fielding."

"How's Ginny?" Andy demanded, giving the younger man's hand a perfunctory shake.

Dr. Fielding smiled and shook his head. "She's an amazing woman, Mr. Johnson. Ginny's just fine and so is the baby. I've called in Dr. Washburn and a pediatrician, but I don't anticipate any problems at all. You did a great job delivering your daughter."

The doctor's lips continued to move, but Andy suddenly found it impossible to concentrate on what he was saying over the weird roaring sound in his ears. He wiped his sweaty forehead with the back of his hand. His stomach took a slow, nauseating roll. He felt his leg muscles going slack, but he couldn't seem to do anything about it.

The last thing he heard before the world went black was the nurse yelling, "Catch him! He's passing out!"

Later that evening Ginny awoke from a nap to the rich, sweet fragrance of roses and the deep, wonderful sound of

Andy's voice talking softly nearby. Smiling, she opened one eye, spotting the flowers—at least two dozen, long-stemmed red ones—overflowing a vase on the bedside table. She opened the other eye and lazily turned her head, searching the hospital room for her husband.

Oh, Lord. A lump formed in her throat at the picture he made, sitting in a chair by the window, having a serious conversation with the baby stretched out on his thighs. He'd changed into jeans and a polo shirt, and it didn't appear to bother him a bit that the infant was sound asleep. Though her arms ached to hold the baby herself, Ginny lay still and shamelessly eavesdropped.

"You sure scared the whey out of your old man, comin' like that," he said, tracing a tiny ear with the tip of his index finger. "And, I suppose you'll scare the whey out of me a lot as you're growin' up. Yeah, you'll probably be a pistol, just like your mom. But I'll always be there for you, little one."

He picked up one of the baby's hands and held it in his palm, his thumb stroking over her delicate fingers. Knowing he'd shut up in a flash if he knew she was listening, Ginny gulped and held her breath, stifling an urge to sniffle.

"You've gotta be the prettiest little thing I've ever seen," he continued, his mouth curved into a tender smile. "But don't think you can wrap me around this little pinky of yours, kid. No way. I'm your dad and I'll always love you, but you're gonna grow up right.

"You'll take piano lessons and dance lessons and learn to swim. Your grandpa'll love teachin' you to ride, and your grandma's gonna try to spoil you rotten. You should've heard her squeal when I called to tell 'em you were here. We're gonna have a great time, baby. Just you wait and see. And you'll go to college and marry some guy I'll know isn't anywhere near good enough for you...."

Ginny closed her eyes and bit her lower lip, wondering if her own father had ever talked to her that way when she'd been born. Had he ever had such plans and hopes and dreams for her? Or had he been angry because she hadn't been another son? Was that why he'd never approved of her? Never told her he loved her? Or was there some other reason—something about her personality or her character, that had disappointed him?

The sniffle came out despite her best efforts to suppress it. Andy jerked his head up and looked at her, a dull red flush climbing his face. The memory of that long, incredibly intimate look they'd shared out at the overlook flitted into her mind, making her feel shy and vulnerable.

"Hi," she said, her voice little more than a whisper.

"Hi, yourself." His voice sounded husky, too, giving her the impression that he was equally aware of the subtle shift in their relationship. "How're you feelin'?"

"Happy. Lazy. Tired." *Incredibly in love with you,* she added silently.

"How long have you been awake?"

"Long enough to know that's one lucky little girl you're holding. You're going to be a wonderful father."

Andy gave her a sheepish grin and shrugged. She reached for the control pad clipped to the bottom sheet and raised the head of her bed.

"Are you going to quit hogging the kid or do I have to come over there and take her away from you?" she asked, wrinkling her nose at him.

Chuckling, he slid one hand under the baby's neck and head, the other under her bottom. Then he shifted her into the cradle of his right arm and brought her to Ginny's bed. Wincing at the tug on her stitches, she scooted over, making room for him to sit beside her. He shot her a concerned frown as he carefully deposited the baby in her arms.

"You all right?"

"Fine. Just a little sore." She unwrapped the baby's blanket, sighing with delight at the sight of that tiny, perfect body. "Isn't she gorgeous?"

He put his arm around Ginny's shoulders and hugged her. "She sure is. Just like her mama. You were wonderful out there today, Gin."

"I thought *you* were." She rested her head in the hollow of his shoulder and sighed again. "I never would have made it without you, Andy. You were so calm—"

His gusty laugh startled the baby. She arched her back, flung her arms out to her sides and let out an ear-splitting wail. Giving Andy a reproving scowl, Ginny cuddled her close.

"It's okay, sweetie," she crooned, stroking the infant's round, fuzzy little head. "That was just your daddy. He didn't mean to scare you." Then she looked at Andy. "What was so funny?"

"Nothing." His face flushed again and he wouldn't meet her gaze.

Convinced he was hiding something, she studied him for a moment. "Uh-huh. Tell me the truth, Johnson."

"I, uh, wouldn't tell the nurses about how calm I was." One side of his mouth twitched in a wry grin.

"What happened?"

"I was worried about you," he said, obviously choosing his words with great care. "And the baby, of course. And it seemed like the doc was taking an awful long time to check you gals out."

"So what did you do?"

"Nothing, until he came out and told me you and the baby were okay."

"And then?" She prompted him when he didn't continue.

"I don't know for sure. From what they tell me, my eyes rolled back in my head and I passed out cold on the floor of the waiting room."

He looked so chagrined, so disgusted, she had to bite the inside of her cheek to stop herself from giggling. He eyed her suspiciously, then shook his head and smiled.

"Hey, the nurses crack up every time they see me. You might as well go ahead and laugh, too. I don't imagine I'll ever live this down if it gets back to Pinedale."

"Oh, Andy." She laid her hand on his thigh and gave it an affectionate squeeze. "It doesn't matter what happened after you got us here. The only thing I care about is that you kept your cool when the baby and I needed you to. I might laugh *with* you when you're ready, but I'd never laugh *at* you, and I won't tell a soul."

Clearing his throat, he covered her hand with his own. "Aw, it's all right. But speaking of the baby, don't you think it's time we gave her a name?"

"What would you like to call her?"

"Well, I know you really like—"

"Don't worry about my list," she interrupted, laying her index finger over his lips. "I want *you* to name her."

Tipping his head to one side, he looked at her as if he couldn't quite believe he'd heard her correctly. She returned his gaze, then nodded in encouragement. A tentative smile spread across his face. "You mean that?"

"Absolutely. I know you love her too much to give her a dumb name."

"Let me have her for a minute." He laid the baby on his lap and studied her tiny face. "After seeing what a scrapper she is today, I'd kinda like to name her after both of my grandmas," he said, stroking her cheek with the back of one finger. "What do you think of Eleanor Rose?"

"Eleanor Rose Johnson," Ginny said quietly, smiling when the baby scrunched up her face, then opened her eyes and blinked rapidly, as if answering to her new name. "I think she likes it, Andy. And I know Bill will love it. His sweetheart's name was Eleanor."

"Think it's too old-fashioned?"

"No, I think it kind of fits her. Everyone will probably call her Ellie, but I like that, too. Don't you?"

"Yeah. I sure do."

He picked up Eleanor Rose, cradled her in his left arm and put his right arm around Ginny. On one hand, Ginny wished someone would come in and take a picture to preserve this golden moment on film for little Ellie to see when she grew up. On the other hand, she was grateful to have this moment at all, and she knew that if a nurse or a visitor entered the room, this intense, wonderful sense of the three of them bonding into a family would be shattered.

She looked at Andy and saw all of the emotions that were filling her chest to bursting, reflected in the blue depths of his eyes. Her throat closed up and her eyes filled with happy tears. He smiled tenderly when he saw them, leaned over and gently kissed them away.

"It's gonna be okay, sweetheart," he murmured, his voice sounding as thick and ragged as her own would if she tried to speak. "Everything's gonna be okay."

Chapter Fifteen

The first month at home with Eleanor Rose was stressful and hectic for Ginny. The day they returned to Pinedale, the baby developed a hideous rash over her entire body, which Pete Sinclair diagnosed as a staph infection she'd probably picked up in the hospital. An antibiotic cleared it up, but the experience scared Ginny half out of her wits.

She'd never been responsible for someone as tiny and helpless as Ellie. She almost drowned the poor kid the first time she'd given her a bath. Every time the baby cried and she had to guess what was wrong, Ginny felt inadequate and inept, terrified that this time her fumbling attempts at motherhood would scar Ellie's psyche for life.

Of course, there were plenty of golden moments, too. Ginny loved to sit by the crib and watch her daughter sleep. When she nursed Ellie, her heart overflowed with a love unlike anything she'd ever known. And she knew with an instinctive, unshakable certainty, that this baby, this miraculous little person would love her back just as much.

As the days passed, Ginny developed more confidence in handling Ellie, but there were two persistent problems that taxed both her energy and her patience. Because of Ellie's premature birth, she needed to nurse more often than a full-term infant. Unfortunately, the days when Ginny could function well on four hours of sleep had vanished.

Pete assured her that Ellie would probably start sleeping all night when she weighed about twelve pounds. Since she already weighed eight pounds, Ginny napped when Ellie did and ignored her exhaustion as much as possible.

The second, and more troubling problem as far as Ginny was concerned, was Andy. He was a wonderful father. He honestly enjoyed spending time with Ellie, and he wasn't the least bit squeamish about changing diapers or doing anything else his daughter needed.

But in his eagerness to play a vital role in Ellie's life, he was driving Ginny nuts. It seemed to her that he was always interfering, offering suggestions for better ways to handle Ellie and pointing out things in the baby books that Ginny had already tried or dismissed as unworkable. And he constantly harped at her that she needed more rest, as if she didn't already know that. He just didn't understand the special bond she felt with Ellie.

Ellie celebrated her sixth-week birthday on the thirtieth of June. Andy came home that night carrying a grocery store sack. The baby had been fussy all day, and Ginny gratefully eyed the bag he set on the work island, assuming he'd picked up something easy and quick for supper.

She brought Ellie over to greet her daddy, peeked into the sack and felt her heart plummet straight down to the soles of her bare feet. Meeting her questioning gaze with a grim smile, Andy reached into the sack and set the baby bottles and cans of powdered infant formula on the counter.

"Why did you buy that stuff?" Ginny demanded, holding Ellie more tightly.

He straightened his shoulders and propped his hands on his hips, assuming the posture that said he meant business.

"I'm taking a week off, and I'm gonna get up with Ellie at night so you can catch up on your sleep."

"That's not necessary, Andy," she said, stepping away from the work island as if it were contaminated with toxic waste. "And you're not feeding my baby that junk."

"If you'd use the breast pump and save some bottles of milk in the freezer, I wouldn't have to. You can't go on like this, Ginny. Don't you know sleep deprivation can be used as a form of torture?"

"I'm *fine*. And I don't mind getting up with Ellie."

"For God's sake, stop trying to be Superwoman. Most women have their mothers come and help for a few weeks when they have a new baby. But you wouldn't let my mom help, or Dani, either. Have you looked in a mirror lately? You're a wreck."

"Well, I'm sorry I'm so ugly. But I'm taking good care of Ellie, so just butt out, okay?"

"No, it's not okay. You're taking good care of Ellie, but you're taking lousy care of Ellie's mother. Who's gonna take care of her if you end up in the hospital?"

Ellie whimpered, no doubt frightened by the angry voices of her parents. Ginny shot Andy a dirty look and cuddled the baby closer. "It's okay, sweetie. Don't cry."

Cursing under his breath, Andy rubbed the back of his neck and turned away. When Ellie quieted, Ginny laid her in the playpen and turned on the music-box mobile to keep her entertained. Then she approached her husband.

"Andy, please. Try to understand," she said quietly. "These infant months go by so fast, I don't want to miss a single second of Ellie's growth and development."

"I think it's more than that, Ginny. It's like you can't stand to share her with anyone. Not even me."

"Maybe I'm being selfish," she conceded. "But she's probably the only baby I'll ever have. Everything she does is precious to me. I just feel this need to give her all the love and attention I never had. Is that so awful?"

"No, of course, it isn't." Andy reached out and caressed er cheek. "But you need a life of your own, too. What bout your painting? Bill's still waiting for his portrait. And aybe I need a little of your attention."

"Are you jealous of your own daughter?" Ginny asked ith an incredulous laugh.

"No more than any other new father. But, honey, if you ake Ellie your whole life, you'll drive her crazy. You don't ave to raise her all alone. You've got to find a little bal-nce here, at least get a few nights' sleep."

"I'll wake up when she cries, anyway."

"And then you can roll over and go back to sleep, just like 've been doing. Once you've caught up, we'll take turns. It on't hurt her."

"How do you know that?"

"Because I asked Pete. Breast milk's the best thing for abies, but there's nothing magic about it. Millions of kids re bottle-fed and they do just fine."

"But—"

"No buts. The decision is out of your hands now, Ginny. mean it. You either let me get up with Ellie, or I'll take her ut to my folks' place for a week."

"That's not fair."

"What you're doing to yourself's not fair, either. To you, o me or to Ellie. Now, what's it gonna be?"

Her head ached and her eyes burned, and she'd never re-ented anyone as much as she resented her implacable hus-and at that moment. He obviously thought he was doing er a huge favor, but it felt more like a punishment. Like a lap across the face—a statement as clear as any billboard logan that he didn't believe she was capable of caring for heir daughter.

Despite all her efforts, her love, her *need* to nurture their aby in every possible way, he'd judged her and found her anting. Just like Charlie. Just like her parents. The bitter aste of defeat coating her mouth, she raised her chin and hose the lesser of the evils he'd presented her.

"You can get up with Ellie. I'll use the breast pump."

Frowning, he studied her face. "Honey, don't take it so hard. I'm not criticizing. I'm only trying to help."

"I know. You're only trying to do the right thing. Isn't that what you always do, Andy? Whether anyone wants you to or not?"

"You're so tired, you're not even rational. Use the breast pump if you want, and go on to bed."

Ginny glared at him, then stomped over to a cupboard, yanked out the breast pump and a sterilized bottle the hospital had given them, and carried them into the bedroom without saying another word. Stripping off her tank top and nursing bra, she marched into the bathroom to scrub her breasts so she wouldn't contaminate the damn pump.

She'd been avoiding mirrors lately, but after what Andy had said, she couldn't resist checking out her reflection while the sink filled with water. Oh, Lord, he was right. Her hair was lank and uncombed, her complexion pallid. The circles under her eyes looked like bruises, and she'd gotten so skinny, she wouldn't have breasts at all if they weren't filled with milk.

She looked worse than a wreck—she looked like hell. No wonder Andy had decided to take over. Maybe she wasn't entirely rational. Well, the sooner she got some sleep, the sooner she could have her baby back. After using the pump, she slipped on a nightgown and carried the bottle to the kitchen. Andy was scrambling eggs at the stove.

"Want some supper?" he asked, his tone as calm and pleasant as if they'd never had an argument.

"No, thanks." She gave him a wry grin. "I think I'm too tired to eat. I'm sorry, Andy."

Setting the skillet off the burner, he came over to the refrigerator, pulled her into his arms and hugged her. "I'm sorry if I was too rough on you. But I didn't know what else to do. I'll take good care of Ellie."

"Yeah, I know."

He turned her toward the doorway and patted her rump. 'Go on, then, and get some rest. We'll be fine.''

Ginny went, pausing by the playpen for a moment, hoping to coax a smile out of Ellie. Andy shooed her out of the room before she could get one, however, and she crawled into bed feeling resentful all over again. Her body ached with exhaustion, but her mind refused to shut down.

She lay there, listening for sounds from the kitchen that might give her an excuse to get up again. Her eyes filled with tears when she heard Andy chuckle and one of Ellie's sweet coos in response. Dammit, she hated being left out. Hated knowing that Ellie was just as happy with Andy as she was with *her.* Hated herself for being so childish and selfish, until her weary body finally took over and demanded the sleep it needed.

Three weeks later, Andy took off his hat, wiped the sweat from his forehead with the back of his wrist and plunked the hat back on again. Damn, but it was hot, even for August. He waited until the ambulance drove George Gregson away, then got into his patrol car.

Gregson was a tourist from Pennsylvania who'd thought he knew everything about hiking. Unfortunately, he hadn't known diddly about the Wind River Mountains. He'd wandered off the trail and gotten lost, and it had taken the search-and-rescue team the better part of two days to find him.

George was exhausted, dehydrated and hungry, and the mosquitoes had made a feast out of him, but he was one of the lucky ones. At least he hadn't broken his leg or fallen off a cliff and gotten himself killed the way that Mason guy from New Jersey had last year.

Muttering under his breath, Andy put the car in gear and headed for Pinedale. Crazy damn tourists drove him buggier every summer. Or maybe this year it just seemed worse than usual because he was still worried about Ginny.

It was the most frustrating situation he'd ever been in, and he was getting pretty damn sick and tired of it. He feared he was losing her, but for the life of him, he couldn't figure out what she wanted or needed from him that he hadn't already given or offered to give her.

He'd hired the Osborn girls from down the street to come in and help with the housework and take turns baby-sitting Ellie for a couple of hours a day. Ginny had caught up on her sleep and appeared to be handling the baby without any problems. She was even painting again.

On the surface, their home life had drastically improved. Ellie was interacting more with them every day. He and Ginny weren't fighting. But the closeness they'd shared when the baby had been born was gone.

They slept in the same bed, ate meals together, played with the baby together. But it just wasn't the same. Their relationship was like spaghetti sauce with no spices, cookies with no chocolate chips, eggs with no salt. It was pleasant. It was polite. It was flatter than hell.

Though she'd supposedly made peace with sharing Ellie more, he knew damn well she still hadn't forgiven him for forcing her to accept some help. Maybe she never would.

Well, he was done crawling. He'd had it with her sulking. With her subtle rebuffs whenever he'd tried to show his affection for her. With her cool withdrawal every time he made a suggestion about the way she took care of the baby.

Ellie was his kid, too. And he'd read as many books about babies as Ginny had. So where did she get off being such a snot about everything? Like *she* was the only one who could decide what was best for Ellie?

Hell, he almost wished they *were* fighting. At least then he'd know she still cared enough to fight. That was what bothered him the most—the fear that she'd given up. On him and on their marriage. He sensed that she was biding her time, waiting for him to screw up somehow and give her an excuse to leave.

He parked in the driveway and climbed out of the car, bending to pet Schnoodle. "Hi there, girl. Yeah, you're always glad to see me, aren't you?" Her canine duty done, Schnoodle raced off after a butterfly.

Looking through the screen door as he tugged off his dirty boots on the back steps, Andy saw Bill sitting at the kitchen table, giving the baby a bottle of water. Ginny stood beside her easel, studying the painting she'd been working on. Lord, she was pretty.

He wanted her so much, his whole body ached with it. But if she was interested in sex these days, she wasn't admitting it to him, even though the doc had told them both it was okay. Discouraged to his toenails, he opened the door and stepped inside.

"Here's your Kitten, Bill. What do you think?" Ginny asked, turning the easel around.

Bill's jaw sagged as he stared at the portrait. A tear dripped down his wrinkled cheek, splashing on Ellie's forehead. The baby swiped at it with her fist, scrunching up her face in preparation for a bellow of protest. Ginny set down her brush again and took Ellie into her arms.

Bill didn't appear to notice. The lines in his face suddenly looked deeper. His throat worked down a swallow and a second tear followed the first one.

"God, wasn't she beautiful?" he whispered. "I still miss her every day, you know? Every night I pray I'll see her again when I get to heaven."

Not wanting to disturb what was obviously a poignant moment, Andy silently crossed the room in his stocking feet. Ginny and Bill were so wrapped up in the painting, neither of them noticed him until he got a clear view of the finished portrait and sucked in a harsh, shocked gasp.

It couldn't be...it just *couldn't* be. He shut his eyes, opened them and looked again, vaguely aware that Ginny and Bill were staring at him instead of the canvas.

Ginny lifted the baby to her shoulder and patted her back. "Is something wrong, Andy?"

"That's Bill's sweetheart?" he asked, still unable to believe what his eyes were telling him.

"Yes, that's Kitten."

"But her real name was Eleanor."

"Yes. But how did you—Oh, that's right, I told you when we named the baby. Andy, what *is* it?"

So many things made sense all of a sudden, Andy was too busy trying to assimilate them all to answer Ginny. Bill's joy at learning Andy had fathered a child. His hanging around Ginny. His doting on the baby. His moving into this neighborhood in the first place. Andy turned to the old man, who was watching him with a wary, hopeful expression.

"You knew who I was all along, didn't you?" Andy demanded. "You bought the house next door on purpose."

Bill nodded. "Yeah. I wanted to get to know you."

"Why, you manipulative, sorry son of a bitch," Andy snarled. "Of all the sneaky, underhanded—"

"What are you talking about, Andy?" Ginny interrupted.

"He's my grandfather," Andy said, spitting out the last word as if it tasted nasty, which it did in this case. "The one who got my grandmother pregnant and deserted her."

Bill shoved himself to his feet, glaring at Andy in righteous indignation. "I never did any such thing. I'd have married her in a minute if her folks would've let me."

"Yeah, I'll *bet*," Andy muttered. "Even if that's true, it didn't give you the right to worm your way into my life, and my dad's without telling us who you were. I'll bet you had one helluva good laugh when Ginny invited you to have Christmas dinner with us."

"It wasn't like that, Andy—"

"The hell it *wasn't*." Andy uttered a contemptuous laugh. "And that was probably nothing compared to the night I told you about Ginny bein' pregnant. You had a lot of gall to get so self-righteous with me, old man. What was it you said? Something like, 'If a woman's good enough to sleep with, she's good enough to marry.'"

"And I meant every word of it. Why, I wanted to make your grandma my wife, so bad it damn near killed me to leave her. But I was just a kid with no money and no prospects, and her dad blacklisted me with every rancher in three counties. Now what could I do against a guy like him?"

"You could've eloped."

"Don't think I didn't try, boy. Once her dad found out about us, he locked that poor girl in her room and posted armed guards around the house. I didn't have a prayer of gettin' her out of there."

"So you just gave up and rode off into the sunset. Now, isn't that romantic?"

"There's no need to be sarcastic, Andy," Ginny protested. "Bill tried to do what was right."

"Oh, sure. Take his side, Ginny. Forget all the pain he caused my grandma and my dad."

"Can't you see he's sorry for that?"

"Ha! He probably took off and never looked back until he got old and figured out he didn't have anybody. So he comes back here and deceives all of us into thinking he's such a nice old coot, we'll take him into the family. Well, I don't buy it and I doubt my dad will, either."

"What do you intend to do?" Bill asked, drawing himself up straight and gazing at Andy with a quiet dignity that almost derailed his anger. Almost, but not quite.

"For starters, you can take that painting and get the hell out of my house. I don't ever want to see you or your damn dog on my property again. And you stay away from my wife and baby. You hear me?"

"Andy—"

Bill shook his head at Ginny. "It's all right, hon. I knew what I was risking when I asked you to paint that picture for me. Andy's got a right to feel the way he does, and I'm gonna respect his feelings. I'm just grateful I got to know you and that precious baby. I'll put a check in the mail for you tomorrow."

With that, he picked up the painting and walked to the door, turning back to face Andy. "I'm sorry. Believe it or not, I looked back plenty of times. I bought a subscription to the newspaper here and read every copy for news of your family. The day you got elected sheriff, was the proudest day of my life."

Then he left, leaving a thick, pulsing silence behind him. Suddenly feeling as if he'd kicked a puppy, Andy opened his mouth to call Bill back. Before he could get out the old man's name, however, Ginny stomped over to the playpen, laid Ellie in it and turned on the mobile.

Marching back to Andy, she braced her fists on her hips and glared at him. "How could you *do* that to him?" she demanded. "He's old and lonely, and he loves you."

"He *lied* to me, dammit. And he lied to you, too."

"Yeah, one of your famous lies by omission? For God's sake, he was probably scared to tell you who he was for fear you'd react exactly the way you did. He's my *friend,* and he's going to stay my friend. If he wants to see Ellie—"

"Stay away from him."

"I won't, and you don't have a thing to say about it."

Her stubborn defense of the old man enraged Andy, not so much because of what she said, but because she seemed to care more about Bill's feelings than she did about his.

"Dammit, Ginny, I haven't asked you for much in this marriage. Not a clean house, or decent meals or even sex since Ellie was born. It seems to me that the least you can do is show a little family loyalty here."

"I haven't had a lot of luck with families, and you're just using that as an excuse to make me feel guilty. Well, forget it. I don't throw away friends like that, and I sure as hell don't throw away relatives."

"You're not related to him."

"Ellie *is.* He's her great-grandpa."

"My dad's her grandpa. Don't you care about him?"

"Of course I do. But how he feels about Bill is his business, not mine or yours. I'll be surprised if he's so damn unforgiving. God, you sounded just like my parents."

"That was a low blow, Ginny."

"No, it was the truth. Come to think if it, you've been almost as bossy as Charlie lately, too."

"I'm not like him or your damn parents."

"Ha! You're critical and nitpicky about every little thing. There's always a right way and a wrong way to do everything, and of course, the right way's always *your* way."

"Now, wait just a minute."

"No, *you* wait. It's *my* turn for a change. Every time I turn around, you're in my face, trying to take more control over Ellie—like I'm incompetent or something. And now you're telling me I can't have Bill for a friend because he made a mistake over sixty years ago? You think you're so perfect? What gives you the right to stand in judgment?"

"Hey, I make mistakes, too—"

"You don't act like it! Tell me something. How perfect does a person have to be before you can love them, Andy? Huh? As perfect as you?"

Her condemnation cut into him like a thousand shards of glass. He studied her for a long, aching moment, wondering how they had reached this awful impasse. Then, fearing he would say something that would destroy what little was left of their relationship, he turned and headed for the door.

"I'm gonna go out and tell my folks about Bill. We can thrash this out when I get back."

He stepped outside, crammed his feet into his boots and got into the patrol car. One thought rode along with him as he drove the familiar back roads—when he'd turned to leave, Ginny hadn't even bothered to ask where he was going.

Shaken by the events of the past half hour, Ginny scooped the baby out of the playpen and carried her into the living

room. She settled into the rocker, holding Ellie close f
comfort. The baby looked up at her with big, serious eyes-
eyes the same color as Andy's.

Ginny stroked the downy fuzz on Ellie's round little hea
which was already turning a coppery red. The baby gave h
a wide, toothless grin, raised her arm and poked her finge
at Ginny's mouth. Ginny kissed those tiny fingers, marve
ing at how much the child had already grown.

She didn't want to deprive Andy of Ellie or Ellie of hin
but the sick feeling in the pit of her stomach told her she'
better face facts. During the past month, Andy had conti
ued to interfere with her mothering efforts, and she'd co
tinued to resent him. It was as if, by allowing him to ord
her to bed that one time, she'd created a monster. Andy ha
decided he liked exercising his authority and he wasn't abo
to give it up.

Whenever he thought she was doing too much with t
baby, he threatened to send her to his folks, and Ginny w
damn tired of living with that kind of a threat hanging ov
her head. Well, nobody was going to get in the way of h
bond with Ellie. Not even Andy.

From the minute he'd insisted on hiring the Osborn girl
despite her vehement protests, it was as if all the love she fe
for him got locked up inside her. She'd been hoping, pra
ing for something to happen that would allow her to chang
her mind and stay with him.

If he'd ever said he loved her, even one more time—to h
face when she was wide awake—well, maybe she would fe
differently. But he hadn't. And now she could see that t
only person he really loved was Ellie. She'd known th
weren't right for each other from the very beginning, but
amazed her that admitting it still hurt so much.

She was tired of feeling as if she didn't quite measure u
and she suspected she would always feel that way with And
If he would judge Bill so harshly, he would eventually jud
her the same way. And what about Ellie? What if he turne

that kind of judgmental attitude on her if she ever disappointed him?

Well, Ginny wasn't willing to risk that. Not for her little girl. No way. Sighing with resignation, she kissed Ellie's soft cheek, then stood, walked into the bedroom and started packing.

The closer Andy got to his parents' ranch, the slower he drove. As he put physical distance between himself and Ginny, he gained emotional distance from the heat of their quarrel. With it, came a painful objectivity that forced him to take a long, hard look at himself.

Pulling over to the side of the road, he ran the argument through his memory again. They'd started out fighting about Bill, but somewhere along the line, the topic had changed to an indictment of Andy's character. Ginny had really lambasted him up one side and down the other.

His first reaction was to deny her charges, but if he did that, he had a strong suspicion that he would miss some message she'd been trying to give him. That last shot she'd taken worried him something fierce. His ears were still ringing with the bitter, hopeless sound of her voice.

How perfect does a person have to be before you can love them, Andy? Huh? As perfect as you?

The only logical conclusion he could come to, was that Ginny believed he didn't love her. Damn. He should have made her sit down and talk to him long before this, but everything had been so chaotic after Ellie was born. And Ginny'd been so distant since things had gotten back to normal, the prospect of discussing his feelings with her had been ... well, he'd just plain turned chicken.

Putting the car in gear, he made a U-turn and drove back to town, his foot riding heavily on the accelerator. Ginny didn't answer when he rushed in the back door and called her name. He saw a light in the hallway and ran toward it, then rocked back on his heels when he saw the closet doors in the bedroom standing open and the empty space where her clothes had hung.

It was an eerily accurate replay of the night Denise had left him. His pride had taken one hell of a beating that night. But seeing the evidence that *Ginny* had left him, was like having a huge chunk of his soul ripped out. It hurt to breathe. His blood thundered in his ears, though how a broken heart could pump that hard was beyond him.

"No," he whispered, taking one step forward.

He hesitated, then turned and walked into the nursery. Ellie's blanket was gone. So was her stuffed rabbit. He didn't have to open the dresser drawers to know they were empty.

Ginny hadn't even left him Schnoodle. Dear God, what had he done? And how could she do this to him after everything they'd shared? After the way she'd loved him?

But *had* she ever really loved him? He'd assumed that she had because of the way she acted toward him. But she'd never actually said the words, any more than he had.

He gulped, then forced himself to return to the kitchen. Surely she wouldn't have gone without leaving him a note. There it was, stuck on the fridge with a magnet.

Dear Andy,
We're at the Circle D. It breaks my heart to admit it, but this marriage isn't going to work. You've been a wonderful husband in many ways, but I need to be free to make my own decisions and my own mistakes. Thanks for everything, especially Ellie. Feel free to come and see her anytime. I'll let you know when I've found a place in town.

Love,
Ginny

"Love?" Andy muttered, furiously crumpling the note. "Yeah, right. What a crock."

Then he smoothed the paper out and read it again. One line jumped out at him—"I need to be free to make my own decisions and my own mistakes." What the hell did she mean by that? He'd never held her prisoner, for God's sake.

Sure, he'd been pretty heavy-handed over the issue of Ginny taking care of herself, but what kind of a man would allow his wife to run herself into the ground? Had she left him because he'd tried to help her? If that were true, the woman was wacko. Maybe she had postpartum depression.

That damn sentence made him feel like some kind of a control freak, and he wasn't. Was he? Denise had told him he was too stubborn and bossy for his own good. That wasn't why she'd left him, but she'd said it more than once. So, maybe he *did* have a little problem with that. He'd never meant any harm by it.

But maybe Ginny didn't see it that way. What had she said tonight when they'd been fighting? *Every time I turn around, you're in my face, trying to take more control over Ellie—like I'm incompetent or something. And now you're telling me I can't have Bill for a friend because he made a mistake over sixty years ago?*

Thinking back over some other times he'd ticked her off with his domineering behavior, Andy winced. Okay, he *did* have a problem with that. And after living with her parents and then with Charlie, Ginny was probably more sensitive to that kind of thing than most people would be.

But he could change, and he *would,* dammit. He'd give her a week to cool off, and then he'd apologize, tell her he loved her and beg her to come home. He'd even promise to stop being so damn bossy. Surely she'd forgive him. She just *had* to.

Because hard as it was to admit, he needed that woman. And he needed his daughter and that dumb dog, too. His life wouldn't be worth spit without them.

Chapter Sixteen

"I don't want to ride this damn horse, Sam. I'm tired," Ginny grumbled, watching her friend swing himself aboard his gray gelding, Smokey.

"Tough. You need some fresh air and sunshine, or your brain's gonna mildew," Sam replied.

"But what if Ellie gives Dani a hard time? She's got her hands full with Kevin."

"She's also got Grandma D and Kim there to help her. Shut up and get goin'."

Shooting a resentful glare at Sam's broad back, Ginny nudged the bay mare with her knees, waiting for the inevitable lecture to start. Just as she'd known he would, Sam had taken her and Ellie in without question. He'd left her alone for the first four days and allowed her to wallow in her misery. But during the past twenty-four hours, she'd sensed that he was growing impatient with her refusal to tell him what had happened to her marriage.

Well, he could torture her all he wanted. She wasn't ready to talk about Andy yet. The pain was still too raw, and she was beginning to suspect it would always be too raw.

Sam didn't say a word, however. He just kept riding across one pasture after another, and then on up into the foothills west of the ranch house. Closing her eyes, Ginny felt the morning sun warming her face. The familiar sounds of creaking saddle leather, horse hooves plodding through the grass, the popping of tiny wings as insects startled into flight gradually soothed her nerves. And the smells—oh, the wonderful smell of freshly cut hay, of the pines, of the horses themselves—took her back to a time when she'd ridden with Sam and life had been much, much simpler.

"Hey, I know you're tired," Sam drawled from off to her left, "but I wouldn't fall asleep in the saddle."

She opened her eyes and smiled at him, her first sincere smile since...she wouldn't think about that now. Perhaps he'd been right to badger her into this ride, though. With the lush valley spread out below her and the Wyoming Range poking holes in that blue sky overhead, she could already feel a measure of peace seeping into her soul.

Sam reined Smokey to a halt, dismounted and held Ginny's mare while she followed suit. He tethered the horses, then led Ginny over to a huge, flat rock. Using the boulder for a backrest, they sat on the ground and watched the animals graze in silence.

"I'm sorry it didn't work out for you and Andy," Sam finally said. "I know you must have tried real hard, Gin, but I guess I wasn't all that surprised when you left him."

Ginny shot him a puzzled glance. "I thought Andy was your friend."

"I like Andy, all right."

"Then what are you trying to say, Sam?"

"Well, you know, he's got quite a temper on him, and I don't suppose he's very good at apologizing."

"He apologizes."

Sam shrugged, then pulled his hat brim down to shade his eyes a little more. "Well, I guess he must be awful demanding, then. He's such a neat freak, he must have yelled all the time about the house bein' messy, huh?"

"Actually, he was pretty patient about that," Ginny admitted. "He'd get a little grumpy sometimes, but if something bothered him, he'd clean it up himself."

"Hmmm." Sam scratched at his earlobe. "Oh, I get it now. He wasn't a good father. Didn't pay any attention to Ellie. Wouldn't change a diaper. Griped when she cried."

"That's not true. Andy adores Ellie. He pitched right in with her and did everything but nurse her."

"I see." Yanking a long weed out of the ground, Sam twisted it around his index finger until it snapped.

"What do you think you see?" Ginny asked when he reached for another weed.

He shot her a pitying glance before answering. "Well, I figure it's got something to do with your sex life, Ginny. I don't want to pry into that. I mean, if he was too kinky or something, I don't really want to know."

Ginny punched him in the shoulder. "There was nothing wrong with our sex life, Sam. Would you knock it off?"

"Hey, Ginny, this is *me* you're talkin' to. I know Andy must have been pure hell to live with in *some* way for you to bail out the way you did. I'm just trying to find out if I need to go beat him up for abusing you."

"He never abused me," Ginny retorted. "For heaven's sake, Sam. Where do you get these weird ideas?"

"You show up here one night, bawlin' your head off. And then you mope around with your chin draggin' the ground for five days. You won't talk to anybody. What am I supposed to think? Was he cheatin' on you?"

"No, of course not."

"Was he drinkin' a lot, then? Bein' mean to your dog? What the hell did he do to you, Gin?"

Ginny scrambled to her feet. Turning her back to Sam, she wrapped her arms around her waist, trying to ward off the chilling ache of regret blossoming deep inside her.

"Andy didn't *do* anything to me. He just didn't love me, Sam. And I couldn't handle it anymore."

Sam stood, rested one hip against the boulder and folded his arms across his chest. "What makes you think he didn't love you?"

"The only time he ever said it was after sex, when he thought I was asleep. I'd have been a fool to believe him then, wouldn't I?"

"Are you tryin' to convince me of that or yourself?"

"What difference does it make? I'm a miserable failure as a wife. Charlie always said so, anyway."

"Andy's not Charlie, Ginny."

"I know that, but—"

"Do you? Do you *really* know that?"

"Of course. But dammit, Sam, you know how judgmental Andy can be. Just like my dad. And just like Charlie. And I knew Andy would reject me sooner or later. So I left."

"Preemptive strike, huh? You blasted him before he could blast you."

"Something like that."

Sam walked up behind her and put both hands on her shoulders. "Well, I think you're forgetting something about Andy. His divorce seemed kinda low-key to most folks, but I know it cut him damn deep. There were lots of gals around town who would've been happy to console him, but he never let anybody get very close to him until you came along."

"What's your point?"

"A guy like Andy doesn't want to fail at marriage. I'll bet he's been as insecure about bein' a husband again as you were about bein' a wife. Maybe he needed a little reassurance and encouragement from you first."

"Well, he was the one who suggested—before the wedding—that we get a divorce after Ellie was born," Ginny muttered.

"What are you talkin' about?"

Turning to face him, Ginny explained the terms of her bargain with Andy. Sam stared at her with an incredulous look on his face, then threw his hands into the air and snorted with disgust.

"For cryin' out loud," he ranted, pacing to the rock and back. "You both went into the marriage expecting it to fail, and now you're whining because it did?"

"I'm not whining!"

"Like hell, you're not! Haven't you ever heard of a self-fulfilling prophecy?"

"Dammit, Sam, don't you yell at me."

"Well, *somebody's* got to. Cripes, woman. Marriage is hard enough when you're both committed to the teeth. And then you add a new baby and all the tension they bring to the mix? Sheesh! What the hell did you expect?"

"Oh, you're *such* an expert."

"I'm doin' a damn sight better than you are. At least Dani and I know if we have a spat, we can trust each other to hang around long enough to make up. You guys killed any hope of that right from the start. You never even gave yourselves a fighting chance to make it."

"How can you say that? We called the deal off before Ellie was born. We *tried*."

"Bull, you tried. Now, be honest with yourself for once. Didja ever really trust Andy to want what was best for you? Or didja hold your cards real close to your chest and wait for him to start actin' like Charlie?"

"You don't know what it was like with Charlie," she wailed, tears suddenly gushing down her cheeks. She dashed them away with the backs of her fists. "He took my self-esteem and flushed it down the toilet. When he died, I swore I'd never let anybody hurt me like that again."

"And just how do you plan to do that, honey? By never loving anybody? Never trusting anybody again?"

"Whatever it takes," she whispered. "I couldn't survive that again."

"Well, I feel sorry for you, but I feel even sorrier for Andy. I know damn well *he* never set out to hurt you."

"I'm telling you, he's a control freak, just like Charlie, dammit. He told me I couldn't be friends with Bill and he won't even let me take care of Ellie like I want to."

Sam rocked back on his heels and held up his hands. "Whoa. Back up there and try to make sense."

Taking a deep breath, Ginny haltingly recounted everything that had happened since they'd brought Ellie home from the hospital. "Now do you see what I mean, Dawson?"

Frowning, Sam shook his head. "I saw Andy and Bill havin' coffee together when I was in town yesterday, Ginny. Looked like they were gettin' along fine to me."

"Andy must have apologized, then. But what about the rest of it? I swear I didn't make anything up. How can I live with a man who thinks I'm too inadequate to take care of my baby?"

"Let's sit down again," he suggested. When they'd resumed their former spots on the ground, he folded his hands between his bent knees and looked her straight in the eye. "Ginny, you know I wouldn't hurt you for the world."

"Of course."

"Well, this might hurt, but I've gotta be honest with you. You're too sensitive and paranoid about criticism."

"I'm not, either."

He raised one eyebrow at her. "If you'll stop bein' defensive, you might learn something important."

"All right. I'm listening."

"Did it ever occur to you that Andy mighta been just as scared when you took Ellie home from the hospital as you were? I drove Dani nuts for the first three months after we brought Kevin home. I was terrified something awful would happen to him.''

''You were?''

''Sure, I was. A man looks at a baby, and they're so little and helpless, you can hardly believe they'll survive. But whenever I'd fuss, I wasn't criticizing Dani. I was just worryin' out loud. I'll bet Andy was doing the same thing. And I don't blame him for makin' you take care of yourself. You're not twenty anymore, Gin. Would you rather he didn't give a damn if you collapsed?''

''No,'' Ginny whispered.

''Well, think about it. You didn't have to take all of that personally. I know Andy can be a little rough around the edges, but that comes with the territory he works in. Shoot, I'd have to say he's bent over backward tryin' to help you and take care of you and Ellie, and all you've done is punish him for things Charlie and your folks did.''

''Oh, Sam . . .'' Ginny gulped, then covered her face with both hands and sobbed. Sam scooted over and pulled her into his arms.

''That's it, Gin,'' he murmured, stroking her hair as she wept against his chest. ''Cry it all out now, honey. You've been tough for a long, long time, but you don't have to be tough anymore. Get it over and done with.''

When she finally quieted, he pulled a handkerchief from his back pocket and mopped up her face as if she were five years old. Then he slid his index finger under her chin and forced her to look at him.

''You gave me some damn good advice one time about letting go of the past. Don'tcha think it's time you took it yourself?''

''I thought I had,'' she said, sniffling. ''But I guess I was wrong. God, I've been doing everything you said. I've been so s-scared. And I've been such a f-fool.''

Tucking her hair behind her ears, Sam gave her a crooked smile. ''Love makes us all a little crazy, Ginny. I never would've had the nerve to take the risk of loving Dani if you hadn't talked to me the way you did.''

"Was it worth the risk?"

"Was it ever. It's still scary as hell, sometimes, but I'd die without her. For the first time since I came home from Vietnam, I feel like I'm really alive.''

Ginny took the handkerchief from him and gave her nose a resounding honk. Then she inhaled a deep breath. "Do you think Andy might be willing to try again?''

"There's only one way to find out. But I want to tell you something first.''

"What's that?''

"You've had some rotten luck with people who were supposed to love you, Gin. And because they didn't, I think they've made you feel like there's something wrong with you—that maybe you're not very lovable. Am I right?''

Ginny nodded. "Yeah. My head tells me that's not true, but my gut doesn't always believe it.''

"Listen to your head this time. I've never lied to you, Bradford, and I'm not lyin' now. You're a fine woman, and there's no reason on this earth that Andy wouldn't love you. And you deserve to be happy just as much as anybody else. Got it?''

"Yes, sir. Anything you say, sir.''

"Smart ass.'' He cuffed her chin, then smiled. "One more thing. You've gotta love and trust yourself before you can love and trust Andy or Ellie or anybody else. Give your folks and Charlie a rest and start fresh right now.''

"Let's go back to the house, Sam. I've got some serious thinking to do.''

Andy stood on Sam Dawson's back steps, fear and impatience roiling in his gut. Shading his eyes with one hand, he watched for a sign of Ginny and Sam's return. He'd planned to give Ginny a full week to cool off, but he'd only been able to tolerate five days—the five loneliest, most miserable days of his life—without seeing her.

The hour he'd spent playing with Ellie had been wonderful, but she was taking a nap now. Dani and Grandma D had threatened to strangle him if he didn't stop pacing. Since he couldn't do that, he'd taken himself outside.

Honest to God, if Ginny didn't come back soon, he was gonna have a heart attack. He'd gone over everything he'd ever said to her and everything she'd ever said to him so many times, he'd sprained his brain. He'd gone from hope to despair and back again at least once an hour since he'd discovered her note on the fridge. Dammit, had they ridden all the way to China or what?

There—was that a trail of dust on the other side of that hill? Yeah, it sure was, and it was just about the right size for two horses. They rode into sight a moment later. The instant she spotted him, Ginny straightened up so fast, her horse stopped walking.

A Stetson shaded her face, making it impossible for Andy to read her expression, but he could feel her intense gaze drilling into him like a laser beam. Then her horse started up again, carrying her closer and closer.

His heart beat faster. His breath locked in his chest. Sweat trickled down his sides and slicked his palms.

She swung down off the bay mare with more speed than grace, tossed the reins to Sam and walked toward Andy, a hesitant smile curving her mouth. Her eyes looked a little red, as if she'd been crying, but there was something new in the way she carried herself—a sureness, or maybe a sense of confidence he'd never noticed before.

"Hi," she said, stopping two feet in front of him. "I'm glad you're here, Andy. We need to talk."

After psyching himself up for a battle to get her to talk to him, her blunt statement took the old starch right out of his shorts. But her smile eased his fears enough to let him smile back at her.

"I'd like that, Ginny. I'd like it a lot."

She glanced at the house, then looked at Andy again. "I need to feed Ellie first. Do you mind waiting?"

"She just finished a bottle and I put her down for a nap," Andy said, sneaking a peek at the front of her shirt. Pressed against the soft cotton, her breasts looked as if they were pretty darn full of milk. He cleared his throat and shoved his hands into his jeans pockets. "Dani didn't seem to think it would be a problem."

"It's not," Ginny assured him. "I'll just, uh, run in and use the breast pump. Give me ten minutes and we can go for a walk."

He couldn't stand not touching her for one more second. Reaching out, he brushed the backs of his knuckles across her sun-kissed cheek. Her eyes glowed and she sighed with such obvious pleasure, he couldn't resist stealing a quick kiss, as well. Her lips clung to his for a brief moment, communicating a whole host of things that pushed his heart into overdrive.

Then she pulled back, gave him a misty smile and whispered, "I'll hurry."

"Yeah. Do that, honey," Andy replied in a husky voice, shoving his hands back into his pockets.

His heart in his throat, he watched her hair bounce around her shoulders and her little tush switch back and forth as she walked to the house. Exhaling a quiet moan of longing, he nearly jumped out of his skin when Sam called to him from the barn door.

"Hey, Johnson. Come here a minute."

Damn. He'd forgotten all about Sam, Andy thought, feeling his face grow hot as he wondered how much of that little exchange the other man had witnessed. Probably the whole darn thing if the grin on his face was anything to judge by. Well, so what?

He stepped through the doorway. "Whaddaya want, Dawson?"

"Catch."

Andy cupped his hands together as a flash of metal arced through the air toward him. "What's this for?" he asked, holding up the key Sam had tossed at him.

"The old foreman's house. You and Ginny can have a little privacy. And here's something else you might need."

Andy held out his hands again and came up with a string of condom packets. He laughed, then stuck them into his pocket. "You keep a stash of those in the barn, huh?"

Sam shrugged and went back to grooming his gelding. "All over the place now that I've got two nosy stepkids underfoot all the time. I'd love to have another baby with Dani, but not just yet."

"Yeah, I know what you mean."

Setting the brush aside, Sam propped an elbow on a stall door and studied Andy with a somber expression. "Don't just tell her you love her, Andy," he said. "Tell her *why* you love her."

"How do you know that's what I'm gonna talk to her about?" Andy asked.

"'Cause you're a damn fool if it's not. And I don't think you're a damn fool. I've been known to be wrong before, but I'd better not be this time."

Shaking his head, Andy chuckled and walked back out into the sunshine. Ginny came out of the house a moment later. He walked across the graveled driveway to meet her, and they set off, strolling along the narrow, dusty path that had brought them together in the first place.

"I've missed you," he said when they'd gone about a quarter of a mile.

She slid her palm against his and gave his hand a tentative squeeze. "I've missed you, too."

Lacing their fingers together, he squeezed back. "I've done a lot of thinking since you left, but I'm not sure how to go about setting things right with you. But I want to, Ginny. I want that more than anything else in this world."

She stopped walking and looked at him, her dark eyes filled with regret. "I was so angry and upset that night, I didn't mean half the things I said."

"Yes, you did, honey," he said, turning to face her. "It all came boilin' right up out of your gut. And I'll admit

ome of the things you said hurt. But that was the most
onest communication we've ever had outside of bed, so
on't apologize and don't back down from telling me what
ou really feel.''

"Well, I didn't have to be so mean about it."

Andy started walking again, tugging on her hand until she
ame along with him. "I'm not so sure about that. I've got
pretty tough hide. Could be, I'm downright insensitive."

"No, you're not."

He smiled at her quick defense of him. "Whatever. But
something's really eatin' at you and I'm not payin' atten-
on, I want you to whack me over the head if you have to,
in. Don't just swallow it down and hate me."

"I don't hate you, Andy. I never did."

"Good. I'm glad to hear that," he said fervently,
queezing her hand again. "'Cause that makes what I want
say a heck of lot easier."

"What's that?"

The old foreman's house had come into view. "Let's sit
own over there and I'll tell you," he said, gesturing to-
ard the front porch with his free hand.

"All right."

They sat on the top step, holding hands like a couple of
enagers. Andy felt just about that nervous, and he sus-
ected Ginny did, too. He cleared his throat, gazed deeply
to her eyes and prayed that the right words would come
ut of his mouth for once in his life.

"Ginny, I know you didn't want this marriage right from
e start, and I know it hasn't worked out as well as we'd
oped it would. And I think I've got a pretty good idea now
f what went wrong."

"Go ahead, Andy. I'm listening."

"Well, see, what you're supposed to do is fall in love, get
arried and then get pregnant. But we did it all backward,
nd the steps didn't work as well in reverse. So we both
nded up feeling like the only reason we were together was
ecause of the baby. Am I right so far?"

"I'd say that's pretty accurate."

"Okay. From here on out, I can only speak for mysel What happened with me, was that when I found myse falling in love with you, I never told you about it because didn't know if you felt the same way about me. We g married so fast, we missed some important steps at the b ginning."

"You mean like, getting to know each other? Building friendship? Trusting each other?" Ginny asked.

"Exactly. We sorta got off on the wrong foot and the Ellie was born and we never had a chance to go back and f things. I know I'm too bossy sometimes and I swear I'll my best to knock it off. Honest to God, if you can forgi me for being such a jerk, I swear—"

She cut him off with a shake of her head. "You werer the only jerk in the house, Andy. Sam pointed out a few my mistakes for me this morning."

He kissed her fingers, then grasped them with his fr hand. "Oh, yeah? Want to tell me what they were?"

"Not really," she said, wrinkling her nose at him. "Bu think if anyone deserves an apology here, it's you. I was, u so scared that you'd turn out to be like Charlie, I . . . well guess what I did was I reacted to almost everything you d as if you *were* Charlie."

"I'm not sure I understand."

"That's probably because I'm not making any sense She laughed, then shook her head and sighed. "Okay, let n try this again. See, every time you made a suggestion abo the baby or picked up stuff around the house, I took it a: personal criticism. Like, you were telling me I wasn't doi: things well enough to suit you. That *I* wasn't good enough

"I didn't mean it that way, Ginny. Honest."

"I know that now. But—" She choked up, gulped, th swiped impatiently at her eyes. "Damn. I swore I was: gonna bawl again."

Andy fished his handkerchief out of his hip pocket a: gave it to her. "Don't worry about it. Go on and finish."

"Okay. I'm fine now. But, see, that's the kind of thing Charlie used to do to me. Only, he'd make a big production out of it and slam around and call me names. And I was so afraid of that happening again, I kept forgetting you weren't like that. It was easier to blame my problems on you than admit that I felt inadequate to be a wife or a mother."

"Aw, Ginny. You're not inadequate in my eyes."

"But I'm such a lousy housekeeper and such a mediocre cook, and I'm not very traditional, you know?"

"And that makes you just about the perfect wife for a guy like me, sweetheart." She shot him an are-you-out-of-your-mind? look that made him laugh. "No, I *mean* it, Gin. I'm too traditional, too play-it-by-the-book, too nitpicky. You've helped me loosen up and figure out what's really important to me."

"What's that, Andy? I really need to know."

Her grip on his hand had tightened to the point of causing pain. The entreaty in her eyes damn near broke his heart. Cupping the side of her face with his palm, he struggled to express himself.

"It's having someone in your life to care about and feel connected to. I love you, Ginny. And it's not just because of Ellie. I think she's the most wonderful baby in the whole world, and I'll always be grateful to you for everything you went through to have her. But besides Ellie, you've given me so much more than you'll ever know."

"Like what for instance?"

"That crazy little dog. I'd never thought about having a pet until you came along, but whenever I come home, there's ol' Schnoodle, wigglin' her hind end off like I'm the best thing that's happened to her all day."

Ginny rolled her eyes and chuckled. "Oh, great, Johnson. I've given you a kid and a wiggly dog. That's supposed to make you love me?"

"Sure it does. And that's not all. I used to come home and brood in the dark when I'd had a bad day. But after you moved in, there was always something interesting going on

at home, and you brought my friends and all those brigh
colors into the house.

"You helped me remember what it was like to be silly an
act like a kid, and that every little thing doesn't have to b
so damn serious all the time."

He jerked his head toward the front door of the house
"You know why I was so lonely the night we made lov
here? 'Cause I didn't have you around to remind me
needed people just as much as the next guy. You've given m
a real home, Ginny, and it's a damn sight better one than
had with Denise or the one I'd made for myself."

"You're gonna make me bawl again."

"That's tough, 'cause I'm not real good about saying th
stuff and I'm on a roll. You'd better listen while the liste
ing's good, woman. Who knows when I'll feel like doir
this again?"

"Okay, okay. I'm listening."

"I like the way you're a good friend to people, like Sa
and Bill. By the way, I apologized to Bill and everything
fine."

"I'm glad, Andy. He loves you so much."

"Yeah, I know. But we'll talk about him later. Have
mentioned sex yet?"

"I think you'd remember if you had," she said dryly.

"See? That's another thing I love about you, Ginny. Yo
tease nice."

"I *tease* nice?"

"Yeah. You can poke fun at me, and I feel flattered by th
attention, you know? You're not mean about it. You ju
show me a different perspective on things I say and do. Yo
make me laugh more than anybody else I know."

"Maybe you'd better get back to sex, Andy."

"I don't have any complaints in that department, excep
that it's been one helluva long time since we made love. On
of my regrets when you left was that we never tried out tho
black satin sheets."

"What black satin sheets?"

"My dad bought us some for our wedding night. They ren't much fun when you're sleeping alone, so I tossed 'em a box and put 'em downstairs."

"What did your mother say when he brought them ome?"

Grinning, Andy put his hands on his hips and tried to nitate his mother's voice. "'Marv, if you ever want to have ookie with me again, you get your butt right back over to laho Falls and buy *us* a set of those sheets!'"

Ginny laughed delightedly, then sighed. "I really love our folks, Andy. They're both such cards, although your ad does a pretty good job of hiding it most of the time."

"They love you, too. They've been almost as upset as I ave. If you don't come home, I'm not sure my dad'll ever peak to me again."

"Oh, Andy, he'll always love you no matter what you do, nd you know it. That's just the kind of man he is."

"And I feel the same way about you, Ginny. You've gotta elieve that, and if you don't tell me you love me pretty oon, I'm gonna shrivel up and die right here on these porch eps."

To his consternation, her eyes filled with tears again.

"I love you, Andy," she said, her voice thick with emo- on. "I have for a long time. But it scares me to death."

His throat constricted with sheer, unadulterated fear. Why, sweetheart? Don't you believe me? I'll say it a mil- on more times if that's what you need."

"What I probably need, is either a good swift kick in the ehind—or a shrink," she said, smiling in spite of her tears. It, uh, seems that I haven't um, gotten over some things om my past as much as I thought I had."

"Like what, Gin?"

"Well, it's not any one specific thing, really. I guess it's ore of a cumulative effect. See, I've never understood why y folks...disliked me so much. And I never understood hy Charlie turned on me the way he did, either. I made up xplanations, but they never made any real sense to me. So,

I figured there must be something wrong with me—som
reason that nobody could love me as anything more than
friend.''

"Ginny, you're the most lovable person I've ever know:
You're generous and kind—our phone rings all day lor
with people wanting to hear your voice or cry on yo'
shoulder. I've never heard you turn anybody down whe
they needed you.''

"You know why?'' she asked, her voice breaking on
sob. "Because I'm terrified that if I don't *give* peop
something, they'll turn away from me like my folks a'
Charlie did. Now, is that sick, or what?''

"Hell, no, it's not sick. It's a survival mechanism ye
must have needed pretty damn bad, honey. Shoot, there's
lot more destructive things you could've done than ;
around befriending people—alcohol and drug abuse, d'
mestic violence, you name it.''

"You really believe that?''

"Damn right. I see it all the time. There aren't many fol
who get through childhood without a few kinks in the
psyches, so don't beat yourself up like this. You don't d
serve it.''

She tipped her head to one side and studied him for
moment. "Okay,'' she said slowly, as if she were still tryin
to absorb what he'd said. "I can accept that. But I think ye
need to understand how I feel about Ellie. I, uh, I know
was pretty obsessive about her. Maybe I always will b
When we come home, you're gonna have to help me keep
under control so I don't smother her.''

He wanted to whoop with triumph at hearing she w
planning to come home, but he restrained himself. "Oka
Go ahead.''

"Ellie represented a fresh start for me, I guess. She w
someone who didn't know about my past sins, whatev
they were. And she was someone who would love me wit
out reservation, you know?''

When Andy nodded, she inhaled a shaky breath, then continued. "You were right that I didn't want to share her with anyone. Not even you. I guess I wanted...or maybe I needed her to love me the most. That sounds pretty selfish, but that's how I felt. I, uh, I guess I thought that since you didn't love me, Ellie could make up for it."

Damn, if she didn't quit soon, he was gonna be the one bawlin' his head off. "Aw, Ginny—"

"No, let me finish. I can see now that that's a pretty heavy burden to put on a little kid. But it's always seemed to me that people only have so much love to give and I'm afraid they'll run out before they get to me."

Andy couldn't stand to see her sitting there for another second, looking small and lost with her shoulders all hunched up. He put his arm around her shoulders and pulled her against his side.

"Real love isn't like that, honey. There's always plenty to go around. I'll always have more than enough for you and Ellie, and I can't even imagine *you* running out of it. With you around as an example, Ellie won't, either. And for Ellie and me, you'll *always* be the first one in line."

"You still want me after hearing all of that?"

"More than ever. If we can talk to each other like this, there's nothing we can't handle. Nothing at all."

He cupped her face in both hands and kissed her then, gently, reverently, tasting the salty tears she'd shed and her own unique sweetness, absorbing the love she offered so freely with her lips. If anyone ever tried to hurt this woman again, they'd have to come through him first, because he needed her like he needed oxygen, food and water.

"Will you come back to me?" he asked when he finally forced himself to release her.

Though her eyes were still a little misty, they took on a mischievous sparkle, and her mouth curved into a teasing grin that assured him *his* Ginny—the one who never let anything keep her down for long—was back with all of her wonderful sass and spirit intact. Thank God.

"Yeah. I think it's the right thing to do, don't you?"

Shaking his head at her, he stood, then pulled her to he feet and into his arms. He crushed her close, loving her Loving the way she returned his embrace, the way her bod matched his in all the right places. "Just don't ever leave m again. I couldn't stand it."

And then their mouths found each other in a wild flurr of kissing and nipping and mating tongues, sighs and moan and searching, hungry hands. When they finally came up fo air, Ginny rested her forehead against Andy's.

"I want you so much, I'm tempted to tear all your clothe off right here on this porch," she said.

"Go ahead, I can take it. Might give Grandma D on heck of a start if she walks by, but I'm willing to risk it if yo are."

"Nope. There's something I want even more."

"Name it and it's yours, honey."

"Just take me home, Andy. Take me and Ellie home, an see if you can find those black satin sheets."

* * * * *

A Note from the Author

The word *grit* doesn't sound very glamorous, but if a Westerner ever says that you have it, stand proud and thank him for the compliment. It means that adversity can drive you to your knees again and again, but you'll always find the gumption to get back on your feet and fight another day. From the moment she came to life in my imagination, Ginny Bradford had plenty of grit.

She survived years of verbal and emotional abuse, but she didn't let that defeat her. She fought off bitterness and self-pity and became a generous, fun-loving, compassionate person, with a rare gift for accepting other people and making them feel good about themselves. I wasn't a bit surprised when Andy Johnson fell in love with her.

Whether we're domestic goddesses or high-powered professionals, women need plenty of grit to survive the stress we face on a daily basis. We need to share our dreams and hopes for better relationships with the special men in our lives. We need to be able to celebrate our strengths, work on our weaknesses and chuckle at our quirks.

Special Edition's That Special Woman! program provides a wonderful arena to help writers and readers do just that. I'm extremely proud that Ginny's story was chosen for the program, and I sincerely hope you've enjoyed it.

New York Times Bestselling Author

Sandra Brown

Tomorrow's Promise

She cherished the memory
of love but was consumed
by a new passion too
fierce to ignore.

For Keely Preston, the memory of her husband
Mark has been frozen in time since the day he was
listed as missing in action. And now, twelve years
later, twenty-six men listed as MIA have been
found.

Keely's torn between hope for Mark and despair
for herself. Because now, after all the years of
waiting, she has met another man!

**Don't miss TOMORROW'S PROMISE by
SANDRA BROWN.**

**Available in June wherever Harlequin
books are sold.**

TP

**Silhouette Books
is proud to present
our best authors,
their best books...
and the best in
your reading pleasure!**

Throughout 1993, look for exciting books
by these top names in contemporary
romance:

CATHERINE COULTER—
Aftershocks in February

FERN MICHAELS—
Nightstar in March

DIANA PALMER—
Heather's Song in March

ELIZABETH LOWELL
Love Song for a Raven in April

SANDRA BROWN
(previously published under
the pseudonym Erin St. Claire)—
Led Astray in April

LINDA HOWARD—
All That Glitters in May

When it comes to passion,
we wrote the book.

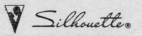

Silhouette®   BOBT1RR

INTIMATE MOMENTS®
10TH
Anniversary

Celebrate our anniversary with a fabulous collection of firsts....

The first Intimate Moments titles written by three of your favorite authors:

NIGHT MOVES	Heather Graham Pozzessere
LADY OF THE NIGHT	Emilie Richards
A STRANGER'S SMILE	Kathleen Korbel

Silhouette Intimate Moments is proud to present a FREE hardbound collection of our authors' firsts—titles that you will treasure in the years to come, from some of the line's founding writers.

This collection will not be sold in retail stores and is available only through this exclusive offer. Look for details in Silhouette Intimate Moments titles available in retail stores in May, June and July.

WHERE WERE YOU WHEN THE LIGHTS WENT OUT?

SILHOUETTE

SUMMER Sizzlers '93

This summer, Silhouette turns up the heat when a midsummer blackout leaves the entire Eastern seaboard in the dark. Who could ask for a more romantic atmosphere? And who can deliver it better than:

**LINDA HOWARD
CAROLE BUCK
SUZANNE CAREY**

Look for it this June at your favorite retail outlet.

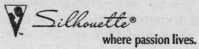

Silhouette®

where passion lives.

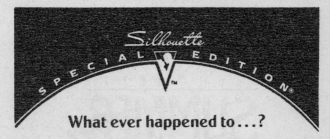